Rotten Apples

by the same author

A Woman's Honor
The Death Trap
The Mark of Lucifer

ROTTEN APPLES

Edith Piñero Green

E. P. Dutton / New York

Copyright © 1977 by Edith Piñero Green
All rights reserved. Printed in the U.S.A.

Library of Congress Cataloging in Publication Data
Green, Edith Piñero.
  Rotten apples.
    I. Title.
PZ4.G78885Ro [PS3557.R367]   813'.5'4
77-7090
ISBN: 0-525-19415-0

Published simultaneously in Canada by Clarke, Irwin & Company
Limited, Toronto and Vancouver

10 9 8 7 6 5 4 3 2 1
First Edition

To my husband, Julie

Rotten Apples

One

Monday, August 8. Arthur Howe was the killer's first victim, but since he was old and crotchety and suffered from cataracts, it raised no eyebrows when he tumbled from his balcony. As a matter of fact, his doctor expressed the opinion that it, or something like it, had been bound to happen sooner or later.

Saturday, August 13. Terence Van Horne's demise was no more suspicious than Arthur's, happening as it had on a sunny Saturday morning before breakfast under benign circumstances. Terence was due at the Wide Rivers Golf Club at noon, an hour before the Seniors' Nine-Hole Tournament. Looking forward to a leisurely breakfast and a few practice strokes on the back lawn, he rose at eight-thirty, a half-hour earlier than usual. He dressed himself in his custom-tailored white knickerbockers and the silk ascot that he considered de rigueur for the greens. He wasn't slender and he puffed as he leaned over his resistant belly to lace his shoes, but his hands were as dexterous as ever and, as he told himself, his eyesight was as keen.

Outside the bedroom doors, the lawn stretched to the line of contoured hedges, beyond which were the swimming pool and tennis courts. A croquet set was arranged immediately under the dining terrace. It was a poor substitute for golf, but Lydia, when she was alive, had always enjoyed it and visitors found it diverting. Now, as

1

Terence dressed, he heard the hollow whack of mallet hitting ball.

"Who's that?" he asked himself. "Certainly not one of the servants." He tied his shoelaces firmly, straightened up, and stretched his back muscles. Then he leaned over, picked up his linen golf cap, and settled it firmly on his head. He stepped through the open doors and strode across the grass. Rounding the corner of the dining terrace, he studied the playing field of patterned wickets. He glanced at the croquet stand on the flagstones at the foot of the terrace steps.

His eyes were drawn to the long drive bordered by oaks that led to the front gates. Quiet. Deserted. Not like the old days. His brain, like a worn gear, disengaged and slipped backward. How often he longed for the lost years, the times when there hadn't been hours enough to do all the things he wanted, those years with Lydia, and even before Lydia, forty years before, when the future, like the oaks lining the drive, stretched before with orderly, reassuring precision. Names crowded his memory, names he hadn't thought about in ages. Dolly Fairchild; Jimmy Bell, the Beekman Place Bard. Fannie Tyler, and the others. What was that group? What had they called themselves? The Rotten Apples. Terence chuckled. But they hadn't been such rotten apples. Young, foolish, a bit promiscuous, perhaps. Arthur Howe, Antoinette, Stella, Vernon Tree, Louise. Poor Louise. Dead all these years. Jack Rogers. What had become of them?

Terence's eyes fixed on the croquet stand and his thoughts snapped back to the present. A mallet and ball were missing. He turned and skimmed his eyes over the smooth lawn. Beyond the last wicket, a few yards from the open pool gate, lay the missing croquet ball, its yellow stripe visible against the green grass.

"Damned careless," he mumbled. He marched across the lawn. "Someone will hear from me." He couldn't see the mallet. He swiveled, trying to spot the telltale yellow handle. Then he heard his name. It had been a whisper. He stood quite still, trying to decide where it had come

2

from, or for that matter whether he had really heard it. Sometimes lately he did hear things, murmurings and buzzings and tiny, indefinable sounds.

"Terence . . ."

He glanced around. It came from the direction of the pool—a low, conspiratorial call. "Terence . . ."

He took a step toward the open gate. Who was it? Harriet didn't rise until eleven. Roger was in Pittsburgh. The servants didn't address him by his given name.

"Terence . . ."

A little more insistent this time. He approached the gate and peered at the pool. He took a tentative step forward and then fell, the fierce blow to his forehead splitting the bone with a sickening crack.

Dearborn ~~dove~~ dived under the blanket and came up holding his pajama bottoms. "Mrs. Woolley, will you kindly ask the laundress not to starch these? They're stiff as cardboard."

"Last time you said they were too limp."

Dearborn unbuttoned his pajama jacket and thrust it at her. "Mrs. Woolley, how old am I?"

"Too old for running around in the altogether."

Dearborn swung himself off the bed and pranced to the window. He turned and stood with his hands on his hips. "Well?"

"Well what? The people across the courtyard are getting an eyeful."

"Over seventy," Dearborn announced triumphantly. "Look at my stomach. Look at my arms. Mrs. Woolley, I have a suggestion."

Mrs. Woolley shook her hennaed head, tucked the pajamas under her arm, and headed for the door. "No more of that, Mr. Pinch."

"You're an attractive woman . . ."

"I'm fifty-seven years old. Too old for nonsense."

"It isn't nonsense I had in mind," Dearborn called after her.

Dearborn sang in the shower, toweled himself vigor-

3

ously, and wrapped himself in a terry bathrobe—red, his favorite color—with his monogram embroidered in brown silk on the breast pocket. When he returned to his bedroom, he found his breakfast tray on the table in front of the window, along with the *New York Times* and a batch of telephone slips. He sat down and drank his juice.

"Frozen? Frozen, Mrs. Woolley," he shouted. Dearborn often addressed himself to Mrs. Woolley even when she wasn't around. "Thought I wouldn't notice? Is that it?"

He glanced at his phone messages, carefully noted in Mrs. Woolley's perpendicular script. "Eleven P.M. Your son Benjamin. Will phone again."

"Nuts to you, Benjamin." Dearborn ripped the slip of paper in half and dropped it on the rug. He tapped his way around the egg in his egg cup and sampled it before continuing with his messages. "I said *three* minutes, Mrs. Woolley. Not *thirty* minutes."

"Eight A.M. Mr. Rothschild. Imp. Please call."

"Otto Rothschild? More complaints? More checks to sign? Too nice a day for that, Mrs. Woolley." Dearborn balled up the note and chucked it through the open window.

"Nine A.M. New York chapter Sons of Britain. About a dinner they're sponsoring."

"Queers. Every mother's son of 'em." Dearborn crumpled the slip of paper and dropped it into his empty orange-juice glass.

"Nine-fifteen A.M. Mrs. August Ormacht. No message."

Mrs. August Ormacht? Who was Mrs. August Ormacht? Dearborn stared at the slip of paper. A Heinie. Probably another big-breasted worthy-cause woman. He'd show her a worthy cause. Dearborn let the slip flutter to the floor and buttered a blueberry muffin.

"Mr. Pinch?" Mrs. Woolley spoke through the closed door.

4

Dearborn wiped a bit of butter from the tip of his nose. "What is it?"

"Someone to see you. A visitor. She says it's important."

"She? Open the door, Mrs. Woolley."

Mrs. Woolley pushed open the door and stuck her face into the crack.

"Why do you persist in talking to me through closed doors, Mrs. Woolley?"

"It's a lady."

Dearborn grunted. "Are you sure she wants me?"

"She asked for Dearborn V. Pinch. She said her name is Mrs. August Ormacht."

"It must be a case of mistaken identity. I don't know any Mrs. August Ormacht."

"And I don't know any other Dearborn V. Pinch. She said to tell you she used to be Antoinette Dill."

Dearborn put down his coffee cup. He gazed at Mrs. Woolley in astonishment. "You don't say? Toni Dill. What does she look like? Small? Blond? Blue-eyed? Good figure?"

Mrs. Woolley relaxed her grip on the doorknob. "I couldn't say if she was ever blond. Her hair's white. She's short and kind of plump. I didn't notice her eyes."

"Toni Dill," Dearborn repeated. "Didn't know she was still around. Thought she'd moved to Portugal." Dearborn picked up his spoon and polished off the rest of his soft-boiled egg. "Legs, Mrs. Woolley," he murmured dreamily. "Slender. Long like a dancer's. A dimple on one knee. Only one, Mrs. Woolley. Unique characteristic."

Mrs. Woolley snorted. "What shall I tell her?"

"I'll see her."

Dearborn skipped his second cup of coffee. He dressed in front of the full-length mirror, choosing gray slacks, a maroon shirt, and a silk paisley ascot, combing his thick, unhighlighted, black hair with care, and dabbing cologne onto his cheeks. He was over six feet tall, less flexible than he had once been, but slender and

5

straight-backed, with an innate sense of style. He admired himself in the mirror—front, profile, and back. Then he started down the hall.

Toni Dill. Not much over five feet tall. High as his chest. What could she want after all these years? Dearborn couldn't even remember if they had parted friends. He approached the library warily.

She was sitting in his easy chair, facing the hall. She held a coffee cup cradled in both hands. Her feet dangled an inch from the floor. "Dearie! Look at you. Is that you?"

It took Dearborn a moment to square this tiny elderly personage with his vision of Antoinette Dill as he remembered her. This one had white hair gathered into a tight bun. Her body was delicate, almost brittle, and her dress, a demure black silk, reached to mid-calf, hiding her once celebrated, now venerable knees. Dearborn covered his dismay by striding across the room to take one of her small hands. He shook it vigorously. "Toni Dill. Well, well, well, well."

"I apologize for barging in on you, Dearie. As I recall, you were never fond of unexpected visitors."

Dearborn lowered himself gingerly onto the couch opposite and took another look. A bit of a jolt, but there it was. Toni was an old woman. Her skin was lined and dry. Her blue eyes were pale, and there were dark blotches on the backs of her hands. Liver spots. None of her was as he remembered. Even her teeth were unfamiliar. "Well, well, well, well. Toni Dill."

"It's Ormacht now."

"What happened to Eddie?"

"He's living in New Canaan, Connecticut. Still in politics and as straightlaced as ever. If he ever knew why I was here . . ." She blushed. "Well, anyway, we were divorced eons ago."

"Might have predicted it. Dull laundry, Eddie. No imagination. Hope the Kraut is an improvement."

"The Kraut? Oh, you mean August. August is dead. I'm a widow."

6

"My condolences . . ."

"He died in 1954."

". . . belated though they may be."

Dearborn waited. Antoinette smiled. Her smile was preoccupied. "You've done well for yourself," she murmured. She nodded toward the Chagall over the mantelpiece and waved at the brandy decanter in its silver filigree basket. "I remember how difficult things were back in '35."

Dearborn shrugged. "I made a few conservative but efficacious investments with what was left of my inheritance. By 1937 I was solvent."

Antoinette lowered her eyes. She seemed to be searching for something in her coffee cup. "I suppose you're wondering what I'm doing here."

"I admit to a certain curiosity."

Antoinette took a sip of her coffee. "I came early to be sure you'd be home. Now that I'm here I don't know how to begin."

"Plunge right in, Toni."

"It *is* difficult."

"Is it money?"

Antoinette shook her head. "No. No. I'm . . . I'm quite well off."

"Then what is it? We haven't laid eyes on one another for . . . it must be twenty, twenty-five years."

"Thirty-nine," Antoinette returned promptly. "I became pregnant with Charlene in 1936. That was the same year Eddie and I moved to Lisbon."

Dearborn was stunned. "Thirty-nine?" he mumbled. "You don't say."

Antoinette wiggled forward in the chair until her feet touched the floor. "As I said, I don't know just how to begin, Dearie. I need help and I can't go to the police."

"Why come to me?"

"I know this is going to sound strange, especially after all this time. But it's partially because of Juanita Froebel's stolen porcelains."

"What? What are you talking about?"

7

"You and Juanita Froebel's porcelains, Dearie. The police never did figure it out. But you did. Remember? And what's more, you got Buzz Beckwith to return them and persuaded Juanita not to press charges. It could have been a dreadful scandal."

"That was over forty years ago."

"And Hal Hamilton. Remember that female he got involved with? You handled that beautifully."

"Hal was a friend of mine. I considered it an obligation."

"I'm a friend, too, Dearie. And I have a problem."

"Are you mixed up in some sort of criminal activity?" Dearborn asked.

Antoinette smoothed her skirt down over her knees. "I'm not sure."

Dearborn was losing patience. "I'm not a mind reader, Toni. What in blue blazes are you talking about?"

Antoinette gazed at him with anxious eyes. "I'm trying to tell you that I think I'm going to be killed. I think that someone intends to murder me."

Two

Dearborn leaned forward. "Are you joking?" He wondered if she were all there. She seemed lucid, but at close range her eyes were peculiarly luminous.

She dug down between the chair cushions and dislodged her pocketbook, a capacious needlepoint tote with bone handles. She snapped the pocketbook open and pulled out a newspaper clipping. "Here. Read this."

Dearborn reached into his pocket for his reading glasses. "Give it to me, Toni."

NOTED HUMANITARIAN DIES

New Rochelle, New York, Tuesday, August 9—Arthur Howe, chairman of the board of Ceilchem Inc. and winner of the fortieth Humanitarian Award in 1972, died yesterday at his home in New Rochelle. Mr. Howe, who was seventy-one years old and suffered from cataracts, apparently lost his footing and plunged to his death from a second-floor balcony . . ."

Dearborn read on impatiently, " . . . blah, blah, blah. 'Services will be held on August 11 at the Blackwell Funeral Home.' So what is this?"

"You remember Arthur Howe, Dearie."

"Filthy little deviate, as I recall. What has this got to do with you?"

"Terence Van Horne was killed two days ago."

Dearborn stared at her blankly.

"You remember Terence Van Horne, Dearie."

"The Horned Toady?"

"The same."

"Married that eyesore, Lydia Brown, the supermarket heiress. Bald, wasn't she?"

Antoinette took a deep breath. "We, all three—Arthur, Terence, and I—have . . . or had . . . something in common."

"I would hate to think so."

"We were all Rotten Apples."

"Arthur was certainly a rotten apple, but I think you're being unnecessarily hard on yourself, Toni."

"Rotten Apples was the name of a group. The Rotten Apple Corps. There were eleven of us: Arthur, Terence, me, Stella Gresham, Jack Rogers, Dolly Fairchild, Louise

9

Cotton, Robert Bright. Let me see. Fannie Tyler, Vernon Tree, and James Bell. Is that eleven?"

Dearborn screwed up his eyes as if trying to see into the past. "Stella Gresham? Didn't she have an affair with that swarthy little Italian? What was his name? Conslavo?"

"Consalvo. Pietro Consalvo."

"And Jack Rogers. Alcoholic, wasn't he? Whatever happened to him?"

Antoinette shook her head. "Who knows? Oh, I suppose he's dead by now. He disappeared after that scandal over Countess Ambeil's nose."

"What scandal was that?"

"Beeswax in her nostrils. Jack lost his medical license."

"Seems to me that incident does ring a bell."

"It was in all the papers. 'RESTORATIVE SURGERY QUACK PROSECUTED.' How could you have forgotten? Anyway, that's not important now. Poor old Jack is long gone."

"Fannie Tyler," Dearborn ruminated. "She retired in the forties, didn't she?"

Antoinette nodded. "She flopped in something or other. The last few things she did, really. The critics weren't very kind."

"The Rotten Apple Corps . . ." Dearborn prodded.

"The eleven of us formed this group which we called The Rotten Apple Corps, because of the basis for membership, which was really, well, rather . . ."

"Rotten?"

"Yes," Antoinette admitted. "It was Bobby Bright's idea. Stella got drunk one night and confided to us that she had just poisoned King Hamburger of Tartan—"

"Who?"

"I'm just making up the name. I don't really remember it. Apparently she did away with a rival's dog on the eve of the Westminster Dog Show . . ."

"Did away?"

"Killed it. Poisoned it with arsenic."

Dearborn was baffled. "Toni, I certainly hope there is some point to all of this."

"Of course there is. Someone else . . . oh, yes . . . Jimmy. Jimmy Bell? He told us that he'd plagiarized a poem, the one that won first prize at the National Poetry Awards. There were scads of money involved and loads of publicity—"

"Toni . . ."

"Everyone tried to top everyone else with stories about the crimes we'd committed. We thought we were awfully clever . . ."

"Awful is the word for it."

"There was Jack and, er, Dolly Fairchild and Bobby Bright . . ."

"The Longevity King Bright?"

"Yes. The Brights lost everything in the crash. Bobby tried to recoup by selling shares in an off-shore drilling operation, entirely nonexistent, of course."

"He got away with it?"

"Not exactly. We dissuaded him from it. He'd been in trouble before and the police were suspicious of him. People were complaining. We—the Rotten Apples— convinced him that he should give back the money. Then we chipped in three thousand dollars apiece so he could buy some property out in Islip. You know, to start the clinic."

"Forty years ago?"

"In '35."

"In '35? But Toni, you and I were still . . ." Dearborn hummed under his breath.

"I know, Dearie. But you were so awfully disapproving of those people. I didn't dare tell you about the Rotten Apples. I kept it from Eddie, too. Come to think of it, you and Eddie thought somewhat alike . . ."

"Only when it came to social parasites, Toni. Otherwise Eddie and I had nothing in common."

"Except me."

"Hmm . . ."

"We held initiation rites," Antoinette went on. "And we all confessed. All of us had something to confess. That is, all except Vernon. He committed a crime to qualify."

"Vernon Tree? He was already practicing law, wasn't he? Always knew him for an ass."

"Oh, Dearie, you're only saying that because he tried to steal Jessamine from you."

"Ridiculous. Jessamine used to say Vernon had ears you could lift him by."

"Vernon broke into a used car lot, stole the week's cash and receipts, and drove off in a used car. Nineteen twenty-nine De Soto, if I remember correctly. Then he didn't know how to get rid of it so he drove it out to New Jersey and pushed it over the Palisades."

"Inspiring," Dearborn muttered. "Most inspiring. And Vernon Tree ended up a judge. An edifying story. And you, Toni? What was your qualification?"

Antoinette looked embarrassed. "I was chairwoman of the planning committee for the Reisler Medical Research Foundation. They were looking for property. They were considering two sites—one on Third Avenue, one on Sixth. I had the deciding vote."

"Unknown to the committee, you owned the property chosen."

Antoinette sighed.

"More unethical than criminal, I would suppose."

"It would have been disastrous if it had come out. Of course, we never thought about the consequences. We didn't mean anyone any harm. But after a while it got to be a bore. I, for one, intended to move to Lisbon. Louise Cotton, I remember, signed a contract with the London Opera . . ."

"Died over there, didn't she?"

"In the Blitz."

"So you disbanded the group?" Dearborn asked. He was annoyed with himself for encouraging her, but she'd piqued his curiosity.

"We held a final meeting and swore ourselves to eternal secrecy. We were so naive. We were sure it would never come back to haunt us."

"Now it has."

"It seems so. I believe someone means us harm. I don't

12

know why. And I don't know who. But Arthur is dead, and so is Terence. Both by accident. Arthur off his balcony, Terence into his swimming pool."

"That's no reason for you to presume that you are in danger."

"Yesterday," Antoinette went on, "I was crossing Madison Avenue and a car swerved toward me. If someone hadn't pulled me out of the way . . ."

"Reckless driver," Dearborn declared.

"It was purposeful. I'm sure of it."

"Did you see the driver?"

"No," Antoinette said. "I was too frightened to notice."

"What kind of car was it?"

She shook her head helplessly. "Dark."

"Big? Little?"

"I'm sorry, Dearie."

"Toni, you have an extremely vivid imagination."

"Perhaps it was someone who holds a grudge. I've even thought it might be Eddie. He was always rather erratic."

"Only in a sociably acceptable way. You said so yourself."

"Perhaps it's a fanatic who thinks we should be punished for our errant ways."

"Asinine. Fanatics kill presidents and kings, not elderly apples, rotten or otherwise."

"It can't be coincidental that Arthur and Terence had accidents in the space of a week and that I was almost killed yesterday."

"Terence Van Horne was always ill-coordinated. I can still recall him knocking himself out with his golf club during a match in Southampton."

"And Arthur?"

"Accidents happen."

"No, Dearie. No, they don't. Not like that."

There was a shuffling noise behind Dearborn. William Rhodes, Dearborn's secretary, stood in the doorway. He smiled timidly and ran spidery fingers along the edges of his seersucker jacket. "It's quarter after eleven. You told

13

me to report to you when I arrived." William handed Dearborn a batch of letters and withdrew.

"I think he's having at Mrs. Woolley," Dearborn muttered. "Spends half his time in the kitchen drinking tea and the other half in the bathroom relieving himself."

Antoinette watched as Dearborn riffled through the envelopes. "What's this? Another letter from the phone company? Damned monopoly. Let them sing for their two thousand sixteen dollars and forty-one cents."

"Dearie," Antoinette whispered, "won't you help? After all, you helped Juanita . . ."

"Toni, I don't know how to help you. Perhaps you should hire a bodyguard."

"You don't take me seriously, do you?"

Dearborn hummed tunelessly. "Frankly, I think it's an attack of nerves."

Antoinette rose and started for the hall. "I must say that you've disappointed me. I thought that of all the people I knew, you would be least likely to let me down. Apparently I was wrong. Well, I shall say good-bye, and I hope you will carry it on your conscience if these are the last words you ever hear from me."

"No need for dramatics," Dearborn called after her. "I have a suggestion to make. A friend, a doctor, Doctor Walter Moltke. Fine fellow. Don't usually hold with psychia . . ."

"Don't bother!"

The front door slammed before Dearborn could unfold his long body and go after her.

Three

Antoinette was sure that her life depended on avoiding isolated places. She went to a movie on Monday evening, at the Paris on Fifty-eighth Street near Fifth Avenue.

The movie was a frothy Italian farce. Antoinette sat through it soberly, not following the plot or even reading the subtitles.

When the film was over, she came out of the theater feeling dizzy and slightly off-balance, as if she'd disembarked from a ship. Dearborn had failed her. How foolish she had been to think he would sympathize. She'd forgotten that Dearborn would not be swayed by sentiment. There was nothing left but to face up to the situation alone.

Antoinette turned south on Fifth Avenue. She crossed Fifty-seventh Street and went into Doubleday's. The store was brightly lit and offered a temporary haven. She browsed among the books, at first the hardcovers, then further back, the paperbacks. Finally she chose a book, *Enter a Murderer* by Ngaio March, smiling at her own sense of the macabre. She carried it to the checkout counter, paid for it, and left. She hesitated outside, not yet ready to face her empty apartment. A good walk might tire her enough to sleep. The traffic light at Fifty-sixth Street turned green as she reached the corner. She rushed across the street and continued crosstown to Park Avenue. She turned south on Park and Fifty-sixth and

15

proceeded downtown. At Fifty-third Street she spotted a few people sitting on the wall in front of the Seagram building, and she crossed the street to join them. She sat down and took a few deep breaths, trying to compose herself.

"Hot night, isn't it?" the woman next to her drawled.

Antoinette turned and said politely, "Yes; yes, it is."

The woman, a dowdy matron in a two-piece jacket-dress and orthopedic shoes, said, "I'm here on a package tour. From Charleston. But, I swear, I'm sorry I ever came."

"Oh?" Antoinette managed without inspiration.

"I used to come here with my late husband. It was different in those days, though."

"Oh?"

"The shows were better. Nowadays the shows are shameful. I wouldn't even go tonight. *Intimate Relations.* Ever hear a title like that? Naked bodies and four-letter words. You live here?"

"What?"

"Are you a New Yorker?"

Antoinette didn't answer. Why did the woman ask her that? She had a sly look. Was the accent real? A faint breeze rippled the surface of the pool, carrying a fine spray that touched Antoinette's face and made her shiver.

"Would you like to go have a cup of coffee? There's a nice place right in this building. My sister Adele and I were in there this afternoon. Almost didn't go in. Thought it was one of those topless places. You know what it's called? The Brassiere! Can you believe it? By the way, my name's Elsie Turner. What's yours?"

Antoinette stood up and smoothed her skirt. "I'm sorry, I must be going."

"You don't want a cup of coffee?"

"I'm sorry. I'm on my way somewhere."

"I wouldn't go in a restaurant by myself. I thought you might like . . ."

"Have a good trip back to—to Charleston."

16

Antoinette hurried across the street and headed back toward Fifth Avenue. The block between Park and Madison was a long one, but she slowed down once she had crossed the street.

A quarter of the way up the block Antoinette became conscious of footsteps behind her, but they were ten or twelve yards away and she didn't turn. She simply stepped up her pace. Halfway up the block the pavement gave way to a wooden walk that snaked its way inward through a construction site for thirty feet or so, bypassing a maze of planks and beams. When Antoinette stepped onto the wooden walk, she was startled to hear the footsteps take up on the wooden planking only a yard or two behind her, and she whirled around.

She had no more than a vague apprehension of the upraised arm, the long, paper-wrapped implement, before it descended. She pitched forward with a small, surprised cry.

When the phone rang, Benjamin groaned and pulled the pillow down over his face. Then, gradually, he swam up out of his grogginess to squint at the clock radio. Ten-thirty. He tried to sit up, but one arm lay heavily across his chest and he couldn't will himself to move it. Then he realized that it wasn't his arm. He pushed the arm to one side and picked up the phone.

"Mr. Pinch?"

"Speaking."

"One moment, please."

Benjamin groaned again. He recognized Miss Simon's prim voice. He waited for Otto Rothschild to pick up.

"Ben?"

"Hello, Otto."

"You sound hoarse. Are you sick?"

Benjamin cleared his throat. "No. I'm okay. What's up?"

"It's your father." Otto sounded agitated.

"What is it? The phone company again? You're paying the bills, aren't you? Can't you get them to lay off?"

"Not the phone company, Ben."

"Abercrombie and Fitch? He's been using the rowing machine again?"

"Not Abercrombie and Fitch."

The owner of the stray arm began to wriggle around under Benjamin's shoulder. Benjamin turned his back. "Okay. What's wrong this time?"

"He went to the police yesterday and told them that a friend of his was murdered."

"What?"

"I'm not kidding. I got a call from some detective. Your father appeared at the police station yesterday afternoon, spouting off about some old lady named Antoinette Ormacht who got clunked over the head Monday night. According to Niccoli—that's the lieutenant down there—your father says the Ormacht woman was murdered. He told Niccoli he got the information on good authority."

"Great. How come the police called you?"

"Your father threatened them with me. How else? They said that if he shows up again they'll ship him to Bellevue."

Benjamin felt a hand creep across his chest. He writhed away. "Otto, you'd better do something. You're his lawyer."

"I inherited the job, Ben. I didn't ask for it."

"He hates me, Otto."

"So who told you to be a basketball player?"

"Not anymore. I'm retired, remember? I'm a thirty-two-year-old former basketball player currently out of work. I've got troubles of my own. I haven't got time to do your job for you. You're his lawyer."

"Look, I don't want to talk about your personal problems. Niccoli said that none of the relatives of the Ormacht woman even know your father. He showed up out of nowhere. I tried to get you last night, but you weren't home. When's the last time you spoke to him?"

Benjamin rubbed his forehead. "Not for a week."

"Well, you better speak to him, baby. You're his son and heir."

"Not his heir, Otto."

"Don't come to me with your troubles."

Benjamin sighed. "Okay, okay, I'll see what I can do."

"And while we're discussing . . ."

"What else?"

"He called Miss Simon a few minutes ago to get some personal information on Robert Bright. You know, the Longevity King? The one with the big clinic out on Long Island. He was my old man's client back in the forties, before Bright decided he needed a corporation lawyer. Anyway, your old man told Miss Simon it was a matter of life or death. It may have something to do with the other thing."

A soft hand slid down Benjamin's back, coming to rest between his thighs. He clamped his legs together. "You made my day, Otto," he said morosely.

Otto's tone was no more cheerful. "That's what friends are for, old buddy."

Benjamin got to the police station at one, and was ushered in to see Lieutenant Niccoli, a burly man with short-cropped hair and tortoise-rimmed glasses. He greeted Benjamin cordially.

"Jesus, you're Benjamin Pinch. What the hell! I saw you at the Garden last winter. Glad to meet you. You came about your father? Hell, if I'd known he was your father I'd have given him the red carpet treatment."

"What's this about, Lieutenant?"

"Your father said the Ormacht woman was premeditated murder and we should look into it."

"What did he give as a reason?"

A knobby little policeman who was hovering nearby sidled over. "She *was* murdered. By somebody. A junkie, probably. He took her wristwatch but left her pocketbook."

Lieutenant Niccoli nodded. "You're one hell of a ball player, you know that?"

"Was," Benjamin said.

"Oh, yeah. You retired this season, didn't you. I kind of thought you might be putting on the old squeeze, holding out for more sugar . . ."

"Mr. Pinch said," the knobby little policeman persisted, "that the lives of innocent people were at stake. He said, 'discretion is the order of the day.' Kind of a cute old guy. And then he was shouting about them other two murders . . ."

"What other two murders?" Benjamin asked.

Lieutenant Niccoli shrugged. "He said two other people were killed. Some guy named Howe up in New Rochelle and Terence Van Horne, the millionaire, out on Long Island."

"Terence Van Horne? He claims that Terence Van Horne was murdered?"

"Yup. Claims he was pushed into his swimming pool."

"Is there any truth to it?"

"He fell into his pool, all right. He was chasing a croquet ball and he tripped. At least that's the official report."

"He drowned?"

"Not drowned," Lieutenant Niccoli said. "Fractured skull. Hit his head on the side of the pool. Coroner said he was dead when he went in."

"And the other man? Howe?"

"Fell off a balcony," the little policeman offered.

"And Mrs. Ormacht?"

"Beaned. By a mugger."

"You mean to say they all died violently?"

"I admit it's a coincidence," Niccoli said. "I guess that's what got your father's imagination working overtime. He picked up the paper, seen where these people all had accidents, and got it into his head that they were murdered. That's what it adds up to."

Benjamin wondered. He wasn't so sure.

"He tried to bribe Stefanich here to give him the Ormacht file."

"Fifty bucks," Officer Stefanich added.

"Then he grabbed the phone and started dialing the *Daily News*."

"Which," Officer Stefanich pointed out, "could of got us a good ass burning from the top brass."

"Look," Lieutenant Niccoli reasoned, "we all got parents. Sometimes when they get a little old, they get, well, you know . . . and we got to watch out for them. Keep them from making trouble. That's what you got to do . . . before your old man ends up in the psycho ward."

"And me along with him," Benjamin muttered. "Okay. I'll clamp the lid on."

"We'd appreciate that."

Benjamin headed for the door.

"Hey," Lieutenant Niccoli called after him, "how tall are you?"

"Six four."

"They don't call you Super Runt for nothing. You're one hell of a basketball player."

Four

At three-fifteen Dearborn, carrying his walking stick and wearing a Panama hat, boarded the Long Island train. His ebony cane with its cobra-head handle was his favorite, and he came close to losing part of it when the car doors closed on the tip. "Fools," he exclaimed, tugging it free. "Irresponsible boobs. Simpletons."

It was an off-hour on a gray day, and the car was almost

empty. Dearborn arranged himself and his belongings on an aisle seat as far from the sooty window as he could get. "Just like Robert to settle in Islip," he mumbled. "Always a hair's breadth off."

The train drew into Islip at twenty to five. The sky had darkened and the wind had risen. Dearborn anchored the brim of his hat, hailed a cab, and gave the clinic address.

Dearborn had been shocked by Antoinette's death, but going to the police had been a wasted effort. The idiots wouldn't cooperate. They behaved as if he were at fault. Nevertheless, the facts were clear. Terence and Arthur had been murdered, and now Antoinette—poor Toni— had been murdered as well. Senseless. Unreasonable. Three people dead and no apparent motive. It was up to him to get to the bottom of it. He owed that much to Toni.

The cab deposited him in front of a high wooden gate set into a stone wall on the outskirts of town. A bronze plaque nailed to the gate read Longevity Clinic, founded by Robert Bright, 1935. By standing on tiptoe Dearborn could peek over the gate into what appeared to be a landscaped park, but when he tried to get in, he found the gate locked. There was an intercom behind a sliding glass panel set into the wall. Dearborn slid the shield to one side, pushed the button, and waited.

After a moment a tinny voice answered. "Who is it?"

The static required that Dearborn shout. "I am here to make some inquiries."

"Name, please," the voice commanded.

Dearborn glanced up and down the road. "Dearborn V. Pinch."

There was a lengthy pause. "Will you state your business?"

Dearborn rattled the gate handle impatiently and put his mouth close to the intercom. "I will state my business after I have been admitted."

There was another pause, then a series of clicks as the

door lock was released. Dearborn, in a huff, stabbed at the door with his cane as it swung closed. He marched up the narrow path that curved right into a clutch of trees. Both sides of the path were hedged by thick foliage, and Dearborn had the uncomfortable sensation that he was being observed. For a commercial hostel the place was strangely deserted. He swiped at a bush or two with his cane and performed a couple of practice lunges at a juniper tree. Somewhere off to his left he heard leaves crackle. He executed a hop, twirl, and feint, ready to defend himself if necessary; then, seeing no one, he continued up the path.

He rounded a bend and emerged onto an open expanse of lawn. The clinic, built on a rise, loomed up ahead of him. It was a Moorish mansion of yellow stucco festooned with shallow balconies and nonfunctional columns. "Taste in his behind," Dearborn murmured.

There was no driveway. As Dearborn approached, the front door opened and a tall gentleman in black trousers and a green bush jacket stepped out. Unaccountably, his jacket was improperly buttoned so that one side hung lower than the other and, although he was otherwise conventionally dressed, he wore bedroom slippers. He was pale, with no eyebrows to speak of, and no hair, except for a few snowy wisps that clung to his head at a point just above his ears.

Dearborn stopped at the foot of the steps and waved his cane. "Robert. I'd have known you anywhere. Still don't know better than to open the door yourself, do you? Missed your calling. You would have made an excellent butler."

"My name is Reid," the gentleman said. "Raymond Reid. I'm the clinic's health director."

Dearborn climbed the steps to take a closer look. "No, you're not Robert, are you? Still, you look familiar. Tell me, where are the cars?" Dearborn pointed toward the grounds. "I don't see any driveway here. The taxi left me at the gate."

"There are garages on the road behind the clinic," Reid informed him. "We have golf carts for going to and from the garages and for pickups at the front gate."

"Why didn't you pick me up at the front gate, then?"

"That service is reserved for guests," Reid replied coolly.

Dearborn looked at Reid more closely. "Have you ever been employed by the New York Athletic Club?"

"Certainly not."

"The Harvard Club? The Stock Exchange?"

Reid shook his head.

"Hmm. I don't suppose you have ever had any connection with the New York Telephone Company?"

"I've been with the clinic for over twenty years."

"Well, well," Dearborn mused, "I know I've met you somewhere. You look like an acquaintance. If you weren't bald as Buddha, I'd guess you were my barber. No matter. It has nothing to do with the matter at hand. I am here to see Robert Bright."

Reid stepped to one side and gestured toward the front door. His gesture, Dearborn thought, was unnecessarily broad, his stance a trifle lopsided.

Dearborn preceded him into the spacious entry hall, a wide gallery about thirty feet square with a marble floor and a curved central staircase leading up to a second floor with a stained-glass window. The window filtered green and rose and blue light onto two giant cacti in wooden tubs on the upper landing.

A parlor opened out to the left of the hall and a dining room to the right. Left of the central stairway, about twenty-five feet from the front door, was an elevator, the kind Dearborn hadn't seen in years, a brass cage in a glass-enclosed shaft.

A young woman in a white halter top, brief white shorts, and a glittering costume bracelet came through a rear archway near the elevator. She was small, slender, and green-eyed, with a blond mane that swept her shoulders and a suspicious expression on her face. "Yes? What is it you want?"

24

"I've come to see Robert Bright," Dearborn announced.

A sudden thunderclap sent Reid scurrying across the hall toward the stairs. He tripped on the bottom step of the wide staircase, recovered his balance, and continued up.

"Mr. Bright isn't here," the girl said.

Dearborn was annoyed by her abrupt tone. "Young lady, I've come a long way. I would like the courtesy of being asked in."

She hesitated, then made a cursory effort to be polite, smiling tightly and motioning him into the parlor. "I'm Nadine Garrett, Mr. Bright's secretary. Most people who want to see Mr. Bright call for an appointment."

Dearborn followed her into the parlor, placed his Panama and cane on one of the tables, and sat down on a straight-backed chair. "I am an old friend," he explained.

"The clinic's closed. It's always closed during August. And Mr. Bright's away."

"The place is empty? Just you and, er . . ."

"Mr. Reid. Yes, that's right."

There was another clap of thunder. "Where is Robert?" Dearborn asked.

"He's in the Orient, on vacation. He should be back about the first week in September."

"I haven't seen Robert for some time," Dearborn informed her. "Quite a number of years, as a matter of fact. I have lost touch with him. Tell me, does he have a family?"

She shook her head. "No. His last wife died."

"Ah, yes," Dearborn said. "Robert was in the habit of marrying. I remember that. No children, then?"

"No."

"Have you worked for him long, Miss Garrett?"

"A couple of years."

"And before that?"

She put her hands on her hips. "I'm sorry if you think I'm rude, but my background's none of your business."

25

"Just making conversation," Dearborn assured her innocently.

"I grew up here. My mother was the housekeeper."

"Then you must know Robert very well."

"Not particularly."

"You mean Robert doesn't fraternize with the help?"

Her lips tightened and she drew herself up stiffly. "That's right."

Dearborn retreated. "When did Mr. Bright leave on his trip?"

"A few weeks ago."

"Did he seem disturbed about anything before he left?"

"What is this? What are you trying to find out? I thought you said you were a friend!"

"Miss Garrett, something of some urgency concerning Mr. Bright has come up. I must get in touch with him. I wonder if you can tell me how I may do so."

She bristled. "His schedule's flexible. I'm not sure where he is now. He may be in Tokyo. Or possibly Hong Kong."

"Will you check his itinerary for me?"

"Look, I don't even know you."

"There isn't anything secret about his whereabouts, is there?"

"No, but . . ."

"He may not be pleased to find out that you refused me the information."

She thought about it for a moment. "All right. Wait here."

"My pleasure."

Dearborn watched her leave the room and then turned his attention to his surroundings. At first glance the room seemed elegant, even luxurious, with clusters of upholstered couches and chairs and a fireplace proportioned to suit a ballroom. But a closer look revealed the underlying shabbiness. The fabrics were frayed and in some cases faded. The woven rattan seat of an occasional

26

chair was broken, and Dearborn noticed that one wall was badly in need of plastering.

He got up and strolled to the open French doors at one side of the room. A flicker of movement caught his eye—a bird or a butterfly flitting across the edge of his vision. But for the second time in the last half-hour he felt uncomfortable. Why did he continue to have the peculiar sensation that he was being watched? He stepped out onto the terrace. Ivy leaves near the corner of the house rustled. Dearborn peered at them. He crossed the flagstones for a closer look. His eyes were drawn to the grass, which needed cutting. And someone had gotten careless with the garden equipment. A hoe gathered rust under a mulberry tree, and a trowel was stuck into the dirt under a rosebush. Dearborn caught the flash of something in motion, someone stooping beyond the terrace wall.

"Who's that?" he called.

Immediately a head appeared over the top of the wall, and Dearborn jumped, startled. He was relieved to see that it was Raymond Reid. "What are you doing skulking in the bushes, Reid?"

"I dropped something," Reid muttered. "There it is." He swooped out of sight and reappeared holding a leather-covered flask. "Fell out of my pocket."

Dearborn crooked his finger. "I wish to speak with you."

Reid came around to the terrace steps. Dearborn noticed that his approach was oblique and that his eyes at close range were not well focused. "Reid, I want to ask you something. Have you ever heard Mr. Bright speak of the Rotten Apple Corps?" Dearborn was becoming more and more conscious of the odor emanating from Reid. Whiskey.

"Rotten apples?" Reid repeated. "Why would he talk about rotten apples?" Reid teetered as if the flagstones had suddenly shifted under his feet.

Dearborn put out a hand to steady him. So that was

27

it—the man was drunk. There was suddenly no point in talking with him.

"What about rotten apples?" Reid persisted.

A gust of wind ruffled Dearborn's hair and a spattering of raindrops bounced off Reid's polished head.

Dearborn sighed. "Forget it. I think we should go inside. I left my hat in there."

"Mr. Pinch?" Miss Garrett was standing in the doorway. "According to his itinerary, Mr. Bright is now en route to Wake Island. I don't know how you can reach him. He's due in Honolulu on August twenty-second. That's next week. There's a note that he'll call me to let me know what hotel he's in."

Dearborn pursed his lips. "I see. I shall call you Monday, then, and in the meantime if you hear from him give him my phone number and ask him to get in touch with me." Dearborn took out his card and handed it to her.

"You'd better get going," Miss Garrett said ungraciously. "It's starting to rain."

"I shall have to brave the elements. I told the taxi to meet me at the gate at six and it is almost that now."

Dearborn went back into the parlor and retrieved his hat and cane. He said good-bye and marched across the lawn toward the gate. Fruitless trip. Typical of Robert to put his affairs in the hands of a skittish young woman and an ineffectual inebriate. Amazing that Robert was able to stay in business, damned fool.

A billow of wind caught Dearborn head on and he leaned into it. A moment later there was a spark of lightning, a thunderclap, and another spate of driving rain. Dearborn tucked his cane under his arm, pulled his Panama low over his forehead, and broke into a sprint, only to pull up short partway down the path. He frowned and murmured aloud, "I wonder. I wonder." Then once again he broke into an energetic trot.

Five

"Mr. Pinch is asleep," Mrs. Woolley informed Benjamin. "He didn't get home until midnight. Didn't even eat supper." Mrs. Woolley tugged at the two strands of prune-sized blue beads that had slipped into the cleavage of her uniform.

Benjamin glanced at his watch. "It's after eleven."

"He doesn't want to be disturbed," Mrs. Woolley said firmly. She stopped fiddling with her beads and folded her arms. "He told me not to bother him."

"Suppose I go down the hall to his—"

"You know your father. He'll have kittens." Mrs. Woolley's red sausage curls bobbed ferociously.

"I'm used to it. I'll just—"

"No, sir! I'll get my head handed to me."

The dilemma was abruptly resolved. "Mrs. Woolley!" a voice shouted from the nether regions of the apartment. "Didn't you hear the bell? What hanky-panky are you up to out there?"

William Rhodes catapulted out of the library, scuttled down the hall, and disappeared through the swinging doors into the kitchen.

"What did I tell you?" Mrs. Woolley left Benjamin and rushed away. Benjamin stepped into the hall, closed the door, straightened his tie, and meandered toward the library.

"Stop!" Dearborn bore down on him, his red robe

flapping, the heels of his scuffs slapping, and his arms churning. "That is far enough, Benjamin."

"Good morning, Dad."

"Apparently I have failed to impress upon you the fact that I do not appreciate these spontaneous social calls."

"You won't talk to me on the phone."

"Straighten your tie."

Benjamin began to reach up and then dropped his hands. "Is everything all right? Mrs. Woolley said you were out all afternoon yesterday, that you didn't get home until midnight. Where were you?"

Dearborn paused in the midst of tying his bathrobe sash. "I'll tell you where I was!" he thundered. "I was locked in a passenger car of the Long Island Railroad, that's where I was."

"You were out on Long Island? What for?"

"None of your business. I spent hours parked on a trestle east of the Jamaica station. They refused to let us debark."

"What was it? A fire?"

"A mechanical failure. The doors wouldn't open. Have you ever seen how those fools operate the doors?"

Benjamin decided to plunge right in. "Dad, you weren't out at Robert Bright's Longevity Clinic, were you?"

Dearborn scowled at him. "Who told you that?"

"Otto. Otto told me you've been to see the police. He said you think a couple of people have been killed—Terence Van Horne, somebody named Arthur Howe, and a woman, Antoinette Ormacht."

"What's it to you?"

Benjamin said exasperatedly, "Dad, maybe you don't realize it, but the police are ready to escort you to the wacko ward."

"Nonsense. I'm as sane as you are. You've come here before breakfast to accuse me of being non compos?"

"*I* don't think you're crazy. As a matter of fact . . ."

A door in the back of the apartment slammed. Mrs. Woolley sailed down the hall. As she passed, Dearborn

30

cupped his hands around his mouth and shouted, "One soft-boiled egg, three minutes. And bring some apple butter."

Mrs. Woolley disappeared wordlessly into the kitchen.

Dearborn elbowed Benjamin out of the way and padded into the library. He went to a cabinet behind his desk, pulled out a telephone directory, and laid it on the desk. "Who is the president of the Long Island Railroad?"

Benjamin ambled into the room behind him. "Now quit it, Dad. Otto says that he got a special delivery letter from the phone company. They're not happy."

"Those dunderheads have dedicated themselves to my lifelong harassment!" Dearborn exploded.

"Okay, okay. Look, Dad, I went to Antoinette Ormacht's funeral . . ."

"What? Who told you to do that?"

"I was looking for you. You won't answer the telephone."

"I forbid you to interfere in my private affairs."

"I overheard the talk. They're convinced she was killed by a mugger. Her wristwatch was missing."

"But *not* her pocketbook, Benjamin. Someone could have intended to make it look like robbery."

"And panicked in the middle of setting it up. I know. I thought of that. I thought it was worth checking up on, so I took a run up to Westchester to check on Arthur Howe. I made a few inquiries. He didn't have any close relatives. His finances were in order. His death didn't have any mysterious elements to it. Cataracts, high blood pressure, dizzy spells. And talking about Van Horne being murdered is pretty heavy going. Still, I figured there must be some reason for you thinking the way you do—"

"Thank you."

"—so I cut over to Wide Rivers. I saw the police there. That is, I went to the police station."

"I could have told you not to waste your time. The police, prize asses that they are, think Terence met with an accident. I spoke with them myself."

"Yeah, but I didn't drop it at that."

31

"Mrs. Woolley!" Dearborn stamped toward the door and met William entering with the breakfast tray. "Where have you been?"

"In the kitchen, Mr. Pinch."

"You think I don't know what's going on out there? You're not so clever as you think."

"Come again?"

"No need for two cups. My son is leaving."

"Oh no I'm not." Benjamin rescued the cup. "What do you want? Cream? Sugar?" He poured the coffee and handed one of the cups to Dearborn. "Dad, what's the connection between those dead people?"

Dearborn didn't answer. He carried his cup back to the desk and began flipping the pages of the telephone directory.

"Were they friends? Business associates? Members of the same club?"

Dearborn hummed the first few notes of "Rhapsody in Blue" and Benjamin nodded to himself. "I drove out to the Van Horne house after I saw the Wide Rivers police. No one was there. Only the housekeeper. I told her I was an insurance investigator. According to the coroner's report, Van Horne took a heavy enough clout to kill a horse. I can't see an old man running fast enough to get up that kind of momentum. I looked around. One of the things I noticed was the croquet set. One of the mallets was missing. The ball was there—yellow striped—but the mallet was gone. It bothered me. I decided to search for it. I found it down near the front gate. It looked innocent enough, except it had no reason for being where I found it. I took it back to the police."

Dearborn was suddenly interested. "And?"

"They weren't impressed," Benjamin admitted. "Or at least they didn't want me to think they were. They wouldn't give me the satisfaction. I hope to hell they give it a good going-over."

"Let me understand you, Benjamin. You came here to tell me that you agree with me? That you think there has been foul play?"

"Possibly."

"In that case," Dearborn reasoned, circling the desk and pointing his finger at Benjamin, "you have nothing to worry about. Now that your mind is relieved you can leave the matter in my hands."

"Are you kidding?"

"There is nothing to concern you here, Benjamin. I am perfectly capable of handling the situation. With or without the police. Most certainly without you."

"The hell with that. I want more than that. I just told you I'm on your side!"

"When I require the services of a man who, at the age of thirty . . ."

"Thirty-two."

". . . . a graduate of Princeton, is still prancing around in his gym shorts—"

"I made a hell of a lot of money prancing around in my gym shorts!"

"What does that nincompoopery mean to me? As I say, when I need an overage adolescent to meddle in my affairs, I shall call on you. Now, if you don't mind, I have other things to attend to. Oh, and Benjamin, please tell Otto that at the first opportunity I wish to talk with him about legal responsibilities as they apply to public-service corporations."

After Benjamin left Dearborn leafed through his personal phone book and dialed a number. "Hello. Miss Wiley? This is Dearborn V. Pinch. I wish to speak with Dr. Moltke. This is an emergency. No ifs, ands, or buts." He waited. "Walter? Won't take up your time. You still a muckety-muck with the screwball set, are you? Fine. Fine. Well, now this is why I called . . ."

Fannie Tyler wasn't listed in the New York telephone directory and it took Dearborn a few hours to track her through Actor's Equity. It turned out that she lived in Englewood, New Jersey. Dearborn didn't intend to undertake another railroad journey, but he didn't want William, whom he suspected of being in cahoots with

Benjamin, to chauffeur him. He tried to borrow William's car, but William informed him that the car had a flat tire. Dearborn contented himself with commandeering William's driver's license.

"Are you sure you know how to drive, Mr. Pinch?" William had ventured nervously.

"You are treading on thin ice, William."

William's license described him as being fifty-eight years old, five foot nine, and gray-haired. The clerk at the auto rental office was polite but skeptical. "Do you have any additional identification, Mr. Rhodes?"

"I do not believe in credit cards," Dearborn replied. "I have no charge accounts and I left my voter registration card at home. What seems to be the problem, Miss . . . er . . ." He read the name on the nameplate. "Miss Menzel."

"Your height, for one thing. You seem taller than five foot nine."

"Five foot nine in stocking feet. That is correct. I wear lifts."

"And your hair?"

Dearborn noticed a poster on the wall suggesting that he support the performing arts. "I am currently playing Hamlet in a little theater production in . . . Nutley," he explained coolly.

He fixed her with a piercing glare, and she stumbled over the next question. "Mr. Rhodes, your driver's license lists you as being fifty . . ." She stole another glance at him and wilted.

"Well?"

"I . . . guess everything is in order. Will you sign here, please?"

Dearborn's foot numbed on the gas pedal and he stalled twice, once on the West Side Highway and once on the George Washington Bridge. But at noon he lurched into the outskirts of Englewood and drew up to a garage to ask directions.

"Cartman Avenue? That's over by Dwight Morrow

High School," the attendant told him. "Go north on Knickerbocker. Past the high school. Turn right at Cartman."

"There is some kind of clicking noise in here," Dearborn muttered irritably, peering at the variety of knobs facing him.

"You got on your directionals."

Dearborn pushed a button that sent a jet of water gushing over the windshield. The attendant reached in through the open window and shut off the directionals. "First Knickerbocker, then Dwight Morrow, then Cartman. Okay?"

"I am not a moron," Dearborn responded.

He drove so slowly up Knickerbocker Road that he stalled again. It was another twenty minutes before he turned onto Cartman Avenue. The house, number Four-sixty-one, had a silver birch in the front yard and window awnings. A woman in maid's uniform was sweeping the sidewalk. Dearborn parked the car and got out. "Is this the Tyler residence?"

The woman leaned on her broom and nodded.

"Is Mrs. Tyler at home?"

"Out back."

"Will you inform her that Dearborn V. Pinch has come to call."

"You can go around back if you want."

Dearborn tut-tutted but said nothing. No use making an issue of it. It was a repeat performance of Miss Garrett's rudeness at the Longevity Clinic. Disrespect seemed to be the order of things nowadays. He circled the house and saw a woman sitting at a card table inside the rear screened porch. She had her back to him.

"Fannie?" he called. "Fannie Tyler?"

She turned. "Who are you?"

"An old acquaintance. Dearborn V. Pinch."

She stretched out her neck and tilted her head to reduce the glare on the screening. "What?" she asked throatily. "Dearborn? What are you doing here?"

35

"Passing through. Thought I'd stop by and say hello."

"Passing through Englewood? Why should you be passing through Englewood?"

Dearborn was not prepared for the third degree. "I shall pass right out again if I am not asked in immediately."

"All right, then. Don't let in the flies."

Dearborn opened the screen door, hopped inside, and pulled the door shut behind him. Fannie stood up. Dearborn was momentarily taken aback. Fannie was wearing a blue silk peignoir and a rope of pearls. He had forgotten how tall she was—almost as tall as he. Her fingernails were long and red, her hair an electrifying canary yellow, and worn as she had always worn it—short and frizzed out at the sides, with bangs that tipped her eyebrows. But, Dearborn noted, there were deep pouches under her still-bright eyes, and the cigarette she held betrayed a slight palsy. She was no longer the imposing first lady of the stage. She was an old—yes, the word was cruel but apt—harridan.

"Time hasn't done you much good either," Fannie observed, responding to his shocked expression.

"We're both still alive, Fannie," Dearborn replied lamely, "which is a point in our favor." He glanced at the card table. It was covered with charts. An empty coffee can held colored pencils and a ruler. Four or five books were piled on a chaise lounge next to Fannie.

Fannie cocked her head. "Strange you coming here, Dearie. I was thinking about you. I read that Toni Ormacht was killed. I was remembering that you and she were lovers."

Dearborn hummed a bit. "That was a long time ago. I'm sure you are the only person who remembers it."

Fannie snorted, dropped her cigarette, and ground it out with the toe of her slipper. "There was a time when you were all that Toni talked about. After all, it was because of you that she and Eddie split up."

Dearborn straightened to his full height. "I do not

assume responsibility for that. I may have been reckless, but I was never a cad."

Fannie's laugh was raucous. "You're still all kinds of an ass, Dearie. Eddie took Toni to Portugal because of you. By the time she got back you had married that dreadful fan dancer and had a son by her."

Dearborn hummed again and tapped his cane on the floor. "Referring to my former wife as a fan dancer," he said finally, "is nothing short of rank, Fannie."

"Thats what she was, wasn't she? She certainly wasn't any Desdemona!"

"No healing old wounds, eh?" Dearborn picked up the books on the chaise lounge and transferred them to the floor. He looked at the titles: *Champion Jockeys*; an enormous tome of encyclopedic dimensions entitled *An Analysis of Thoroughbred Blood Lines*; and another smaller book, *The Harness Money*.

Fannie studied him with amused eyes. "That's right. I'm still the last of the big-time gamblers."

"So I see."

"I lost twenty-four thousand dollars on a horse in '37. Did you ever hear that story?"

"The Derby?"

Fannie nodded. "Pompoon to win. Can you imagine? Twenty-four thousand dollars on the nose. The smart money," she added wryly, "was on War Admiral."

"Speaking of losers," Dearborn said, "I hear that Terence Van Horne pulled the short straw last week."

Fannie nodded. "So I heard."

"Nasty accident. Fell into his swimming pool. Hit his head on the tiles . . . or at least that's what they say."

"I'd really rather not talk about it."

"Arthur Howe, too," Dearborn said.

"Arthur Howe what?"

"Arthur Howe is dead. He died a few weeks ago. Also an accident. Fell off his balcony."

Fannie frowned. "Toni, Terence, and Arthur?"

"Odd, isn't it?" Dearborn suggested cautiously.

"What do you mean?" She looked at him curiously.

"The Rotten Apples. That's what I mean."

"What do you know about the Rotten Apples?"

"Toni told me about the group," Dearborn said. "She came to see me before she was killed. She anticipated her death. She thought someone was going to kill her. She said she thought it had something to do with the Rotten Apples, that someone is bent on killing off the entire group."

Fannie reached for the back of her chair and guided herself to the seat. She sat down heavily. "Why did Toni think someone wants to kill us?"

Dearborn shook his head. "She didn't know why. I am trying to find out why."

"From me?" Fannie's voice rose to a high pitch. "Why from me?"

"From all of you," Dearborn returned shortly. "From all of you or from any one of you who might know the answer. That is, from those who still . . . remain."

Fannie looked at him with apprehension. "Who would even know about us? It was a secret group. No one has ever known about it . . . except . . . except . . ." Her eyes opened wide and her eyebrows disappeared under the frizzle of bangs. She lifted a trembling forefinger and pointed to Dearborn.

"Are you deranged, Fannie?"

She grabbed *An Analysis of Thoroughbred Blood Lines* and struggled to her feet. "If that's it, then go ahead." She thrust the heavy volume into Dearborn's hands. "Here. Here's the perfect weapon."

"You are starting to get my goat, Fannie. This is not a Wednesday matinee and I have no intention of playing Jacques Damala to your Sarah Bernhardt."

Fannie shrugged, put the book on the table, and sat down. "The point is," she said matter-of-factly, "that I do not wish to be killed."

"I accept that as a reasonable expression of your feelings. Now, if the performance has ended, perhaps we can get down to business."

"What *is* business?"

"Catching the murderer."

"How do we do that?"

"To begin with, I want you to concentrate on all the people you know or have ever known who might have learned about the Rotten Apples and who might, for one reason or another, rational or irrational, have developed a desire to see you dead."

Six

"The clinic is closed," the snappish voice rasped over the intercom. There was no opportunity to explain his business before the receiver clicked off. Benjamin rang again, quickly explaining that he was a Long Island Lighting Company inspector, and the gate lock clicked.

Benjamin pushed the gate open and went through. Once inside, he walked up the winding path toward the clinic, following a progression of wooden arrows nailed to every fifth or sixth tree. When he caught sight of Nadine Garrett, she was crouched next to a clump of bushes tugging at something.

"Just a second," she said irritably.

She was wearing a short-sleeved tennis dress; her blond hair was pinned by a barrette into a sloppy top-knot, a few loose tendrils clinging damply to her neck. She was, Benjamin noted appreciatively, extremely pretty.

"I'm looking for Robert Bright," he said.

"I thought you came to read the meter."

"Yeah, well, that wasn't exactly the truth."

"What is the truth, then?" She slipped off her sunglasses. Her eyes were green and cool under golden brown lashes. She kept pulling at the bushes.

"What's wrong in there?"

"My bracelet fell off. It's caught on a branch. Wait a minute—I've got it." She pulled the bracelet loose and examined it. "Damn. I broke the safety catch."

"That's what you get for wearing diamonds when you're greeting meter readers."

"Diamonds? Don't I wish." She shook the bracelet carelessly and shoved it into a pocket. "I'm Nadine Garrett, Mr. Bright's secretary. What's this all about?"

Benjamin thrust out his hand. "I'm Ben Pinch. Glad to meet you."

She ignored the hand and said impatiently, "The clinic's closed for the summer. You'd better come back in a couple of weeks." She ran speculative eyes over Benjamin, then repeated curiously, "Ben Pinch? You mean *the* Ben Pinch?"

Benjamin gave her his celebrity smile. "That's me."

"I read about you in *New York* magazine. One of the Big Apple's twenty most eligible bachelors. You look better in the flesh."

"You look pretty terrific in the flesh yourself," Benjamin returned.

"Thanks a lot. Now if you don't mind, I've things to do."

Benjamin tackled the subject directly. "My father was here yesterday. I'm trying to find out why."

"Your father? Who do you mean? That old man? Oh, Mr. Pinch. Of course. I didn't make the connection."

"Could you tell me what my father wanted?"

"Don't you know?"

"No."

"What difference does it make?"

"That's a little hard to explain," Benjamin told her.

"It's something personal. Couldn't you just tell me what he wanted?"

"Why should I? Ask him if you want to know."

"I'm not trying to put you on the spot. Maybe I could talk to Mr. Bright."

"Like I told your father, Mr. Bright's not here. He's away."

"Did my father mention any names to you?"

"What do you mean, names?"

"Arthur Howe? Terence Van Horne? Antoinette Ormacht?"

"No, he didn't."

Benjamin looked past her to a turn in the path. "Who's that?"

Raymond Reid ambled up to them. He scrutinized Benjamin from head to toe, taking in his poplin suit, cotton oxford shirt, and silk tie. "You're from Lilco?" he challenged.

Benjamin returned the scrutiny. The man, he thought, looked like a lush. He had the puckered, puffy-eyed look. "As a matter of fact, no."

"His name is Benjamin Pinch," Nadine Garrett said. "He's the son of that Mr. Pinch who was here the other afternoon. This is Raymond Reid, our health director."

"What's he want?"

"That's what I'm trying to find out."

"I guess I'd better lay it on the line," Benjamin said bluntly. "Three people have died during the last few weeks. They were all elderly. Two of them were supposedly killed in accidents. One was attacked by a mugger, or at least that's the police theory. My father's got some idea that their deaths are connected and that the deaths weren't accidental."

"What?" she exclaimed. "That's crazy!"

"My father went to the police. They weren't convinced, either."

"What are you talking about?" Reid burst out. "What

41

do you mean, three people were killed! What three people?"

"Their names are Arthur Howe, Terence Van Horne, and Antoinette Ormacht."

Reid grunted with astonishment.

"Do you know them?"

"I told you we don't know them," Nadine Garrett declared impatiently.

"*Do* you know them, Mr. Reid?" Benjamin persisted.

Reid reached into his pocket, fumbled around, and extracted a small, leather-covered flask. "Yes."

"What?" Miss Garrett shot out. "That's ridiculous! How could you know them?"

"Everybody knows who Terence Van Horne is," Reid muttered. He unscrewed the top of the flask, tilted it to his lips, and took a deep draught.

"But you don't know them personally," Benjamin said disappointedly.

"What have they got to do with Mr. Bright?" Miss Garrett interrupted.

"That's what I'm trying to figure out. I think it might have something to do with membership in some organization."

"Mr. Bright doesn't belong to any organizations."

"Murder," Reid said in an awe-struck voice.

"I know," Benjamin said. "It sounds far-fetched to me, too. But my father's obviously got some reason for thinking it."

"How did they die?" Reid asked thickly.

"Supposedly Arthur Howe fell off a balcony, Van Horne hit his head on the side of his swimming pool, and Mrs. Ormacht was killed by a mugger."

Reid shook his head and took another pull at his flask.

"The truth is that I'm afraid my father's gotten himself into deep water. But he won't tell me what's going on and I'm having a hell of a job trying to figure it out on my own. Right now Robert Bright is the only clue I've got."

"Would it make you feel any better if you could take a look at the files?" Miss Garrett suddenly asked.

42

"Would it be too much trouble?"

"What's the difference? You're going to say yes, aren't you?"

"I'd appreciate it."

"Raymond," she said, addressing herself to the unsteady Reid, "maybe you'd better come up to the kitchen and get some coffee."

"I don't want it," Reid muttered. He looked as though he were still trying to digest the information Benjamin had just given him.

Miss Garrett shrugged and gestured to Benjamin to follow her. They left Reid standing on the path, swaying back and forth and gazing blearily into space.

"He drinks too much," Miss Garrett commented superfluously when they were out of earshot.

"Is he always this bad?"

"Not always," she conceded, "but often enough."

"How come Bright keeps him on?"

"I haven't any idea, Mr. Pinch."

"Do you think you could call me by my given name?"

"Why not?" She led him into the clinic through the back entrance. The kitchen was big and desolate, with cold ovens and bare cupboards. The twenty-foot counter was swept clean, and the doors to one of the two restaurant-sized refrigerators stood open and empty.

"I grew up here," she said. "My mother was the housekeeper until she died a few years back."

"What about Bright?" Benjamin asked. "Is he married? He doesn't publicize his private life much."

"He's not married now. He was married. Four times, as a matter of fact."

"Pretty old geezer by now, isn't he?"

"Seventy-three."

"Doesn't sound like the liveliest person to work for."

"He pays well."

"Still," Benjamin insisted, "there's a big world outside those gates."

"I've been out," Nadine returned. "Two years in Europe. After my mother died. When the money ran

43

out, I came back. Look, the files are in the basement. Want to follow me?"

She led Benjamin into the hall, past a couple of rooms, one of which was marked Infirmary, to a glass elevator shaft. She pressed the button. From overhead they heard a noisy clanking and grinding. A moment later the elevator descended. It was an antique, its brass cage replete with bas-relief flowers and curling ivy. She opened the door and they got in. She pushed a button marked B. "I know what's in all the files for the last couple of years," she explained, "but there may be something in the pre-1971 files in the basement."

The elevator stopped. There was a ray of light hitting them from above, but the rest of the cellar was black. Nadine reached out to wave her hand. She contacted the light chain and yanked on it. Pale light flooded the hall from the single, dangling bulb.

Benjamin looked around. They were in a narrow hall that ran about twenty feet in either direction. There were two doors opposite one another in the hall to their left and an archway leading to a room on their right.

"What's in there?" Benjamin asked.

"Wine cellar. The files are over here in the recess." She led him to a row of four file cabinets. "One of these," she explained, "has all the permanent records. The other three go back ten years from 1971 to 1961. Every year we eliminate the earliest files." She opened a drawer labeled '70-'71 and began reading off the labels. "Accounts; client, household, personal; Corbett, Rubin, and Bonnell; Expenses." She took out the Expenses folder and looked through it. "Nothing here about any club or organization. It couldn't have been a club that collected dues. Let me take the folders one by one. Maybe there's a specific one."

Benjamin leaned over one of the file cabinets and watched as she flipped through the folders with practiced skill, finishing one drawer and patiently going on to the next. The whole procedure took about fifteen minutes. She finished with the top file drawer nearest to

Benjamin. "Advertising Promotion, Contracts, Registry Lists, Tax Information," she said.

"Did you say registry lists? Could we take a look at those?"

Nadine pulled out a folder and laid it on top of the file. "This is for 1960," she pointed out.

"Let's have a look." Benjamin ran his finger down the lists of names and addresses. "How about the other folders?"

One by one they went through the folders.

"What are you hoping to find?"

"Some connection between Bright and one of those people who were killed. Maybe one of them stayed at the clinic sometime or another."

But there was nothing to indicate that any of them had.

"Well, that's that," Nadine said when they had finished.

"Not really. I've got to keep on digging."

"Not here, I hope."

Benjamin smiled engagingly. "From my point of view that would be ideal."

She caught the tip of her finger in the drawer as she shoved it closed. "Damn!"

"You okay?"

"I broke a nail."

"Something I said?"

She pointed to the elevator and Benjamin got in. "I thought you might be getting ready to make a pass." She pulled the light cord and the cellar was once again enveloped in darkness.

"And you'd rather I didn't?"

"That's right."

"You're rejecting me hands down?" Benjamin asked solemnly. "Do you have any idea what rejection does to me?"

The elevator bounced to a stop on the first floor and Nadine squinted up at him. "You thrive on it?"

"Yup."

"I might have guessed."

Seven

On impulse Benjamin turned off the East Side Highway at Ninety-sixth Street and headed toward Park Avenue. It was probably useless, but he'd give it one more try. Maybe he could still persuade his father to open up.

By the time he got to Dearborn's apartment, it was after six. He ran into William coming out of the apartment door.

"Hold the elevator!" William shouted.

Benjamin turned back but the elevator door had already closed. "What's wrong?"

"He was in an accident!"

"Who? My father?"

William nodded excitedly.

"Was he hurt?"

"No. He's all right." William passed Benjamin, dashed to the elevator, and pressed the button. "I've got to get over there!"

"Where?"

"Englewood."

"Englewood? I don't get it."

William had a slip of paper clutched in one hand. He banged on the elevator button with the other. "He swore he could drive," William declared. "He took my license."

"Why didn't you drive him?"

"He suspects."

"That you're filling me in on what he's up to?"

"Spying," William said succinctly. "That's his word for it."

"But he's not hurt? You're sure?"

"He isn't hurt. She told me she put him on a bus to New York."

"Who the hell is *she*?"

William consulted the slip of paper. "Mrs. Fannie Tyler."

"Here, let me see that." Benjamin grabbed the piece of paper. "Mrs. Fannie Tyler, Four-sixty-one Cartman Avenue, Englewood."

The elevator arrived and the doors opened. The two men rushed inside. "Mr. Pinch was visiting her. Then he left and she heard a noise and ran outside. The car was up on somebody's lawn. He knocked over a mailbox. Then he backed up and crashed into somebody's stoop. He had my license. I'll probably get arrested."

"Where is he now?"

"She got her maid to drive him to the bus stop."

"He left the scene of the accident?" Benjamin asked incredulously.

"It's my license," William reminded him desperately. "I'm the one they're after!"

The doors opened and they tore through the lobby. "Wait a minute," Benjamin puffed, "how are you going to get there?"

"Bus."

"I'll drive you to the bus terminal."

"I knew it," William lamented as Benjamin guided him to the curb. "I knew it would end up with me going to jail."

On Friday Dearborn wasn't up to snuff. He hadn't yet revived from Thursday. First there had been the difficulty with Fannie. Then there was the disconcerting incident with the car. Then, to add insult to injury, there was the indignity of having to crouch on the floor of Fannie's Oldsmobile while the maid drove him to the bus station, and the irritating fact that when he had crossed paths with Rhodes in the bus terminal, Rhodes told him that Benjamin knew all.

It could have been worse. Rhodes had told the police his license and wallet had been stolen, and Dearborn had made it home and into his bedroom before Benjamin caught up with him. Nevertheless, it hadn't been one of his more successful days.

He reflected on his visit to Fannie. Fannie had said she could think of no one who might know about the Rotten Apples except for the Rotten Apples themselves. Her husband Hugh was dead. She had an uneasy but predictable relationship with her daughter and son-in-law. She said that she had never confided in any of her close friends; indeed, had insisted that she had no close friends.

Dearborn had made her take a pen and write down the names of all her gambling cronies past and present, people she'd disliked and people who disliked her, and then had waited while she crossed each name off the list. "Dead; lives in France; rich as Midas and over a hundred; dead; state governor; dead," and so on through that list and through the lists of her social acquaintances, her business contacts, and even her lovers. She had remained adamant. Her maid was a gem, her hairdresser too fastidious, her doctor a saint. She had never spoken to anyone about the Rotten Apples and she could think of no motive for anyone wanting to eliminate them. Dearborn was going to have to look for suspects in someone else's life.

So be it. Dearborn dressed at noon and set off at two-thirty for a visit to Vernon Tree. Tree had been listed in the telephone directory, and Dearborn had phoned before going there.

"Dearborn Pinch?" Vernon had exclaimed. "What do you want with me after all these years? Still alive, are you? Can't say I'm overjoyed to hear from you. I won't refuse, of course. Never let it be said that I'm a poor sport."

Lincolnside II was one half of a matched pair of concrete columns on the West Side a few blocks from Lincoln

Center. The circular drive led to a chrome and glass lobby carpeted with green indoor-outdoor carpeting. The doorman wore gold epaulets and space shoes.

"I am calling on Mr. Vernon Tree," Dearborn informed him. "Name's Pinch."

The doorman jammed a button on the phone panel, shouted into the receiver, "Juan, somebody for Tree," listened, then hung up. "He's in the health club."

"Where is that?"

"Down the hall to your left. There's a sign on the door."

Dearborn, swinging his cobra-head cane, proceeded down the corridor. At the end of the hall was a door marked Scandia Health Club. A blowzy woman sat at a desk just inside. She flashed a toothy smile. Her ample figure strained at the seams of her white uniform. Her black hair was arranged in an intricate knot, and she wore a plastic name tag like a single headlight on the bosom of her dress. She pointed to it. "I'm Sugar. Come on in. Do you have an appointment?"

"No, I do not. I am here to meet Mr. Vernon Tree."

"Well . . ." She glanced at the wall clock. "Mr. Bauer's late. I guess Goldie could take you."

"I do not wish to be taken. I am not a customer, Madame. If you will inform Mr. Tree that I'm here, that will be quite sufficient."

She snapped off her smile. "Mr. Tree should be done soon."

"I haven't all day."

Dearborn stood impatiently tapping his cane on the floor. He was just getting ready to charge the door to the inner sanctum when an old gentleman in gray, carrying a black cane and adjusting a hearing aid, emerged. "Dearborn?" he said in a feeble voice, "that you?"

"What?" Dearborn exclaimed absently. "Who are you?"

The gentleman stared hard at Dearborn. "It is you, isn't it?" he demanded in a tremolo.

"Vernon?" It couldn't be Vernon Tree. It was a

49

wizened caricature of the dapper Tree, the Lothario who had once, with the twitch of an eyebrow, set the ladies atwitter. The shrunken little man with the crumpled face was a travesty of the Vernon Tree Dearborn remembered.

"Dyeing your hair, I see, Dearborn," Vernon noted, proving his identity by a show of the old acerbity. "Why not? No harm in it. I couldn't see doing it myself . . ."

Dearborn fought to retain his sangfroid. "You're looking . . . good, Vernon."

"What did you say?" Vernon crackled, cupping his hand behind his ear.

"Good!" Dearborn repeated loudly.

"Thanks to Scandia," Vernon replied, winking lasciviously at Sugar. "Come. Shall we go upstairs?"

Vernon lived on the eleventh floor. He unlocked the door to his apartment and fluttered his hands at Dearborn. "Put your cane in the umbrella stand." He dropped his own cane an inch behind the stand and it clattered to the floor. He didn't bother to retrieve it. "Your stick's a nice wood, Dearborn. Where'd you find it?"

"Ceylon," Dearborn replied. "Hand carved. Impossible to duplicate."

"H'mm." Vernon eyed Dearborn's cane avariciously.

Dearborn noticed the look. Same old Vernon after all. As greedy as ever.

"What's this all about?" Vernon asked a few minutes later as he waved Dearborn to the couch and lowered himself carefully onto the other end. "You haven't dared show your face to me in the last thirty, thirty-five years."

"Dared?" Dearborn repeated. "I think 'cared' is the better word."

"Haven't seen one another since you made off with Jessamine."

"I didn't come here to discuss Jessamine."

"It was an underhanded trick, but you paid the piper, didn't you, Dearborn?"

"I am not interested in discussing a thirty-five-year-old romance."

"You're the only one would have married her."

"Nonsense."

"Eh? Speak up."

"I said that the last time I heard of Jessamine she was divorcing her fifth husband, which does not suggest that I was the only man who would marry her."

"I never married, you know," Vernon rattled on. "It always ends nastily. Divorce, alimony, custody proceedings. I saw a lot of it when I sat on the bench. Never made the mistake myself. I hear you have a son."

Dearborn acknowledged Benjamin with a stiff nod.

"Not much in the brains department, I hear. Professional ball player of some sort. Am I right?"

"He is a Princeton graduate," Dearborn replied through tight lips. "Summa cum laude."

"What's he doing playing ball?"

"Vernon, I am not here for social purposes."

Vernon's houseboy came in with two glasses and a bottle of brandy on a tray.

"Why are you here?"

"I am here," Dearborn stated flatly, "to talk about murder."

"Murder?"

The houseboy put down the tray and darted curious eyes at Dearborn.

"That's all, Juan." Juan scuttled away.

"Murder?" Vernon repeated in an unimpressed voice.

He and Dearborn were seated on a tufted couch in front of a teakwood coffee table. The room, a characterless box, had resisted the imposition of fleur-de-lis wallpaper, velvet draperies, and Persian rugs, and remained an L-shaped nonentity. Basically, Dearborn decided, Vernon was as unimaginative as ever. Even when it came to something like murder. "That's right," Dearborn said, "murder."

Vernon reached out to the coffee table and opened an ebony cigarette box.

"Do you know what I'm talking about?" Dearborn pressed.

"What?"

"I said, do you know what I'm talking about?"

"You're talking about murder," Vernon replied. "I have practiced law and I have served as a district court judge. I assure you that I am acquainted with the subject of murder. Do you want some brandy?"

"Vernon, I am talking about murder in a specific context."

"You are. Well, I wish you'd get on with it, then."

"Toni—Antoinette Dill—came to me before she died and asked me to help her."

Vernon leaned forward to cup his hand behind his ear. "To do what?"

"Help her!" Dearborn shouted. "She was convinced that the Rotten Apples were being murdered—*are* being murdered—one by one."

"What rotten apples?"

"Damn it, Vernon! I'm talking about *the* Rotten Apples. Toni believed that the group was being victimized—*is* being victimized! Arthur Howe and Terence Van Horne were already dead when she came to me. Arthur went off a balcony; Terence was killed by a blow to the head. Now all three are dead. Toni was struck down by someone who tried to pass himself off as a mugger. And all within a week of one another!"

Vernon tried to insert his cigarette into an ivory holder he had pulled out of his pocket. He couldn't get the end of the cigarette and the end of the holder to meet. He made a few delicate stabs and then tried ramming them together.

"Here. Give me that!" Dearborn took the cigarette and the holder and connected them.

Vernon leaned back against the couch cushion. "Who told you about the Rotten Apples?"

"Toni." Dearborn didn't take his eyes off Vernon's face, and Vernon returned his gaze with calm unconcern. "Well?" Dearborn asked.

"Well what?"

"What do you make of the situation?"

Vernon exhaled a long, narrow stream of smoke. "Nothing."

"Look here. You don't seem impressed by what I'm telling you. Toni and Arthur and Terence were murdered."

"Eh?"

"I said," Dearborn yelled, "murdered! Murdered!"

"Says who?"

"Never mind who. The point is that you may be in danger and I'm trying to help you."

"What?"

"Vernon, turn up that blasted receiver!"

Vernon opened his jacket and fiddled with the mechanism pinned to his shirt front. "Can I offer you some brandy, Dearborn?" Crackling sounds issued from under his tie.

"As a member of that disgusting social club, you are inextricably tied into this intrigue." Dearborn was beginning to suspect that Vernon might be playing the fool deliberately. "Is there anyone you know who might be mixed up in this? Can you think of anyone unbalanced enough to commit murder? Can you give me a list of the names of people you've talked to over the years about the Rotten Apples?"

"What for?" Vernon asked. "No one has tried to kill me. Here I am, hale and hearty as ever."

Dearborn hummed a little. Vernon had certainly cultivated self-deception to a fine point. "You mean to say that there is no one who might wish you and the others dead?"

"There may be people who, from time to time, have wished me dead. It wouldn't surprise me if you were one of them, Dearborn. But I never told anyone about the Rotten Apples. It's not something I'd talk about. As a matter of fact, during the last forty years, you're the first outsider who has ever mentioned it in my presence. The thought that a deranged person would want to kill off the Rotten Apples is preposterous."

"Preposterous? Toni, Terence, and Arthur are dead

within a week of one another and you call that preposterous?"

"I must be honest, Dearborn. I have always looked on you as slightly preposterous. Your behavior is as outlandish as ever. Anyone who would go so far as to marry a belly dancer just to show up a rival—"

Dearborn was incensed. "Vernon, you are a half-wit! Are you going to continue this stupid verbal duel or are you going to listen to reason?"

"I am not in any danger," Vernon insisted. "And frankly, I have no intention of casting my lot with yours no matter what the adventure."

Dearborn felt his face redden. He took his card case from his pocket, extracted a card, and slapped it down on the coffee table. Then got up from the couch and stalked to the front door. "If you change your mind you know where you can find me." He opened the door, started out, then pushed his head back in to shout, "Watch out, Vernon, or you may be the next victim!" He left, slamming the door behind him.

Vernon's houseboy came out into the hall. "Anything wrong, Mr. Tree?"

"Not at all, Juan."

Vernon cackled wickedly and shook a forefinger at the door. "Forgot your cane, Dearborn. Too bad, isn't it? You know what I say: finders keepers."

54

Eight

Stella Gresham lived in Riverdale. Dearborn got the address from the American Kennel Club records, and on Saturday afternoon William, flat tire repaired, drove him there. Stella's house was built on a cliff overlooking the Hudson, the grounds sloping steeply down to a narrow private road. Closed iron gates protected the driveway, and a sign on one of the two stone pillars that flanked the entrance read The Highlands.

"Stop here, Rhodes. Pull over and wait. And confound it, stop behaving in that idiotic hangdog fashion."

William had been moping ever since the Englewood incident. He handled the car lethargically, drawing up to the side of the road so gradually that they were ten yards beyond the gates before the car stopped.

Dearborn got out of the car, slammed the door, and poked his head back through the open window. "I do not like cranky people, Rhodes, snap out of it!"

He marched away from the car swinging his second best cane, a Malacca, and used it to push his way through one of the iron gates. An asphalt walk ran parallel to the driveway, and Dearborn could see, straight ahead, a square, three-storied, white-brick house with a balustraded roof. As he approached, he heard a medley of barks and looked around, trying to locate the dogs. He saw nothing but an unadorned lawn stretching away to the stone walls that bordered the grounds. He discovered the source of the barks when he rang the doorbell. The yelps intensified, and some of them turned into growls.

"Stop that, Clydie. Dundee Boy, get down. Macduff, mind your manners."

The door opened and Dearborn found himself facing a crowd of Scottish terriers. In their midst was a long-limbed woman wearing baggy dungarees and a paint-stained workshirt. Her short, white hair was cut into a Dutch bob, and she had a leathery, outdoor face, pleasant and healthy-looking. Except for the sparkling emerald ring on her finger, she looked like a simple farm woman.

"Stella?" Dearborn inquired.

"Dearie," she said immediately. "Dearie Pinch."

"You recognized me, eh?"

"Of course. Why shouldn't I? As a matter of fact, I picked up an old *Life* magazine a few weeks back and saw a picture of you and your son in it. Taken ages ago, of course. It was something about your son. He's a baseball player or a football player or some such, isn't he?"

"Some such," Dearborn admitted.

A fierce little terrier leaped forward to nip at Dearborn's shoe.

"Miss Dee, stop it! Come in, Dearie. They won't bother you."

Dearborn eyed the dogs warily. One of them snarled and Dearborn poked at it with his cane.

"Whoosh!" Stella cried, waving her hands. The dogs, sliding and tumbling, spilled rowdily into the adjoining rooms. "Come into the kitchen." She headed for the back of the house. Dearborn, describing a wide arc with his cane, peered into the rooms on either side of the hall as he followed. Everything was a shambles. The living room furniture was raggedy. There were pillows on the floor and an overturned lamp. The dining room table was thick with dust, and the library rug was polka-dotted with saucer-sized stains.

Stella pushed open a swinging door and held it for

Dearborn. She came in after him and closed the door quickly before any of the scotties could slip through. Two rows of identical aluminum bowls rested on a large butcher-block table in the center of the room. An enamel basin on the table was piled high with ground hamburger.

"Who is in charge of these beasts?"

"I am, of course. Here, sit down." She pulled out a kitchen chair and held it for him. The seat was covered with crumbs. Dearborn shook his head. "Is there no kennel master? No handyman? Is there no houseman?"

"Men? Why men? Why should a man be more capable of handling the dogs? Or the house?"

"Good lord, Stella, do you keep those animals here in the house with you?"

"No. At least not all of them, at once. I'm painting the kennels this week. As soon as I've finished I'll put the dogs back out."

"*You* are painting the kennels?"

"Haven't you heard? We women are quite capable of handling a paintbrush, Dearie."

"Don't tell me you're one of those women's libbers, Stella. At your age?"

"Age has nothing to do with it. It's a question of pride and self-respect. It just so happens I'm president of the local chapter of NOW."

"If you don't mind, Stella, I'm not in the mood to discuss women's rights. That's not why I'm here."

"Why are you here, Dearie? Want to buy a scottie? Nobody else wants to. It's a sheep-dog market this year." As she spoke, she unbuttoned her shirt sleeves, rolled them up, and began scooping lumps of hamburger out of the enamel basin and into the aluminum bowls.

"I am here because of Toni Ormacht. She charged me with an unpleasant but necessary task, and although I declined the request initially—"

"Toni? How is Toni? Last time I saw her was on a visit from Portugal in—let me see—'61, I think it was. Came in

57

to get her varicose veins fixed. Ran into her quite by chance at the hospital. I was there for a gallbladder operation."

"You are unaware of the fact that Toni is dead?"

Stella's hamburger-filled hand paused in mid-air. "Dead? I had no idea. When did she die?"

"Last Monday. She was killed."

"Killed? What do you mean by killed, Dearie?"

"She was accosted on a street in Manhattan, knocked over the head, and robbed."

"Oh, no."

Dearborn pulled a handkerchief out of his breast pocket, flicked the crumbs off the chair, and perched himself gingerly on the edge of the seat. He rested his weight on the tortoiseshell cane between his knees. "She's not the only one who has died in the last month. Arthur Howe and Terence Van Horne are dead, too—Arthur off a balcony, Terence into his pool."

Stella was holding the fistful of hamburger and staring at him.

"Stella, why don't you take off that ridiculous ring while you're fishing around in the chopmeat?"

"I can't. I haven't been able to pry it off in eight years. I guess I've put on some weight."

"You see, Stella," Dearborn went on, averting his eyes from the hamburger, "Toni came to me and told me about the Rotten Apples. In strictest confidence, of course. She said she thought the Rotten Apples are being victimized by some person, who has it in for the members. A few days after she visited me, Toni herself was killed. Three so-called accidents within a month—too many to be coincidental."

Stella looked at the lump of hamburger she was holding, put it into one of the empty bowls, and wiped her hands on her dungarees. She strode to the counter and opened a drawer. It was filled with small kitchen implements, scraps of paper, balls of twine. She rummaged around in the drawer until she found what she was looking for. "Here. Look at this." She handed him a scrap of cloth. "I was at the vet's with Lady Doon last night. She was vomiting and walking strangely. I was afraid it might be leptospirosis. I took her down about ten o'clock. I got back at one. I found that on the floor when I came into the house. It was near the window in the living room."

Dearborn examined it. It was a ragged scrap of cotton fabric, yellow-and-red plaid. "Part of a shirttail," he murmured. "You can see the hem is rounded."

"Yes," Stella concurred. "That's what I think."

"Someone was in your house."

"Yes. The window was open. A vase had been knocked over. The dogs were in a frenzy. The flower bed in front was trampled."

"You didn't call the police?"

"No. I wasn't thinking about murder, Dearie. And I figured no sneak thief is going to bother with this place twice."

Dearborn tucked the swatch into his breast pocket. "You're in danger, Stella. It might be wise to call the police."

"No, Dearie. No. I wouldn't do that."

"Because of that asinine group?"

"I would have to admit too much. I won't do it."

"You are being very foolish." He waved the piece of cloth in front of her. "Contrary to what you believe, the intruder is very apt to return."

"Dearie, have you contacted any of the others? Have there been any other incidents?"

"I saw Fannie. She had nothing to tell me—no suspicious people lurking around, no near-accidents. Kept insisting that no one she's ever known could be responsible for the attacks. She doesn't want any publicity. Won't consider calling in the police. Afraid of what may come out."

"I suppose Toni told you about the qualifications for becoming a Rotten Apple?"

"She did."

"I'm surprised."

"Under the circumstances, it was necessary."

59

Stella nodded resignedly. "Then you know what we're hiding?"

"Fannie fixed a horse race, didn't she?"

"Not *a* race. *The* race. In '31, or was it '32 or '33? I can't recall. Fortunes were made and lost on that race. Billy Bottoms killed himself."

"Good-for-nothing that he was," Dearborn murmured. He drummed his fingertips on the tabletop. "I tried to see Robert Bright. He is out of the country. I shall contact him next week. I succeeded in interviewing Vernon Tree."

"I'm sure he was no more eager for publicity than Fannie," Stella said. "Or me, for that matter. Do you have any idea how many Bests in Show I've taken over the years? If it ever got out that I had . . . well, I'd rather not be reminded of it, Dearie. I did something terrible. I'll never forgive myself for it . . ."

"It's ridiculous. That happened almost half a century ago. There is a statute of limitations."

"Not to scandal, Dearie. And it was so . . . so . . . demeaning."

"Everybody knows you can't hold a woman responsible for everything she does."

"Dearie!"

"All right, all right. This is no time to take offense. Can you think of anyone who might wish to kill you?"

She shook her head. "No, not really."

"As I understand it," Dearborn went on, "there are five Rotten Apples remaining now that Arthur, Terence, and Toni are . . . gone."

"Yes. Louise Cotton is dead," Stella mused. "And who else? Who were the others?"

"Jack Rogers."

"Oh, yes. Jack Rogers, the surgeon. He disappeared after that mess concerning Caroline Ambeil's operation. I see very few of the old crowd," Stella went on. "I have my dogs and my work for the cause. That's enough. Times have been a little difficult these last few years. I'm not so well off as I was. I haven't spoken about or even

60

thought about the Rotten Apples in years. That's a closed chapter; something I'm not proud of, that I've tried to forget. I wouldn't like it dredged up now."

Dearborn took out his card case, removed a card, and laid it on the table. "Stella, give it some thought. Call if anything occurs to you. In the meantime I suggest that you protect yourself. Get someone to stay here with you. Do not open the door to strangers. Keep your front gates locked. And above all, give me your word that you will not mention anything about this piece of fabric you found."

"I promise. What do you intend to do next, Dearie?"

"I'm going to visit Dolly Fairchild and James Bell," Dearborn answered. "See if they've got anything worthwhile to offer."

He rose and pushed on the swinging door. Two wet, black noses slipped into the breech. Dearborn, holding his cane like a billiard cue, popped one black nose back out through the crack in the door. The second disappeared before he could take aim. "I am equal to most challenges," he offered calmly. "Not easily intimidated. I shall speak with you soon, Stella." So saying, he disappeared through the door amidst a chorus of yelps.

"I don't know what you're talking about, Mr. Pinch. Murder? It sounds like *Eight for Strychnine*, a lurid little play I did in '42. I played a fortune teller. Not a bad part. Unfortunately, the director was totally inept."

Benjamin was frustrated. He'd arrived at Fannie Tyler's at ten in the morning. It was now eleven-fifteen and he didn't know any more than he had an hour before. "Mrs. Tyler, if my father didn't come here to discuss a threat to your life, can you tell me why he *was* here?"

Fannie lifted her hands and spread her long fingers supplicatingly. "You tell me, darling. He said something about passing through Englewood."

Benjamin knew she was lying. During the last forty minutes she hadn't left off fussing with the soft silk tie of her peignoir. "Mrs. Tyler, have you ever heard of Arthur

61

Howe or Terence Van Horne or Antoinette Ormacht?"

"I was acquainted with them at one time or another through the years."

"Did they have any special relationship to you?"

"What do you mean?"

"I mean did you share something in common? Did all of you belong to a particular group?"

Fannie pursed her lips. "Not that I can recall."

"I'm laying my cards on the table. My father claims that those three people were murdered."

"How perfectly mad."

"I'm not so sure. They all died within a short span of time. My father thinks their deaths are connected. If he's right then they must have been involved in something—a scandal, a crime, some sort of provocative activity. A shady deal, maybe. And from the way my father has been dogging it all over town, I've got a feeling those three aren't the only ones involved."

"It sounds very sinister."

"He went to see Robert Bright last week. Do you know Robert Bright?"

Fannie, resplendent in her peach lace peignoir, reclined on a love seat upholstered in red velvet. "Robert Bright?" she answered vaguely. "Oh, yes. He runs that clinic for the elderly, doesn't he?"

"Is that all you know about him?"

"I've met him once or twice."

Benjamin wasn't getting anywhere. "I'm afraid you may be in danger. My father, too."

"Why your father? He's not one of the group."

"What?"

Fannie got pink. "That is, didn't you say . . . I mean, I thought I understood . . ."

"What group, Mrs. Tyler?"

She was annoyed with herself for having let it slip. "Mr. Pinch, I'm not going to talk to you any further. It's obvious that your father hasn't confided in you and I don't see any reason why I should."

62

"My father doesn't have much faith in me, I admit. At least so far. But I'm working on him."

"You remind me of Jessamine," Fannie shot out suddenly. "Not in looks. In some other indefinable way."

"You know my mother?"

"I did once. She was a beauty."

"She still is," Benjamin found himself drawn to say.

"Your father adored her. She hurt him terribly, though. When he was courting her she used to drive him to distraction by breaking engagements with him to see other men, especially that deplorable Vernon Tree..."

"Yes, well, Mrs. Tyler—"

"... Vernon Tree and your father despised one another. Then after your father and Jessamine married, she ran off a couple of times without so much as a by-your-leave, not that anyone would expect a by-your-leave for adultery..." Fannie drew in her breath. "Oh, I'm sorry. How tactless of me."

Benjamin realized that Fannie was purposefully diverting him. "Mrs. Tyler..."

"You don't look anything like her," said Fannie. "You're the spitting image of Dearborn. Same nose. Same black hair. Same mouth. Lucky, too. Dearborn was very bitter toward Jessamine after she left."

"Mrs. Tyler—"

"But he did adore her. We thought it so odd. I mean, wanting to have an affair was one thing. But he actually married her..." Fannie bit her lip. "Oh my, I didn't mean—"

"Mrs. Tyler, it'll help if you'd stop pretending you don't know what I'm talking about."

Fannie sighed and suddenly dropped her hands into her lap. "If it will make it any easier, I'll tell you that this situation doesn't really involve your father. He isn't in any danger. Beyond that I have nothing to say."

Benjamin realized that she would never relent. At least he had learned there was a group and that Fannie Tyler was part of it. Armed with that, he might be able to confront his father and persuade him to talk. He nodded resignedly. "If you change your mind, will you call me?"

She uncurled from the couch. "You're a nice young man. I hope I didn't say anything to hurt your feelings." She patted his arm solicitously. "Tell Dearborn I was asking for him. Tell him I said you don't look anything like Jessamine."

Nine

Dearborn wanted his best cane. He had called Vernon five times and each time Vernon's houseboy had told him Vernon was out. Nothing was left but for Dearborn to storm Vernon's apartment and take his cane by force.

But first he had to see Dolly Fairchild. He hurried through his morning exercises. Mrs. Woolley, in pink, with a string of yellow enamel daisies, arrived with the breakfast tray at eight-thirty.

"Mr. Rothschild called. He wants you to call him back. The note's on the tray."

"No time, Mrs. Woolley. I have an appointment." Dearborn scanned the contents of the tray. "On the other hand, there is time to have breakfast." He leered at Mrs. Woolley. "Care to join me? A succulent fruit, a morsel of sweet bun? An interlude of . . . social intercourse?"

"Two policemen were here before."

"What? This morning? Why?"

"They didn't say. They wanted you and they were

rude. So I told them you were away for the weekend."

"Exactly right, Mrs. Woolley."

"You'd think they'd remember you didn't contribute to whatever it is they were collecting for last year."

"H'mm. Collecting? Yes indeed. I suppose that was it. Mrs. Woolley, there's enough coffee here for two . . ."

Mrs. Woolley headed for the door. "The exterminator's due at nine-thirty. I haven't made out the grocery list and Ralph's coming up from the basement to unstick the window in the living room. I've no time for foolish talk." She left, enamel daisies and sausage curls bouncing.

"Peculiar woman," Dearborn mused in her wake. "Can't figure her out."

The brownstone on Eleventh Street was easy to locate. The door was opened by a butler, a long-faced, sober gentleman in dark trousers and an alpaca jacket. "I'll inform Mrs. Fairchild of your arrival."

The hall was paneled in dark oak. The intricately inlaid parquet floor glowed. There was a mahogany hall chair with a gilt-framed mirror hanging over it, and on the opposite wall a John Singer Sargent. Dearborn squinted at the brass nameplate tacked to its lower frame: Abigail Honore Fairchild. 1887-1959.

The butler returned. "May I show you into the library, Mr. Pinch? Mrs. Fairchild will join you."

Dearborn followed the butler into the Victorian library and occupied himself by perusing a set of old photographs on the wall until a whirring sound behind him made him turn. It was an electric wheelchair steered by an old woman in silk lounging pajamas and a matching silk head scarf. Tendrils of wispy white hair, like pulled threads, stuck out from under the scarf. "Dearie. Dearie Pinch."

"Hello, Dolly. How good of you to receive me."

"How are you, Dearie? How long has it been?" She glided to the couch. There was a sewing basket and a half-finished quilt lying on one of the cushions. She picked up the quilt and extracted a threaded needle from the sewing basket. "I'm a little nervous, Dearie. I feel better when I'm sewing. I hope you don't think it's impolite."

"Not at all."

"I'm not so well able to cope as I once was . . ."

"Go right ahead, Dolly."

She poked the needle into the fabric of the quilt and began stitching. "Your phone call truly set me off. I've been recalling the old times, Dearie. Thinking about what a gallant you were, back when that sort of thing was in fashion."

"That sort of thing, as you put it, was never in fashion. If it were, I never should have practiced it."

"Do you remember the time you bought out all the seats at the Bayliss Theater on Thirty-second Street," Dolly went on reminiscently, "so that Jassamine could perform Desdemona?"

Dearborn hummed a little snatch of something under his breath. "Vaguely. Only vaguely."

"She was beautiful. Fannie Tyler was green with envy. Positively furious. Remember? I think at the time Fannie was between plays and, what's more to the point, between lovers."

"Dolly, the reason I've come—"

"I know why you've come, Dearie. But do you remember *Othello*?"

"I've all but forgotten the episode," Dearborn insisted.

"You even brought in the press. They weren't kind. But then critics never are."

"You say you know why I've come?"

"You've come about the murders."

Dearborn was astonished. "You know about them?"

Dolly's voice was suddenly unsteady. "Stella Gresham called me right after you did."

"She did? What did she say?"

"She told me everything. Arthur, Terence, Toni. Everything."

"About her, too?"

"What do you mean, Dearie?"

"Did she say anything had happened to her?"

"She said that someone broke into her house. That her dogs chased away an intruder and that it might have something to do with the murders."

"That's all? Nothing about clues or evidence or anything of that nature?"

"You're confusing me, Dearie."

Dearborn patted his breast pocket containing the piece of yellow-and-red plaid. "You realize, Dolly, how urgent it is that you—all of you—determine who is responsible and take steps to see that he is stopped before—"

"Oh Dearie, please! Don't say it." She took three or four nervous stitches without looking up.

Dearborn frowned. "Stella didn't tell me that you and she are friendly. As a matter of fact, she led me to believe that she travels in a very different crowd these days."

"We haven't seen one another in twenty years. She called because she wanted to know whether or not I would agree to call in the police once you proposed it."

"And?"

The doorbell rang.

"Hilton?" Dolly called. Her voice carried no further than the end of her arm, but Hilton appeared in the doorway almost immediately.

"Yes, Madame." He went to the front door, and a moment later voices mumbled in the hall. Hilton reappeared, leading a rotund little gentleman in a straw boater.

"Where is he?" the gentleman demanded, ignoring Dolly and advancing on Dearborn. "Ah, there you are. Have you seen the morning *Times*?"

"Who are you?" Dearborn demanded.

"Why, he's Jimmy," Dolly declared. "Jimmy Bell. I took the liberty of calling him and telling him you were coming."

"Have you seen the morning *Times*?" Jimmy Bell repeated.

"No," Dearborn replied. "Why?"

" 'That flesh is but the glass, which holds the dust that measures all our time, which also shall be crumbled into dust.' "

"What are you saying, Jimmy?" Dolly asked diffidently. "You're trying to tell us something."

"Take hold of yourself, Dolly," Jimmy cautioned.

"Don't keep us in suspense!"

"All right, then. Here it goes. Vernon Tree is kaput. Finished. Through. In a word, dead."

"Dead, you say?" Dearborn declared. "When? Where?"

"Do you have the paper, Dolly?" James asked.

"I don't read the paper. You know that. It's too upsetting. But I can send Hilton for a copy."

"I'm sure James can tell us what the paper says," Dearborn suggested.

James swept off his hat, dislodging the Byronesque toupee underneath. Dolly wriggled her finger at his head and he reached up to set it right. Resting his weight on one leg and thrusting the other forward, he declaimed, " 'Here is my journey's end, here is my butt and very sea mark of my utmost sail.' " He turned to Dearborn and held out his hand. "How are you, Dearborn? Haven't seen you since I moved to Hartford. Must be twenty, twenty-five years. How long has it been, Dolly? I keep a suite at the Pierre. Get in fairly often."

"Yes, yes," Dearborn acknowledged shortly. "Now what about Vernon?"

"Apparently Vernon was accosted by someone in the hallway of his apartment building last night, struck over the head, and tossed onto a stair landing. His body was discovered at about ten last evening."

"How terrible," Dolly whispered. "How perfectly awful."

"They have a lead," James said. "They didn't name names but it seems that Vernon had a visitor the day before and that his houseboy overheard the visitor threaten to kill him."

"A visitor?" Dearborn reflected interestedly.

"A gentleman," James replied. "Elderly. Not an intruder."

"I think I will send Hilton for the paper, after all," Dolly said. She set her wheelchair in motion, rolled out of the room, and disappeared down the hall.

Dearborn and James sized one another up. "Well, Dearborn," James said finally, "I'm not sure why you allowed yourself to get involved in this, but I must admit that I'm glad you are. I remember how you handled the Juanita Froebel incident. It might have been the scandal of the decade."

"It seems to me," commented Dearborn drily, "that while your trust in me is justified, your concern is misplaced."

"What does that mean?"

"Three—pardon me—four of your group have been, shall we say, dispatched. The remaining five are in imminent danger. Yet none of you is as interested in the possibility of being killed as you are in avoiding scandal. What good is a sterling name to a corpse?"

" 'Nothing can we call our own but death, and that small model of the barren earth which serves as paste and cover to our bones.' Marked for extinction and for no reason that we comprehend."

"You are begging the issue, James. You are more concerned about being embarrassed than about being killed."

James lowered his plump buttocks onto the other end of the couch. "We've kept our secrets well. To have them exposed would be more than a humiliation; it would be a disgrace. All the more so because of who we are and what we have become. My own crime was not so grave as to have any legal consequences now, but I would ..." James examined his polished pink nails, "I would become an object of ridicule. I *am* senior editor of *Poesy Personified*; not an illustrious position, perhaps, but one which I cherish. I was a member of the voting committee for the National Poetry Plaudits last year. I was—"

69

"You have made your point," Dearborn interrupted.

"I sent for the paper," Dolly informed them, gliding back into the room.

"For forty years," Dearborn said, "your group has kept its secrets. For forty years there has been no hint of scandal, no attempts at extortion, no leaks to the press. If it weren't for Toni coming to me, I wouldn't have known anything myself, and yet Toni and I were once . . . ahem . . ."

"Sweethearts," Dolly supplied. She leaned forward to lay a gentle hand on James's arm.

"There is some catalyst at work," Dearborn went on, "some factor relevant to the group that makes you vulnerable where you were not vulnerable before. The motive for killing the members lies in an alteration of the dormant character of the group."

"I don't understand," Dolly said.

"He means, my dear, that something we did or said back then may be having repercussions now," James explained. "Although I fail to see how people we offended forty years ago would still harbor a grudge."

"I think we must look for a practical motive," Dearborn said. "Self-protection, or personal gain, perhaps. Before we explore the possibilities, I must discuss again the advisability of calling in the police. After all, I am not a professional inves—"

"No," Dolly exclaimed. "Not the police!"

"Not to put too fine a point on it, Dolly," Dearborn reminded her, "it may come down to your reputation or your life." He rose from the couch and rocked back and forth on his heels absentmindedly for a moment. "So long as we're being candid, I wonder if it is merely protection from the past that interests you. Are you certain there is nothing else you are interested in protecting?"

"Whatever do you mean, Dearie?" Dolly asked.

Dearborn tried to put it delicately. "You and James seem to, er, know one another rather well. That is to say, I wonder if you are afraid that your friendship might be in jeopardy?"

"Now see here," James returned, "I am a married man. I am not at liberty, no matter what my inclinations, to form any romantic attachments." He reached out to pat Dolly's hand.

Dolly began tucking stray wisps of hair up under her silk head scarf. She had become very pink in the face.

"Think what you wish," James went on. "Whether our decision meets with your approval or not, we are determined to have this affair—"

"Situation," Dolly corrected.

". . . this situation kept confidential. If you refuse to help us, then we shall go it alone."

Dearborn sighed resignedly. He nodded, took his seat, and stretched his long legs out in front of him. "All right, then. Discretion it is. At whatever cost."

Ten

Whoever was on the other end of the telephone wire wouldn't give up. Benjamin rolled over and slid his head under the pillow. It muffled the ring of the telephone but it also inhibited his breathing. He rolled back and lunged for the receiver. "Hello!"

Otto's hoarse voice came over the wire. "Ben? Where's your father?"

Benjamin sat up and swung his feet to the floor. "What do you mean, where's my father?"

"He's not there? The police didn't call you?"

"What the hell are you talking about?"

"What's he doing to me, Ben? Now the cops are after him."

"What are you talking about?"

"Another murder," Otto declared. "Some old geezer over on the West Side. Somebody bashed him over the head and threw him down a flight of stairs. The cops have an idea your father knows something about it."

Benjamin was conscious of aching eyelids and a dull band of pain over his eyebrows. "Who was it you talked with, Otto?"

"Lieutenant Niccoli. Down at Homicide. The one your father went to see about that Ormacht woman. He just called me. The cops went to the apartment. Mrs. Woolley told them your father's away for the weekend."

"Is he?"

"No. He's there but he won't talk to me." Otto sounded desperate. "Ben, you'd better call Niccoli and straighten this out. I'll be in the office all day if you need me."

"Why should I need you?"

"To arrange bail."

Whatever color Benjamin had in his face drained away. "Wait a minute, Otto. Start again."

"According to them, your father visited this guy, Vernon Tree, on Friday. The houseboy says they had an argument and your father threatened to kill him."

"Vernon Tree?" Benjamin pressed his fingers against his eyelids. "Where have I heard that name?"

"A judge. A former judge," Otto said. "I remember him."

Fannie Tyler's words came back to Benjamin. "*Vernon Tree and your father despised one another.*" Benjamin groaned.

"What's wrong?"

"Nothing. I'll call Niccoli. I'll keep in touch."

Benjamin made it downtown by twelve-thirty and was once again ushered into Lieutenant Niccoli's office. Niccoli needed a haircut. He also looked like he needed some sleep. He directed Benjamin to a chair next to his desk, poured two cups of coffee out of a dented coffee pot into two styrofoam containers, and handed him one. "Milk?"

"Black is fine."

"Where were you?" Lieutenant Niccoli asked. "I sent a man over there about three this morning."

"I didn't get home until four."

"You jocks lead a hell of a life."

"So they tell me."

"Anyway, about your father. You know where he is?"

"I don't know any more than you do, Lieutenant. As a matter of fact, I know a lot less. Otto Rothschild said you think my father's mixed up in the death of someone named Vernon Tree."

"Ever heard of him?"

"No," Benjamin lied.

"You don't know your father's whereabouts?"

"No. And I'm not going to try to figure it out until you tell me what you think he's done."

Lieutenant Niccoli rested one thick ankle on the opposite knee. "Judge Tree was killed last night. The super of his building found his body on a stair landing a little after ten. The coroner said he probably died about nine-thirty. His houseboy said he went out to eat about six. The doorman said he came back about twenty past nine. He took the elevator upstairs to his apartment on the eleventh floor. But he never went into his apartment. Whoever killed him cornered him in the hall."

"It wasn't robbery?"

"No way. He had his wallet on him and he was wearing a ring and a wristwatch. He was lying on the weapon. A black cane with a cobra-head handle."

Benjamin put down his coffee container carefully. Even so, a little of the coffee sloshed over the edge.

"Your father was carrying that cane when he came down here to visit me last week."

Benjamin wasn't aware of saying anything, but he must have made some sound.

"Sorry, Mr. Pinch. But that's it. We've taken prints.

There's blood on the handle. The shape of the handle fits the wound. Juan García, the houseboy, made an official statement. Here it is." Niccoli handed Benjamin a sheet of paper.

Benjamin read it reluctantly. Old man, black hair, black cane with cobra-head handle, talk of murder, last words a threat.

"There are a lot of old men with black hair—"

"And canes with snake heads for handles?" Niccoli reached out to the desk and flipped over a card. "He left this at the apartment when he visited Tree."

Benjamin didn't touch it. He could see it from where he sat: the name Dearborn V. Pinch engraved in black on a thick, cream-colored rectangle.

"Lieutenant," Benjamin argued, "my father called on you for help. Why would he have come to you if he were involved?"

"Oldest story in the world," Lieutenant Niccoli assured him. "He wanted to get noticed. He's an old man. No one pays any attention to him. His son is famous. Probably never has time to visit him—"

"Nothing could be further from the truth. If you knew my father—"

"Come on, Mr. Pinch. I appreciate your feelings. I got a father myself. I know how I'd feel if the old coot flipped out. But facts are facts. Now I'm telling you we got to get him off the streets before he . . ." Lieutenant Niccoli squinted at a crack in the ceiling. Benjamin realized he was trying to put it tactfully. "We got to get him off the streets before he, well, hell, you know!"

"Yeah, I know."

"Don't get sore. We're looking to you for help. Do you think you could find him?"

Benjamin got up and headed for the door. "I'll try."

"I knew you'd cooperate. Believe me, it's the only thing to do. Want me to send a man with you?"

"No thanks," Benjamin said drily. "I'll handle it alone."

* * *

It wasn't until Hilton brought back the paper and Dearborn read the account of the murder firsthand that he realized whom the police suspected.

"What's the matter, Dearborn?" James asked. "You look positively bilious."

"There has been a misunderstanding," Dearborn muttered. "The police seem to think that I am somehow mixed up in this business."

"Why should they?" Dolly asked.

"I visited Vernon on Friday. That is a matter of record. We had words. That is a matter of record. I absent-mindedly left without my cane. Vernon, as I suspected, appropriated it. And the murderer, with what was for him a remarkable stroke of luck, utilized it."

"How ghastly!" Dolly exclaimed.

"It seems that I am a hunted man. They are probably watching the airports and the train and bus depots by now. I can't return to my apartment. I can't even risk checking into a hotel."

"You can stay with me," Dolly offered. "I have a guest room. No one would think of looking for you here."

"Thank you, Dolly," Dearborn replied. "It would be unwise. The police, incompetent though they are, might find out about it and accuse you of being an accomplice."

"He's right, Dolly," James said.

"You could disguise yourself," Dolly suggested tentatively. "Bleach your hair. Wear a false moustache."

Dearborn shook his head. "I'm afraid even those idiots might see through a disguise."

"Not every disguise," Dolly persisted. "You might dress as a woman."

"Or wear a uniform," said James.

Dearborn strode to the library door and peered out into the hall. "Your man, Hilton. How tall is he?"

"About six feet, I think."

"A possible solution," Dearborn said. "Do you think you could prevail upon him to cooperate, Dolly?"

"Marvelous. Yes, of course." Dolly put down her quilt-

75

ing, pushed the starter button on her wheelchair, and rolled out of the room.

"I must find a base of operation," Dearborn mused. "As soon as I leave, I want you to call Fannie and Stella and tell them again to take all precautions. Tell them not to leave their homes. Tell them not to answer the door but to wait to hear from me. We will observe the utmost precaution. As soon as I am settled, I will contact you. Is that clear?"

"Perfectly."

Dolly returned with Hilton, who was willing to help perpetrate "a small practical joke on an unsuspecting friend." Dearborn soon learned that a sharp schism separated Hilton's business and private lives. His taste in dress ran to flowered sports shirts, bell-bottomed trousers, and yellow-checked jockey caps. The only item that promised anything near inconspicuousness was Hilton's goggles, which hid half of Dearborn's face.

"You look like Baron von Richtofen," James commented when Dearborn returned to the parlor.

"You look splendid," Dolly said. "Very . . . what is the word? Oh yes. Distingué."

They sent him off with pats on the back and promises to remain at the ready. "Simply give us the signal if you need us," James instructed.

"Any hour of the day or night," Dolly added.

It wasn't so bad on Eighth Street, but walking uptown Dearborn felt foolish beyond measure. He fervently hoped that none of his neighbors would recognize him. The closer he got to his block, the more tense he became.

He stopped at the newsstand nearest his building. Hector ("The Hound") Toole, impresario of the establishment, peered at him warily. "What you got on there, Mr. Pinch? You look crazy."

"Never mind how I look, Toole. I need your assistance."

"What do you want this time?"

Dearborn waited until a passing customer paid for his

76

newspaper and walked away. "I want a place to stay for a few days."

"Sure. What's the matter? Had a fight with your son?"

Dearborn scowled at him. "My personal affairs needn't concern you, Toole. I am calling on you because I thought you would be the least likely person to require an explanation."

"Why? Because I been in jail? I'm sorry I ever told you that. First you asked me to tail your lawyer. Then you tried to get me to steal somebody's phonograph . . ."

"A justifiable measure, I assure you."

"Then you wanted me to sabotage Burger King. I come to this country thirty years ago. Since I left Liverpool I been straight. What do you want from my life? You seen too many movie pictures."

"I need a place to stay, Toole."

"How much?"

"What would you consider a fair price?"

Hector cocked his head and studied Dearborn out of half-closed eyes. "A C-note."

"Twenty-five dollars," Dearborn bargained.

"Fifty."

Dearborn nodded. "Agreed."

Dearborn glanced up and down the street. "I shall return in half an hour. If anyone should ask about me, say you know nothing."

Dearborn thought it best to enter his building through the service entrance. He passed under the canopy, keeping his head averted from George, the doorman, and loitered near the corner of the building, pretending to tie his shoe. Once he knew the coast was clear, he slipped into the alley and through the service door.

There were two garden apartments on the ground level. Dearborn heard a swishing sound coming from the laundry room to his right and paused at the angle of the hall to peer at the laundry-room door. A string mop swished back and forth across the floor, passing in and out of his field of vision with metronomic regularity. The pail, resting in a puddle of soapy water, was outside the

77

door, and Dearborn tiptoed quickly to the elevator, praying that the car was not somewhere on an upper floor.

He pushed the button and raised his head to read the floor indicator. The car was on the second floor and moving downward. He heard it stop above him in the lobby and then start down again. When the doors opened he leaped inside. Dearborn's apartment was on the sixteenth floor. He didn't know if the police had posted lookouts in the hall, and it seemed wisest to take the last three flights—there was no thirteenth floor—on foot. He pushed the twelfth-floor button and held his forefinger against it until the doors closed.

When he arrived at the twelfth floor, he peered out of the elevator before stepping into the hall. Since there were only four apartments on each floor, he'd be hard put to explain his presence if he were to run into any of the twelfth-floor tenants—especially, he thought, decked out in Hilton's Sunday best. He slipped out of the elevator and crossed to the glass-doored emergency exit opposite. Behind him the elevator descended.

Dearborn pushed open the door and began tiptoeing up the cement stairs. He looked through the glass door on the fourteenth floor. The hall was empty, but he could see, from the elevator indicator, that the elevator was once again on its way up. He waited to see where it stopped. The arrow circled the dial—nine, ten, eleven, twelve. It reached fourteen and kept going. Dearborn looked through the rectangular window in the elevator door as it passed, but he couldn't see any passengers.

The elevator stopped on the fifteenth floor. Dearborn waited and watched. After a moment the elevator started down. He pulled his watch out of Hilton's trousers' pocket. Three thirty-five. Probably Alberta Ryland, coming home from school. In another two or three minutes the Ryland stereo speakers would begin blasting. Pity Hector had refused to cooperate with Dearborn. He could have made himself considerably richer by relieving the Rylands of that diabolical piece of equipment.

Dearborn moved stealthily upward. When he reached

the fifteenth floor, he noticed that the foyer door was closing. He glanced at it in time to see it slip quietly into place. Alberta must have given it a casual push while she was waiting for the housekeeper to answer her ring. Dearborn looked through the door at the elevator indicator. The elevator was at the lobby level. He started up the last flight of stairs.

A quarter of the way up, he stopped. He heard something, a faint, shuffling sound, out of place in the empty stairwell. He peered upward, but the stairs turned and he couldn't see the sixteenth-floor landing. He strained to catch another sound but heard nothing. He stood with his hand on the bannister, one toe on the next step up. He took another step and stopped to listen. Nothing. But he had a sharp impression that he wasn't alone. Someone, standing as still as he, breathing as shallowly, was on the stairs above him.

The police? Dearborn didn't wait to find out. He began to back down the stairs, then miscalculated the width of the step behind him and tripped. Over the sound of his near-fall, he heard another sound, an indrawn breath. He turned and ran. Above him he heard the sound of feet pounding down the steps behind him. It was difficult to see in the dim hallway, especially through the tinted sunglasses, but Dearborn squinted through the fifteenth-floor door at the elevator indicator as he streaked past. It was on the fifth floor and moving upward. He kept going. Halfway down to the fourteenth-floor landing he tripped again and, without stopping, pulled off the sunglasses and threw them against the wall.

At the fourteenth-floor landing Dearborn saw that the elevator was passing the eleventh floor. If only he could stop it as it reached the twelfth. But there wasn't time. Dearborn was out of breath and his pursuer was on the fifteenth-floor landing right behind him.

He jerked open the glass door on fourteen and threw himself into the foyer. He was trembling from the exertion and leaned his full weight against the door and looked hopelessly at the elevator indicator. The elevator

79

had already stopped on twelve and was once again on its way down.

"Why, Mr. Pinch? Is something the matter? My, who was that?"

Miss Helen La Motte, fourteen A, had come out of her apartment, stopped short, and was staring in consternation first at Dearborn and then at the glass door behind him.

"What was what?" Dearborn gasped.

"Somebody just went by."

"Where?"

"Behind you. Somebody ran down the stairs."

Dearborn's legs were unsteady. Only the presence of Miss La Motte kept him from sliding to the floor.

"Are you all right, Mr. Pinch?"

"Male or female?" Dearborn wheezed.

"I don't know. Just a person. Probably little Alberta Ryland, now that I think of it. Mr. Pinch, are you sure there's nothing wrong?"

Dearborn shook his head and attempted a weak smile. "Not at all."

Miss La Motte looked dubious. She eyed Dearborn's clothes curiously.

"I'm just on my way to the basement," Dearborn improvised.

Miss La Motte raised her eyebrows.

"To get my bicycle."

She nodded.

"To go for a ride in the park."

"Oh?"

"Exercise, Miss La Motte. Nothing like it. Nothing better for keeping in trim." Dearborn straightened up, tested his knees, and made the shaky crossing to the elevator.

Eleven

Benjamin and Otto spent the afternoon checking Dearborn's contacts, then spoke with one another at four.

"We've got to get him to turn himself in, Ben," Otto insisted. "They'll get him sooner or later and it'll look a lot better if he goes in under his own steam."

"I talked with Mrs. Woolley," Ben said. "She swears he was home Sunday evening. She'll alibi him. Still, it's her word against the evidence."

"First we've got to find him. Then we can talk alibis. What about his doctor?"

"Nothing. Did you call his banks?"

"He hasn't been near any of them," Otto said. "Did you check the NYAC?"

"The Athletic Club, the Harvard Club, Uncle Matthew, his friend Abbott Noble . . ."

"I hit the hotels, fourteen of them, his insurance broker, and Mimi Olmster."

"Who the hell is Mimi Olmster?"

"You know. The old broad who wanted to sue him for alienation last year."

"He wouldn't be *there*, for Christ's sake!" Benjamin said.

Benjamin wasn't able to reach Fannie Tyler until evening.

"No, I have not heard from him since he was here. I have my own problems. Creme de Cliquot. Beautiful miler. Five-horse race. Inside position. Beaten by a neck."

"What?" Benjamin asked in a mystified voice. "Creamed what?"

"As for Dearborn, who knows where he is or what he's up to. Certainly not I."

When the thought of the Longevity Clinic first occurred to Benjamin, he rejected it. His immediate reaction had been that Dearborn wouldn't return to the clinic with Bright away. It wasn't until early evening, after Benjamin had exhausted every other possibility, that he reconsidered. Robert Bright could have returned or Dearborn could have decided to go there and wait for him. The clinic had its advantages. Dearborn, on the basis of his friendship and concern for Bright, could probably talk Nadine Garrett and Raymond Reid into letting him stay there, and it certainly was an ideal hideout.

Benjamin ate a quick ham sandwich, changed into chinos, sneakers, and a denim shirt, and snapped on his automatic answering device. It was a fortunate accident that he glanced out his window before he left. He hadn't had much practical experience with the police, but he recognized one of the two men lounging against the hood of an old Chevy across the street. He had seen the man down at Homicide. He took the elevator to the basement, then tipped his garage man two dollars to drive his Ferrari around the block and leave it while he escaped through the basement door. He climbed over the fence that separated the courtyard of his building from the one that backed on it and emerged on the next block a few yards from the spot where his car was parked.

By eight o'clock he was in Islip and by eight-fifteen he was standing in front of the Longevity Clinic gate. "Here goes nothing," he murmured. He pushed the intercom button.

Nadine's voice, slightly apprehensive, answered. "Yes? Who's there?"

"Nadine?"

"Who is this?"

"Ben Pinch."

"Ben Pinch? What are you doing here?"

"I have to see you."

There was silence at the other end. Then the gate clicked open.

If the place was dismal during the daytime, Benjamin thought, it was even more so at night. The path was narrow and sloped upward, winding through and around overgrown bushes and trees that were badly in need of pruning and that brushed against Benjamin's head and shoulders as he walked under them. When he reached the front stoop, the door opened and Nadine stepped outside.

"Hello, Ben. I didn't expect you back so soon."

She was wearing white slacks and a V-necked white silk blouse and looked, Benjamin noted appreciatively, as beautiful as he'd anticipated.

"Come in." She led him down the hall to a small room with a sign on the door saying Private.

"This is the employees' lounge. Right now, except for Raymond and me, there isn't anyone here."

"Who runs the switchboard? What do you do about phone calls?"

"When everyone's away we plug in some of the switchboard cords so the calls come and go direct."

Nadine sat down yogi-fashion at one end of a long couch facing the unlit fireplace. She pushed aside the newspaper and reached out to turn off the television set. "You want a drink? The liquor cabinet's behind you, in the bookcase."

Benjamin shook his head and sat down next to her. "Where's what's his name?"

"Upstairs. Why?"

"Nobody else around?"

She cocked her head curiously. "Mr. Bright's still away, if that's what you mean."

"That's not what I mean." Benjamin nodded toward the paper. "Is that today's paper?"

"Yes. Want to see it?"

"No. I want you to. Page twelve."

Nadine picked up the paper and flipped through it. "What in particular? 'Student Wounded in Riot'? 'Nassau Realtor Indicted for Payoffs'? 'Former District Court Judge Found Murdered'?"

"That's the one. Former District et cetera."

Benjamin studied her face as she read. There was no change of expression. "Am I supposed to know him?" she asked when she'd finished.

"It might help if you did. But it's not the victim you should notice. It's the suspect."

Nadine scanned the article. "A tall, elderly man with black hair . . . a walking stick matching the description of the murder weapon . . . an ebony cane with a cobra-head handle." She frowned and shook her head. "I don't know anybody like that."

Benjamin said flatly, "It's my father."

"Your father?" She crumpled the paper in her lap. "You're joking!"

"What's that?" The voice came from behind them. They turned to look over the back of the couch. Raymond Reid was standing in the doorway. "You still looking for your father?"

Benjamin nodded.

Reid crossed to the liquor cabinet and took out a bottle of Scotch.

"You don't know where he is?" Nadine pressed.

"I was hoping you might."

She regarded Benjamin uncomprehendingly.

Benjamin shrugged. "I thought he might have come here. I knew he wanted to see Bright."

"But I told you that Mr. Bright's away."

"I know. I thought my father would figure this as a good hiding place anyway."

"Why?"

"It's out of the way. He could wait for Bright here."

Reid had poured himself a drink. He didn't seem as

84

drunk as he had the first time Benjamin saw him, but, Benjamin judged by the half-full tumbler, he was on his way.

"Hiding place?" Reid repeated harshly. "What are you talking about?"

"There's been another murder, a man named Vernon Tree."

"Vernon Tree!" Reid exclaimed in a shocked voice.

"You know him?" Benjamin asked.

Reid rattled the ice cubes in his glass. "I heard of him. A judge."

Nadine shifted her attention from Reid to Benjamin. "It isn't true, is it?"

"Of course not."

The phone rang suddenly. It was resting on a bookcase shelf behind Reid, and he turned and picked up the receiver. "Yes," he said. "This is the Longevity Clinic. No, he's not here. Who?" Reid fixed Benjamin with a surprised look. "Yes. I do know who Dearborn V. Pinch is. Who is this?"

Benjamin got up. He went to the phone and took it out of Reid's hand. "Who is this?"

"Stella Gresham," the voice answered. "Who is this?"

"My name is Benjamin Pinch."

"Oh, yes. I know who you are. Dolly Fairchild called me. She told me what happened. The murder. Vernon Tree. Has your father shown up there?" Her voice was sharp with anxiety.

"No," Benjamin replied cautiously. "Does . . . er . . ." He tried to make it sound as if he'd heard of her. "Does Dolly Fairchild have any idea where he is?"

"I called Dearie's apartment after I spoke with Dolly. The housekeeper said he's not there. It wasn't until Dolly called me that I knew what was going on."

Benjamin suppressed his inclination to shout, "What is going on!" Instead he grunted noncommittally.

"Frankly, I'm not happy about staying here after what happened to Vernon. There are only five of us left now

85

—Dolly, Bobby Bright, Fannie, James Bell, and me. I'm simply too frightened to stay. I know it's what Dearie wants but . . ."

"Fannie?" Benjamin remarked. "You mean Fannie Tyler?"

"Yes, of course."

"Have you called the police?"

She caught her breath. "No. Of course not. None of us wants that. Not until we know what that maniac is after."

Benjamin reached up to rub his forehead. His head was aching again. "Do you think I could talk to you face to face? Where do you live?"

"Riverdale. The Highlands Kennels."

"Look, maybe I could come over there."

"I'm not staying. I don't care what Dearie advises. I'm getting out. I was trying to reach Dearie to tell him that. I called someone to stay with the dogs and I'm leaving."

"Where will you go?"

Her voice was strained. "I'm not sure. Just tell Dearie I've gone, will you?"

"Miss Gresham, if you run out on my father now, he may wind up in jail."

"Dearie will be all right."

"He's got the whole damned homicide squad after him."

"I'm packing now. I'll be leaving first thing in the morning. Tell Dearie I'm sorry. I know he'll understand." Stella hung up.

Benjamin held the receiver for a moment longer, then replaced it in its cradle.

"Who was that?" Nadine asked.

"Another one of the infamous group," said Benjamin. "Woman by the name of Stella Gresham. She says she's running away. She heard about Vernon Tree. She just told me there are five people mixed up in this. Her, somebody named Dolly Fairchild, a guy named James something or other, Robert Bright, and Fannie Tyler."

"I heard you say the name Fannie Tyler to her as if you knew the woman," Nadine noted.

86

"Yeah, I did meet her. A lot of good it did me. She's as closemouthed as my father."

"What about your father?" Nadine asked. "What are you going to do to help him?"

"You tell me. There are five people here who may be knocked off any minute. And one old man who's got a murder charge hanging over his head. What am I supposed to do about any of it?"

Reid had finished his drink and was pouring himself another. "Bring them all here," he suggested in a thick voice.

Nadine gasped, "Here? Oh no!"

"What good would that do?" Benjamin returned.

"For one thing," Reid said, "there's safety in numbers. For another, the clinic's out of the way. You said so yourself. Your father's probably going to show up here anyway."

"We can't be sure of that."

"You came here on the strength of it, didn't you? And that Gresham woman called here looking for him."

"There's no guarantee."

"Make sure, then," Reid declared. "Let him know everybody else is here and he'll come, too."

"How?" Nadine asked.

"I *could* call the housekeeper," Benjamin said, playing with the idea. "If he calls home, Mrs. Woolley will let him know that we're all here. Besides, didn't you say Dad told you he'd be in touch with you this week, Nadine?"

"How will you persuade those people to come here?" Nadine asked. "They won't come. Not unless your father tells them to come."

Reid was still thinking all right, but his speech was becoming more and more slurred. "Simple," he said. "Call that woman back and tell her your father is on his way here. Say you just spoke to him."

"And the others? I could call Fannie Tyler, but I don't know where to reach the others."

"She can call them—this Miss Gresham."

Nadine got up and walked over to Benjamin. "I don't

mean to be a spoilsport, but what about Raymond and me? What's going to happen to us? What have we got to do with this mess?"

Benjamin regarded them both thoughtfully. "You're right. How can I let you get involved in it?"

"We're already involved," Reid broke in.

"I don't see that," Benjamin interrupted.

"Mr. Bright's involved, and we work for him."

"It's not the same," Benjamin argued. "Look, the police are swarming all over my apartment building . . ."

"They are?" Nadine asked in a stunned voice. "I had no idea . . ."

"Which only goes to show you how hairy the setup could be."

"Wait," Nadine said, holding up her hand. "Let me think a minute." She stared into space sorting out her thoughts, then said with sudden resolve, "Raymond's right. We've got to clear things up before Mr. Bright gets back. If anything happens to him, we'll never forgive ourselves."

"If I hadn't come here, you'd never have known."

"You did come."

Benjamin nodded. It was true; it was too late for any of them to turn back. "I'm still not convinced," he said. "I admit the plan has its advantages . . . but suppose we get that bunch down here and then my father doesn't show?"

"What's the alternative?" Reid asked. "What's your next move?"

Benjamin shrugged. "God only knows."

"It's settled," Nadine said firmly. She picked up the phone and handed it to Benjamin. "For better or worse, we're in it together now."

Twelve

"Otto?"

"Where are you?"

"Don't ask."

"Why?"

"The police are watching my apartment."

"So where are you?"

"They can't make you tell what you don't know, Otto. I managed to sneak out last night, but I'm going to have to stay put for a few days, at least until I straighten out this mess."

"By this mess," Otto said sarcastically, "I assume you're talking about your old man?"

"I've thought of a couple of things. The first one's personal. I've got a date tomorrow night that I can't keep. Caroline Gilman, Plaza Hotel. Have Miss Simon call, will you?"

"You're passing up a date with Caroline Gilman, Hollywood's hottest property since Marilyn Monroe? You're in hiding, all right."

"Have Miss Simon call her, will you?"

"And that's another thing. You're either going to have to start paying half Simon's salary or get your own secretary."

"My father rented a car last week. I'm wondering if he might have done it again . . ."

"With whose license?"

"You don't think he could get hold of one?"

"I'll check the rental agencies," Otto agreed. "And listen, I got a call from Mrs. Woolley. She says a guy named Hector called the apartment this morning. He told her your father wanted to rent his pad and he was trying to find him to give him the keys."

"Come again?"

"Your father wanted to rent his pad."

"When?"

"Yesterday afternoon. Your father said he was going home to get some money. He was supposed to be right back but he never showed."

"Right back where?"

"Search me. I don't know who Hector is. Neither does Mrs. Woolley. All she could tell me was that he had a hoarse voice and a trace of an accent. Maybe Cockney."

"Cockney?" Benjamin repeated the name. "Hector? That's all she gave you? Just Hector?"

"That's all."

"Look, Otto, you'd better find him."

"Find him?" Otto declared incredulously. "Now I'm supposed to run around town looking for a hoarse-voiced Cockney named Hector?"

"Somebody's got to do it and I sure as hell can't. I'll call you first chance I get. In the meantime, see what you can dig up. Okay?"

"Shit."

"Okay?"

"Okay."

Stella Gresham arrived first. She called from the front gate to explain that she had driven and that her car was parked in the road. Raymond Reid, hung over but resolutely sober, went down to direct her around back to the garage. They had no sooner walked into the house than the intercom jangled and Reid left again to drive the golf cart down to the front gate for Dolly Fairchild and James Bell.

Benjamin and Nadine ushered Stella into the parlor.

90

Benjamin was surprised by her. He had expected a fragile old lady. Instead she turned out to be almost as tall as he, thin and vigorous, with lively eyes and a quick, broad smile. She was dressed in faded dungarees; work boots; a jersey pullover; a small, floppy, cotton cap; and wore a very large emerald ring. She was carrying a leather pouch shoulderbag and a small leather overnight case.

"Is he here?" she asked without preliminary. "Did he get here yet?"

"No, not yet," Benjamin answered cautiously. "Soon, I hope. Miss Gresham, I'm Benjamin Pinch and this is Nadine Garrett, Robert Bright's secretary."

"Mr. Pinch. Miss Garrett." Stella cocked her head and studied Benjamin's face. "You look like Dearie, you know. You must be about the same age now as he was the last time I saw him. Thirty? Thirty-one?"

"Thirty-two," Benjamin acknowledged.

"That's about right, I guess. And Miss Garrett. Tell me, where is Bobby? Mr. Bright, I mean. Mr. Reid said that he's away."

"Yes," Nadine replied. "On a vacation trip."

"What about the others? I got tied up on the West Side Highway or I'd have been here at nine. I normally get up at six. This morning I outdid myself and got up at five-thirty."

"Stella. Stella Gresham!" The voice was soft but it carried. Dolly Fairchild, ensconced in her wheelchair and holding a carpetbag from which protruded a corner of her patchwork quilt, motored into the room. Behind her were Reid and James Bell, jaunty in a blue blazer, white flannel slacks, and a straw boater.

"Stella," Dolly cooed, "we're delighted to see you. Aren't we, Jimmy? You remember Jimmy, don't you? And this must be Dearborn's son. There's no mistaking the resemblance."

"Where's Bobby?" James asked.

Nadine explained.

"And Dearie?" Dolly inquired.

"He'll be here soon," Benjamin reassured her.

"I hope so. We were very dubious about sending him off yesterday, especially in that outrageous costume."

Benjamin was caught off-guard. "Sending him off?" he echoed. "Sending him off where?"

Dolly frowned. "To wherever he is, of course. Wherever he ended up. Where *is* he, by the way?"

Benjamin pulled himself together. "On his way. In transit. He'll be here anytime now."

"I suppose no one guessed it was Dearie in that cap or in those sunglasses. But I was worried about hoodlums. I'm not sure Dearie is well equipped to deal with street types."

"And we forgot to ask him if he needed money," James interrupted. "If he's anything like me he doesn't travel around the city with much cash in his pocket. Of course, there are always credit cards."

"He doesn't carry credit cards," Benjamin said gloomily. "Says it's a form of usury."

"He'll be fine," Stella put in reassuringly.

"I wonder where the other lady is?" Nadine murmured. "Mrs. Tyler, is it?"

"Wants to make a grand entrance, I expect," Stella said.

Dolly nodded. "Fannie is always the actress."

"Not the final word in talent, Dolly," James added.

"But with all the trappings, Jimmy. Temperament, ambition, showmanship. I remember Louise Cotton once telling me she'd give her eyeteeth for a fraction of Fannie's style, and you know how truly talented Louise was."

"Louise Cotton, the opera star?" Benjamin asked. "You knew her?"

"She was a Rotten Apple," Stella replied. "She'd be here today if she were alive. Remember, Jimmy? She set the fire that killed William Kirland's child."

"Be fair, Stella," Dolly chided. "Louise was in a jealous rage and she never meant to hurt the child."

"But she did set the fire."

"And Fannie did fix the Kentucky Derby," James chimed in.

"Was it the Kentucky Derby, Jimmy?"

"Maybe not, come to think of it. I can't recall. It was one of the big ones, though."

Benjamin was trying desperately to relate what they were saying to their predicament. There was obviously a connection somewhere.

"The point is," Dolly was saying quietly, "that none of us was lily pure. If we had been we wouldn't have been members of the Rotten Apple Corps."

"Or," Dolly finished, "dumped into this pretty kettle of fish."

"Robert's was mail fraud, wasn't it?" Stella reminisced.

"No, not that," James corrected. "It was a con game. Selling phony shares in something or other."

Stella nodded. "I remember that Toni was mixed up in some kind of graft. An unethical real-estate deal."

James nodded. "And remember Jack Rogers? He was the only one who didn't get away with it. Lost his medical license."

"Do you think we should be talking about these things?" Dolly asked. "I suspect they're better off forgotten."

"Vernon actually committed a crime to get into the group," Stella went on, ignoring Dolly's reticence. "What about you, Dolly? For the life of me I can't remember what you did. I remember that Arthur Howe molested women in elevators and that Terence was a bigamist . . ."

"I prefer not to talk about my past," Dolly said in a prim voice.

"To think how we women have allowed ourselves to be exploited," Stella sighed. "You did a little borrowing from some obscure Elizabethan poet, didn't you, Jimmy?"

James puffed out his chest. "The whim of a moment," he defended. "A childish indulgence. A question of sheer prankishness. A good deal less violent than poisoning helpless animals." He scratched his head, dislodging his toupee. Dolly pointed to his head and he reached up to adjust his coiffure.

Stella shrugged. "I'm afraid we were a spoiled and useless lot."

Dolly sighed, pushed the starter on the arm of her wheelchair, and rolled to the front window. James followed and stood behind her solicitously.

Benjamin had listened to the conversation with the concentration of a United Nations interpreter. The Rotten Apple Corps was, he gathered, a club as well as a character profile. This knowledge didn't explain why anyone would want to kill the members—though it did explain why they weren't anxious to call in the police. And why, collectively, they were looking so down in the mouth.

"Good heavens," Dolly murmured. "Is that Fannie?"

Both Dolly and James were staring intently out the window.

"Good Lord!" James boomed. "What has happened to the woman?"

Benjamin, with Nadine and Stella behind him, ran over. Rushing toward the front stoop with a lopsided gait and a face of pure terror was Fannie Tyler. Her clothes were disheveled. Her yellow hair was unkempt. She had a rip in one stocking. The hem of her green silk dress was torn. She was holding her pocketbook clutched tightly in one hand and she was gripping the heel of one of her shoes in the other.

Benjamin dashed into the hall, threw open the front door, and leaped out. Raymond, who had just yielded to temptation and taken a surreptitious swallow from his flask, followed.

"What happened?" Benjamin shouted.

"Chase . . . chase . . . chased!" Fannie spluttered helplessly, flinging her arm out to indicate the path behind her.

Benjamin grabbed her as she began to sag and half-carried, half-dragged her up the steps into the hall.

94

"Fannie, what is it?" Stella cried.

In the stress of the moment, James, who had removed his straw hat when he first arrived, slammed it back on his head. "Here. Bring her in here. Easy now. Her ankle's bent. Grab her there under the arm. Watch out for her pocketbook."

"How did she get in?" Nadine asked Benjamin as he dragged her toward the couch.

"Get in?"

"Yes. Get in the gate. Wasn't the gate closed?"

Benjamin released his hands and straightened up, letting Fannie crumple to the floor.

"Hell, I don't know. I'd better go see." He raced out the door, Reid hard on his heels.

Fannie, halfway between the parlor door and the couch, waved her arms agitatedly and Nadine tried unsuccessfully to hoist her to her feet.

"Leave me here," Fannie gasped. "Let me catch my breath." She leaned her back against a table leg and stuck out her thin legs. Nadine noticed that the one shoe she was wearing was green silk with what looked like a four-inch heel. It was amazing she hadn't broken a leg running on the soft ground.

After a few minutes Benjamin and Reid returned. Benjamin informed them that they had seen no one. "No sign of trespassers. The gate's locked. There are dozens of places to hide, though. We'll take another look later."

"I'd like to be moved," Fannie announced from her spot on the floor.

Benjamin picked her up and carried her to the couch. He lowered her gently onto the cushions.

Dolly revved up her wheelchair and steered over to Fannie. She began rubbing Fannie's hands. "Are you all right now?"

Stella asked calmly, "Nothing sprained or broken, is there?"

Fannie shook her head.

"What happened?" Benjamin asked.

"Did you see my luggage at the gate?"

"Yes. We'll pick it up for you. But could you tell us what happened?"

"Someone was chasing me!" Fannie snapped out shortly. "That's what happened!"

Benjamin hesitated. "You're sure?"

Fannie glared at him. "The woman who works for me drove me here. She parked on the road and carried my suitcases to the gate . . ."

"Suitcases?" Stella murmured. "How many suitcases did you bring?"

"The gate was ajar," Fannie went on, ignoring Stella. "I was afraid to leave the car unattended, so I told Agnes to put down my luggage and leave. She left and I started to walk up the path. The path is narrow and hilly. The bushes are overgrown. I couldn't see the house. I didn't know how far I'd have to walk. Partway up the path I heard something, like someone giggling off to one side, in the bushes, where I couldn't see."

"Giggling?" James repeated. "Are you sure it was giggling?"

Fannie had regained her composure. She made a stab at imitating the sound, a muted, high-pitched vibrato. "I called out. I said 'Who's that?' and I pushed away some branches. Then I saw a face. It was about as far from me as you are." She pointed to Stella, who hovered over her.

"Was it a man?" Stella prompted.

"It was a face," Fannie stated flatly. "A hideous white face like a doll, smooth and shiny with white fuzz instead of hair and a terrible leering smile."

"A mask?" Dolly suggested tentatively.

Fannie stared at her uncomprehendingly for a moment. "A mask? You mean like a Halloween mask? No, of course not. It was a face." She sat up and began gesticulating. "I started to run. Then I heard him following me—the sound of him rushing through the bushes. I looked around but he wasn't on the path. He was running alongside me behind the trees. When I looked back I tripped and fell. The heel came off my shoe. While I was getting up I heard him giggle again." Once more Fannie imitated the sound.

96

"Fannie, dear," Dolly suggested nervously, "could you stop making that sound?"

"I got up," Fannie went on dramatically, "and I began running. I could hear him running alongside me. Then I saw the house—"

"Just in the nick of time!" James exclaimed. " 'Ah, fear not in a world like this, And thou shalt know ere long, know how sublime a thing it is, to suffer and be strong.' "

Fannie scowled at him. "Jimmy? Good Lord, you're as big a bore as ever!" She drew a deep breath. "I saw the house and, gathering my strength, I ran as fast as I could across the lawn. Behind me, once more, I heard that laugh . . ."

"Please," Dolly interjected, holding up a warning hand.

Fannie refrained from further sound effects. "And then Mr. Pinch opened the door . . . and here I am."

"Bravo," muttered Stella.

"I'll take another look around," Benjamin said.

"And while you're doing that," Dolly said, "Jimmy will phone for a taxi."

Fannie nodded and gripped her pocketbook more tightly. "We never should have come."

"I have my car," Stella offered. "I'll be glad to drop you all off."

Unexpectedly it was Reid who intervened. He walked to the parlor doors and placed himself dead center. "As Mr. Bright's proxy, I feel I have a vote in this matter. Or at least the right to offer an opinion. It's my opinion that there shouldn't be any hasty decisions. There's probably a simple explanation for what happened. It could have been pranksters. It happens every August. The neighborhood children get bored and begin making mischief. Mrs. Tyler says she heard giggling. That doesn't sound sinister to me."

"It did to me," Dolly said promptly.

"Pranksters?" Fannie cried. "It certainly didn't look like a prankster to me. It looked like a maniac!"

"Our lives *are* in danger," Stella reminded Reid.

"If your lives are in danger," Reid suggested, "then leaving will do more harm than good. Once you scatter you're more vulnerable than ever."

Benjamin's glances kept shifting to Nadine, who was standing apart from the group, her arms wrapped tightly around herself as if she were cold. It was unfair to drag her into this mess. He walked over to her. "You've got to make up your mind if you want to go through with this," he said softly. "I'll understand if you change your mind."

"I haven't changed my mind," she answered. "And I won't."

Fannie was regarding Benjamin with a thoughtful expression. "What are *you* doing here?" she asked suddenly. "When did your father decide to let you in on what's going on?"

Benjamin had anticipated the question coming sooner or later. "I convinced him that he needs a good right-hand man."

"And he told you everything?"

"Everything," Benjamin replied recklessly.

"Dearie did arrange our coming here," Dolly mused. "I had forgotten that. He must have a good reason."

"He thinks we should work out our problems in concert," Jimmy said. "He may be right."

"I do think," Stella added, "That we're either going to find the murderer or take the consequences."

Dolly shook her head disconsolately. "I've racked my brain and I haven't the faintest idea who it might be."

"We need an objective and clever party for that," Stella said.

"Namely Dearie," Fannie said.

"So we stay, then?" James asked.

"We'd best stay, Jimmy," Dolly proposed. "At least for another hour or two."

"I've had to go to the toilet ever since I got here," Stella announced.

"I'll show you to your rooms," Reid suggested.

"While you're doing that," Benjamin said, "I'll make another search of the grounds."

"No," Nadine declared. "You've already looked once. If anybody was there, he isn't there now. Wait until later. I think it's better if there's an able-bodied man in the house for now." She looked apprehensive and Benjamin felt another twinge of guilt.

"She's right," Reid said. "We can look around after lunch."

Unconsciously Reid patted the pocket containing the flask. Benjamin wondered if Reid would be functioning after lunch. But the growling sensation in the pit of his stomach was increasing and so was his reluctance to beat the bushes.

"Okay," he agreed. "Later on, then."

Thirteen

Reid didn't join them at lunch. Instead, confirming Benjamin's worst suspicions, he furtively slipped away with an excuse about a headache.

The rooms were all in the south wing. Robert Bright's suite was at the far end of the hall. Next to it on the right was Nadine's room, and between her room and Reid's, the elevator. Nadine had placed Stella on the far side of Reid and beyond Stella, Benjamin. On the left were Fannie, Dolly, and James. The rooms were large and comfortable, arranged for utmost adaptability, with a series of connecting baths.

Stella insisted on helping Nadine with lunch. "We'll make a more equitable arrangement once we get settled.

No reason the men shouldn't shoulder their share of the culinary burden."

The result of the partnership was an assembly line of runny poached eggs and lumpy home-fried potatoes, although Nadine rescued the brandied peaches before Stella could slap them onto the plates with the eggs.

"Well, my boy," James remarked chattily at the table, "you are a basketball player, I believe."

"Was," Benjamin corrected. "I retired at the end of last season."

"You've retired?" Dolly said in amazement. "So young?"

"Why should he work?" Fannie declared. "No son of Dearborn's need worry about money."

"Thirty-two may be young for a businessman," Benjamin explained, "but it's a ripe old age for a basketball player."

"An unusual choice of profession," James interposed.

"It's not a profession at all," Fannie sniffed. "It's a pastime."

"Now really, Fannie," Stella rebuked, "you were an entertainer yourself."

Fannie bristled. "I *am* an actress," she returned. "That is a God-given talent. It is not in any way dependent upon one's muscle tone."

Dolly shook her head and made vague clicking sounds with her tongue and the roof of her mouth.

Benjamin tried not to be insulted. "You should get together with my father, Mrs. Tyler. He feels the same way about it."

"I'm not surprised," Fannie stated unequivocably. "I'd think less of him if he didn't."

"Fannie," Dolly appealed, "I think you're becoming the least little bit . . . rude. After all, Benjamin is Dearie's son."

"Where is Dearie?" Stella asked. "I'm beginning to worry."

"Why don't we talk about your situation," Benjamin

said, trying to distract Stella from speculating about Dearborn. "This might be a good time to compare notes."

"I want to wait for Dearie," Dolly insisted.

"Oh, I don't know," Stella said, "we're not going to sit here with our mouths clamped shut, and I for one couldn't bear a lot of small talk. Let's at least make sure we all have the same information."

Fannie nodded. "I want to know what's behind those deaths and I mean to find out before I'm killed myself! Now let's see—Arthur was killed at the beginning of August. Terence was killed Saturday before last. Toni was killed a week ago Monday . . ."

"And before she was killed," Stella picked up, "she visited Dearie and told him she suspected the Rotten Apples were all in danger."

"Why did she think that?" Benjamin asked.

"Because of Arthur and Terence's deaths, of course. She told your father somebody had already tried to kill her by running her over with an automobile. Surely Dearie told you that?"

"Sure he did," Benjamin hurriedly assured her.

Fannie regarded Benjamin with suspicion. "Dearie had told you all this, hadn't he? You said he had."

"He had. He had."

"Vernon was killed Sunday night," Stella went on. "I spoke with Dolly the next morning."

"That's right," Dolly picked up. "Then Dearie came to visit me and Jimmy was there too and then Dearie realized he was suspected by the police . . ."

"Why?" Fannie demanded.

"Because he had been to see Vernon the day before Vernon was killed and he'd left his cane in Vernon's apartment and Vernon was killed by a blow from Dearie's cane."

"My God!" Fannie exclaimed in horror.

"So Dearie took off," James concluded.

"Have any of you had any trouble?" Stella asked. "I

101

told Dolly that someone broke into my house. Of course, I can't be positive that the incident was related to our difficulties, but Dearie seems to think it was."

"When did that happen?" Fannie asked.

"Two days ago."

Benjamin silently digested the information, trying to maintain a nonchalant appearance but feeling anything but calm. The old man was in way over his head this time.

"Has anything . . ." Stella asked Fannie, ". . . has anything out of the ordinary happened to you?"

"No," Fannie replied. "Not until today. What about you, Dolly?"

"No," Dolly replied. "Not to me. Not to Jimmy, either."

"Robert Bright has been away, so I guess he couldn't have been having any trouble," Benjamin said to Nadine.

"I have no idea."

"It's a crazy setup," Benjamin reflected. "The big question is who and why."

"As we told Dearborn," James said, "Dolly and I can't think of anyone who might have a specific reason for wanting us all dead."

"Nor can I," Fannie declared.

"If you want to talk about who and why," Stella advised, "then you've either got to talk about no one or everyone. That is, I'm sure we can all think of people we've known who might wish us ill, but wishing you ill is not the same as murder."

Benjamin said patiently, "You know, besides your own personal troubles, my father's in serious trouble now, too. Unless he's willing to expose you people, he can't explain to the police how he came to be mixed up in this situation. Maybe you ought to think about that."

"Dearie will handle it," Stella said with maddening trust.

"Not single-handedly he won't. He's going to need help. It's lucky I tumbled to what's going on myself . . ."

"Tumbled?" Fannie picked up. "There's something peculiar here. What do you mean by tumbled? I thought Dearie asked you to help us."

"Where *is* Dearie?" Stella asked.

"Wait a minute," James put in. "Your father is coming here, isn't he?"

"Of course he is." Benjamin's eyes darted around the table and came to rest pleadingly on Nadine.

"That's what Benjamin told me," she said.

"Then why did you use the word *tumbled*?" Fannie demanded.

"Well, I—"

"Have you inveigled us here under false pretences of some sort?"

James rose from the table, dabbed at his lips with his napkin, pulled down the corners of his blazer, and fixed Benjamin with a stern gaze. " 'O, what a tangled web we weave, when first we practice . . .' "

"Sit down, Jimmy," Stella instructed. "You're behaving like a fool."

"Look," Benjamin said, "I'm not trying to put anything over on anybody. You're in trouble and so's my father. If you'll just let me—"

"I'm beginning to think," Fannie announced, "that Dearie hasn't the least intention of coming here!"

Nadine suddenly reached out and deliberately tipped over her water glass. It fell against her plate and broke. Fannie shrieked and the table was thrown into momentary confusion. Benjamin squeezed Nadine's hand gratefully as he reached over to help pick up the pieces of broken glass.

As he was dumping the pieces into the garbage pail, the back door opened and Raymond Reid, looking sheepish, came in.

"Raymond!" Nadine cried. "What happened to you?"

"You're bleeding," Benjamin said.

"I am?" Reid reached up to pat his cheek.

"What happened?" James asked. "We thought you were upstairs."

"You didn't fall out the window, did you?" asked Stella.

"Nonsense," Fannie cried. She struggled to her feet, pushing herself away from the table and drawing herself

103

up majestically. "He has been attacked! Attacked by that maniac!"

Stella put a restraining hand on Fannie's arm. "Don't jump to conclusions. Let's hear what happened."

Reid was a mess. Besides the cut on his cheek, he had a bruise under his eye and a swollen right hand. "It's nothing," he insisted. "I remembered that Mrs. Tyler's luggage was down at the gate. I thought I would pick it up before I took a nap. I drove the golf cart down there and on the way I had a small accident. I missed a turn and hit a tree."

"What happened to the golf cart?" Fannie asked.

"Nothing."

Fannie was unconvinced. "Are you quite sure?"

"I promise you that it was a simple accident. Nothing more. Your luggage is in the cart, Mrs. Tyler."

Benjamin eyed Reid skeptically. "I'm going to take a look around."

"It's a waste of time," Reid insisted. "There's no one out there."

"Let's call it a matter of precaution."

"I'll go with you, Benjamin," James offered bravely. "That is, if you think you need me."

"I'll go with Mr. Pinch," Reid said. "If he's bent on searching the grounds, then I'm the logical one to go with him. Though there's no reason on my account."

"Wait!" Fannie bellowed. "I do not intend to stay here alone!"

"Nor do I," Dolly murmured. She started her motor and circled the table. "Perhaps we'd all better go."

"Hold it," Benjamin declared. "We don't need the whole gang out there kicking up the dirt. If Mr. Reid wants to go, fine. The rest of you wait here. Are you feeling up to it, Mr. Reid?"

"Certainly."

"Sure?"

"It was a minor accident."

"All right then." Benjamin motioned Reid to follow and they went out the kitchen door. The golf cart was parked near the back door, four suitcases piled into the back. Reid and Benjamin circled the cart and strode across the back lawn.

"Want to make a clean breast of it?" Benjamin tried lightly once they were out of earshot. "You didn't actually have an accident with the golf cart, did you?"

Reid was adamant. "I drove over a stone and was jolted out of the driver's seat. Why should I lie?"

Something in Reid's manner, a faint aura of hostility, kept Benjamin from pursuing the subject. "Okay, give me the grand tour then. How big is the place?"

"Not large. Fifteen acres."

Benjamin looked around. Beyond the wide lawn was a border of trees. To the right and left, north and south, the trees were dense, but directly out back the trees were sparse, with well-defined clearings among them. Benjamin noticed a canvas-sided tennis court and a swimming pool. To the left of the swimming pool was a concrete-block building. "What's that over there?"

"It's a tool shed."

"Is that the only outbuilding on the grounds?"

"That's all," Reid replied. "The rest of the grounds are woods and lawn. We keep most of our equipment in the cellar."

"Don't you think we should take a look at the shed?"

"I already have," Reid informed him. "It's locked."

"So you did check around."

Reid shrugged. "The shed is the one likely place a person might hide."

They circled the main building and tramped toward the front gate. When they got there, they found the gate securely closed with no signs of anyone having tried to force the lock. Benjamin opened and closed the gate a few times. Each time he closed it, it fell into place with a definite click.

"If you want the gate to stay open," Reid said, "you have to ease it against the jamb so it won't lock." He demonstrated, opening the gate and then carefully closing it without letting it lock.

"Yeah, I see that. It's an automatic spring lock. Where does this path lead?"

Reid pointed to the right. "The path circles the grounds and comes out back of the garages. If you cut off the path, you'll hit the wall about fifty feet back."

"Let's take a look."

They left the path, skirting the white birches, Russian olive trees, willows, and scrub pine, pushing their way through the bushes, carefully holding back the brambles, until the woods opened a little. They went on for a few more yards and stopped.

"Nothing here," Benjamin muttered.

"Why should there be?" Reid asked.

"This is the thickest part of the woods. I figured it was a possibility." Benjamin held up his hand. "Ssh," he hissed suddenly. He cocked his head. There was a crackling sound behind them. They turned and peered in the direction of the path. The crackling sound was repeated.

"It's nothing," Reid said. "A rabbit or a squirrel."

"Ssh." Benjamin started back, parting the leaves and tree branches cautiously and holding them for Reid. It was fourteen or fifteen noisy yards back to the gate. Benjamin realized the uselessness of trying to take anyone by surprise. "Hey!" he called out.

The shout did take Reid by surprise. His knees buckled and he pitched forward. By the time he recovered Benjamin was already hurdling the bushes as if they were ocean waves, going up, over, and through them with awkward, high-kneed leaps.

Somewhere up ahead there was an explosion of sound as whoever it was tried to escape. When Benjamin reached the path, he saw a man cresting the west hill. Benjamin broke into a fast, easy trot and quickly closed the gap until he was close enough to see the trespasser, a tall, thin man running with a stiff-legged gait.

When Benjamin was within a few yards of him, the man tried to avert capture by dodging into the woods. He was hampered by a pair of flared slacks that flapped around his legs and then caught on a piece of loose tree bark as he ran past. Thrown off balance, he fell. Benjamin, at the same instant, executed a flying tackle that carried him a few feet beyond his target and dropped him, screeching with pain, into a blackberry bush.

Reid, arriving at that moment, stopped short and croaked, "Grab him! Grab him! Don't let him get away!" while the trespasser, already on his knees, lifted his head to inquire in a weak voice, "Is that you, Benjamin? I might have known it would be you I'd have to thank for this mortification!"

Fourteen

Dearborn had wrenched his ankle when he fell. Reid went for the golf cart and drove him back to the house with Benjamin, still picking thorns out of his shirt, following at a quick pace. When they reached the house, Benjamin and Reid gripped one another's wrists to form a sling and carried Dearborn up the front steps.

Nadine met them at the door. "What happened?"

Behind her a cacophony of cries greeted them.

"Dearborn!"

"Dearie!"

"It's about time!"

" 'See the conquering hero comes!' "

Dearborn was stunned. "What is this?" he quavered, the vibrato resulting from his bouncing ascent. "What are you doing here?"

Benjamin and Reid carried him into the main parlor and deposited him onto a straight-backed chair.

"What kept you?" Fannie exclaimed. She kneaded her pocketbook between nervous fingers. "We were beginning to think you weren't coming."

"I misplaced my invitation," Dearborn said sarcastically.

"Dad," Benjamin asked, "how did you get onto the grounds?"

"Through the front gate, of course. How else would I get in? I no sooner stepped through the gate than you and . . . er . . ." Dearborn waved his finger at Reid, "what's-his-name there began chasing me."

"We left the gate open," Benjamin said to Reid, "when we were fooling around with it."

"I take it," Dearborn declared contentiously, "that no one knows that any of *you* are here?"

"Somebody knows," Fannie declared pointedly.

"If you mean the police, Dearie," Stella assured him, "the answer is no. Your son relayed your message last night and we came separately this morning."

"He relayed my message?" Dearborn twisted his head and glared at Benjamin. "You are reading minds now, Benjamin?"

James nodded to Benjamin. "Apologies are in order, young man. I'm afraid we were carried away earlier."

"Yes," Dolly agreed. "We should have known better than to doubt you."

"We're impressed, Dearborn," James said. "Your son is a chip off the old block. He carried out your instructions to the letter."

Dearborn muttered something unintelligible.

"We were all worried about you, Dad. How *did* you get here?"

"I bicycled as far as Massapequa Park," Dearborn said. "Then my tire went flat. I came the rest of the way in a bakery truck."

"You hitchhiked?" Nadine asked in astonishment.

108

"Benjamin," Fannie broke in, "did you see the intruder?"

"No," Benjamin replied.

"What intruder?" Dearborn demanded.

"No intruder," Reid cut in. "I had a small accident about an hour ago and for some reason it was assumed that I was attacked."

"For some reason?" Fannie returned indignantly. "I suppose I wasn't chased all over Kingdom Come this morning? Dearborn, I think I was followed here."

"What are you gabbling about?"

"I'd better explain," Benjamin said. He gestured for quiet, then undertook to fill in the gaps.

"That's it, Dad," he concluded. "The next thing that happened was that we heard you come in, thought you might be the guy we were looking for, and went after you."

"It's so good to see you, Dearie!" Stella burst out. "I feel as if everything will be resolved with you—"

Dearborn held up his hand. "There are still certain aspects of this affair which, I must admit, elude me . . ." He scowled at Benjamin. "However, now that I have arrived, the investigation of this unfortunate situation can commence."

"Hear! Hear!" James declared.

"We shall make a concerted effort to track down the person responsible for your . . . plight. We shall pool our information and . . ."

"Hope for the best," Stella concluded matter-of-factly.

"We shall, I promise you, do more than hope for the best."

"Speaking of hope," James announced, "it may not be so difficult as it seems. I've been waiting for you, Dearborn, before saying this, but I've been thinking things over and I have a theory."

Dearborn looked at James with a skeptical eye. "What is it?"

"Hope."

"Hope?" Dearborn repeated. "What is that? Dramatic hyperbole?"

Dolly began making delicate clucking sounds and waggling her fingers at James. For a moment he misunderstood and reached up to wrestle with his toupee. Then he realized what she was trying to tell him.

"Never mind, Dolly," he said manfully, "this is not the time for delicacy. Dearborn, Hope is my wife."

Benjamin, who had edged over to stand next to Nadine, heard her exhale with a soft whoosh. He knew how she felt.

Dearborn was undismayed. "I understand why your wife might take a dim view of your friendship with Dolly . . ."

All eyes darted from James to Dolly.

". . . but how do you explain her vindictiveness toward Arthur, Terence, Toni, and Vernon?"

"Simple," James snapped. "They were killed as a smoke screen to hide Hope's real objective."

"You're overlooking the most basic fact," Dearborn pointed out. "So far as the police are concerned, there's no link between you, Arthur, Terence, Toni, or Vernon."

"So much for smoke screens," Nadine whispered.

"Fortunately," Stella reflected, "I have no family who would benefit from my death."

"God knows my family has nothing to gain," Fannie added.

"My children and I are close," Dolly murmured. "I wouldn't dream of suspecting them."

"I think we can assume," Dearborn said, "that family greed plays no part in this. Putting aside the unlikelihood of James's theory or the question of how much or how little would be gained from your individual deaths, there is still the question of age."

"How so?" Benjamin asked.

"It is unlikely that any heir would conceive of so elaborate a plan as James suggests in order to murder one person who, we can safely assume, will accommodate his

110

heirs by dying anyway within a reasonable span of time."

"Dearborn!" Fannie cried, "how can you talk like that?"

"He's right," Stella said. "If they didn't kill us twenty years ago, they're not apt to do it now."

"No," Dearborn went on, "I think we may eliminate family greed as the motive. And judging by the single-mindedness of the killer, I think we may eliminate the possibility that the murders are the work of a senseless madman. The murders have, so far, been quick, clean, and efficient. There is a reason for them, no doubt a simple reason, albeit a reason that has so far escaped me. But we will discover that reason, and when we do, we shall have our murderer."

"What about that crazy person hiding out there?" Fannie interposed.

"If he had meant to kill you," Dearborn speculated, "he would have done so. I think we must assume that you were set upon by pranksters."

"I tried to tell her that," Reid said.

"Though," Dearborn added immediately, "it is also to be assumed that none of you is safe, even here, so long as the killer is at large. Now, Miss Garrett, have you heard from Robert?"

"No."

"When is the last time you heard from him? Or have you heard from him at all?"

"Oh, yes. Of course. I . . . he . . . well, not phone calls, but we've written to him and he's written to us."

Dearborn hummed. "When did you last receive a communication?"

Nadine glanced at Reid. "When was it? Day before yesterday?"

Reid nodded. "There were some documents to be signed. Nadine mailed them to Mr. Bright and he returned them."

"I'd like to see his latest letter to you, Miss Garrett."

"There wasn't any letter. Just the papers with his signature."

111

"You saw them?"

"Yes. I took them to his lawyer yesterday."

"What was in those papers, Miss Garrett?" Dearborn asked.

"I'm sorry. They're confidential."

"Who is Robert's lawyer?"

"Corbett, Rubin, and Bonnell. Mr. Bonnell. I had to go to my bank . . . it's in the same building . . . I got there just before closing and then I took the papers upstairs and delivered them. About three-thirty."

"Justin Bonnell? Fat? Cast in one eye? Why couldn't Miss Simon tell me that?"

"Mr. Pinch," Nadine asked. "Wouldn't you like to wash up?"

Dearborn examined his hands and clothing. "I would like to change my clothes. Robert is about my size, isn't he?"

"Raymond will find you something," Nadine said.

"Reid," Dearborn said, "how much does a health director know about sprains? I'd like you to take a look at my ankle."

Reid, who had been caressing his pocket and running his tongue over his lips, said, "What?" and got up from the couch. He knelt next to Dearborn's chair, unlaced Dearborn's shoe, and eased it off, then rolled down Dearborn's sock and, holding the bottom of his foot with one hand, slipped the sock carefully over Dearborn's foot. He manipulated the flesh at the base of Dearborn's ankle and cautiously wiggled the foot. "A little swollen. Not critical. How does it feel?"

Dearborn leaned over and rubbed his shinbone. "I can't tell."

"Try to put your weight on it."

Dearborn got up and tried resting his weight on the injured foot. He sat down again with a grunt and pointed a finger at Benjamin. "I hold you responsible for this, Benjamin."

"It doesn't seem too bad," Reid said. "A slight strain. You'll be able to walk on it in a day or two."

112

"Until then what? Are there any crutches around here?"

"I don't think so," Nadine said.

Reid shook his head.

"Can you bandage it, Reid?"

He nodded. "The bandages are in the infirmary. I'll get them." He started out of the room. As he went through the door, Benjamin caught a glimpse of him reaching into his pocket and pulling out his flask. He'd never make it through the afternoon.

"How am I to get upstairs?" Dearborn demanded.

"I'll carry you," Benjamin offered. "There's an elevator here so there shouldn't be any problem with steps."

"Carry me? How? Piggyback?"

"Why not?"

"I'm not Tiny Tim."

"You could sit in a blanket," Stella suggested. "We'll all take an end. Benjamin, me, Miss Garrett, Fannie . . ."

"I do not intend to be carried by women."

"That is a classic example of the male chauvinist ego!" Stella declared.

"I have the solution," Dolly said suddenly. "I'll give you my chair." Before anyone could protest she got up, circled the wheelchair, and pushed it toward Dearborn.

There was a stunned silence. Fannie was the first to recover. "You can walk?"

"Why not? I'm not paralyzed."

"Then why . . . is it your heart?"

Dolly exchanged a sly glance with James. "At times I get dizzy spells . . . especially when I'm upset."

"Then you'd better not—"

"It's quite all right. I'm perfectly well at the moment. And poor Dearborn is not. He needs it more than I do."

Fifteen

After dinner the group gathered in the parlor and by ten were deep into conversation and brandy.

"It was a Packard, a Packard Eight."

"It was a 1929 De Soto."

"I don't know why, but I have a Reo in mind. A 1925 Reo."

"Vernon was a fool," Dearborn intoned.

Benjamin, Nadine, and Reid sat a little to one side. The others were clustered in front of the fireplace. Dearborn, ensconced in Dolly's wheelchair, held center stage.

James had a fresh handkerchief in his blazer pocket; Dolly had added a pearl choker to her blue linen sheath; Stella's workshirt was fresh and crisp. Fannie had applied a curling iron to her already frizzled coiffure and was wearing a white sharkskin dinner skirt with a blue silk middy blouse embroidered with anchors and a matching blue silk scarf tied at the throat. Dearborn was sartorially transformed, having outfitted himself in a summer suit belonging to Robert Bright, beige shantung, with a pale blue linen shirt and midnight blue silk tie.

"How could Vernon admit to anything, Dearie?" Stella asked. "His position as a retired judge was even more delicate than ours."

"I disagree, Stella," James piped up. "He had no more to lose than we."

114

"Had he cooperated," Dearborn declared, "he wouldn't be lying on a slab in the city morgue."

"Oh, Dearie," Dolly whispered. "How morbid."

Benjamin broke into the conversation. "Dad, you've got to persuade these people to go to the police."

Dearborn waved an impatient hand. "The police are inept fools."

"Nevertheless . . ." Benjamin persisted.

"Nevertheless," Dearborn picked up, with a warning scowl at Benjamin, "contacting the police might be strategically sound and it's my duty to remind everyone of that fact."

"Never!" Fannie cried. "We've been through this already, Dearie. We will call the police when we know who the murderer is and not before!"

"There. You see?" Dearborn said smugly. "They won't do it, Benjamin."

Benjamin said sternly, "It's not only their lives at stake, Dad . . ."

"I take it that you are not disturbed by the prospect of your father being arrested for murder?" Dearborn returned. Dismissing Benjamin, he turned to James. "James, when was the last time you published a book of poems?"

"Why?" James asked. "What has that got to do with any of this?"

"When?"

"Nineteen forty-seven. *Pagan Parables*."

"And you think the public would be interested in knowing that James Bell, obscure poet—"

"Obscure?"

"—plagiarized a poem in 1934?"

"Three. '33," James corrected.

"Do you think anyone would know or care who you are?"

"Cruel, Dearborn," James murmured. " 'Man's inhumanity to man, makes countless thousands mourn!' "

"Robert Burns," Dearborn declared. "*You* don't even quote yourself, James."

115

"Dearie, you're outrageous," Fannie remarked in an amused voice.

"And you," Dearborn said, switching attention to Fannie. "What celebrated reputation do you suppose you're protecting? 'Fannie Tyler, who for those readers who are not grandparents, was a stage personality of the twenties, and now resides in Englewood, New Jersey, admits to having fixed the Belmont Stakes race in 1925' . . ."

"Wrong on three counts, Dearie! The race is wrong, the year is wrong, and the characterization is wrong! I'll have you know that I was approached only last month with an offer to play Amanda Wingfield in *The Glass Menagerie!*"

"Dearie," Stella remonstrated, "you are being a bit ruthless."

"And you, Stella," Dearborn went on relentlessly. "It pains me to suggest that your ego has magnified your own peccadillo out of all proportion."

"On the contrary," Stella argued. "Exposure would mean my ruin. I'd be dropped from the AKC and I could never lift my head again at NOW."

Dearborn studied Dolly thoughtfully. "Toni didn't tell me what it was you did to qualify as a Rotten Apple, Dolly."

Dolly, like fragile Dresden, was packed into a large armchair and surrounded by pillows. She held her patchwork quilt on her lap and was making swift little stabs at it with her needle. "I prefer not to discuss the subject," she answered primly.

"She skewered a lady with an icepick," Fannie informed Dearborn promptly.

"An icepick?" Nadine whispered from the sidelines.

"Is that true, Dolly?" Dearborn demanded. "I don't seem to recall the incident."

"It is not true," James declared. He leaned over the back of Dolly's chair and patted her shoulder.

"It *is* true," Fannie insisted, maliciously. "Dolly thought the woman was after Patrick."

116

Dolly's lips tightened. "It was a flesh wound. I only meant to frighten her. She didn't press charges." Her eyes darted from one to another nervously. "I'm not going to talk about it."

"Who was the woman?" Dearborn asked with interest. "Anyone I know?"

Dolly suddenly leaned forward and gestured at Reid. "Mr. Reid," she gushed in an unnatural voice, "you know, I've been studying you ever since we arrived. I've been trying to place you."

Reid, who had been in a soporific state since dinner, made a valiant attempt to straighten up in his chair.

"But now I have it," she prattled. "John Gilbert. Doesn't he look like John Gilbert, Jimmy?"

Everyone, James included, obligingly studied the bleary-eyed, slack-jawed Reid.

"I knew John Gilbert," Fannie remarked finally, "and I must say that I fail to see the likeness. For one thing, John Gilbert had hair."

Dolly tilted her head. "John Gilbert in *Flesh and the Devil*," she mused, ignoring Fannie. She gave a sidelong glance at Dearborn to see if she had succeeded in diverting him.

"Wasn't Barbara Sharp, was it?" Dearborn asked Dolly. "Was that the one after Patrick? I always thought she was a wild one."

"Dearborn," James intervened, "what's to be gained by raking up old coals?"

Dearborn abandoned the subject reluctantly. "I had hoped that you could regard the past with more equanimity."

"You should go to the police," Benjamin cut in again.

"Stop harping on that," Dearborn remonstrated.

"Somebody has to!" Benjamin insisted.

"I have already suggested the police as an alternative."

"Alternative?" Benjamin repeated incredulously. "Alternative to what?"

"To my undertaking an investigation, of course."

117

"You mean you intend to play detective?"

"*Play*, Benjamin? May I remind you that we are dealing with a life-and-death situation. This is no time to play at anything."

"But you're not—"

"Don't interfere. I shall put it to the principals." He faced the group. "Well? What shall it be? The police?"

"We've just been over that," Fannie declared.

"We are determined not to give in," Dolly said with dignity.

"No police!" Fannie said in a strident tone.

"Only as a last resort," Stella added firmly.

"I wouldn't talk to the police," James stated coldly.

"If that is your final decision, then I want you to begin thinking about the possibilities."

"Frankly, I don't know where to begin," Stella said.

"Dad, listen," Benjamin interjected, "this isn't going to work. You've already gotten yourself into one hell of a mess. Don't make it any worse—"

"One thought comes to mind," Dearborn plowed ahead stubbornly. "Did you, as a group, have any assets?"

"What do you mean, Dearie?" Stella asked.

"Did you collect dues? Levy fines? Did you maintain a treasury? Did you salt away money or valuables?"

"You mean in a private vault?" James asked.

"Exactly."

"If we had, I can assure you that we'd have recovered the so-called assets long ago," Fannie replied.

"You were a profligate group."

"Profligate, but not careless."

"Well, then," Dearborn asked, "do you share some bit of intelligence, some information damaging to a third party?"

"Only to one another," James replied.

"Would your deaths benefit anyone other than your immediate families?"

They shook their heads.

"It's so discouraging," Dolly murmured, pushing her

needle in and out of her quilt with precise drill-hammer stitches. She came to the end of the piece, broke off the thread, and looked up. She gave a small, startled cry.

"Stick yourself, my dear?" asked James.

She patted his hand. "Jimmy, I think Mr. Reid is unwell."

Everyone looked at Reid. He was still slumped in his chair but had begun slowly tilting forward. Benjamin, who was closest to him, grabbed him before he toppled to the floor.

"Oh, my," Dolly exclaimed. "He *is* unwell."

"Swacked out of his mind," Benjamin said grimly.

There was general chaos while Benjamin and James worked at rousing Reid and getting him upstairs.

It was decided to postpone the discussion until morning. The interruption had served as a reminder that they were all tired and that it was getting late. By ten-thirty the parlor was empty, the last two members of the group, Benjamin and Dearborn, switching off the lights and going up in the elevator.

"I want you to call Otto," Dearborn commanded.

Benjamin sat on a chair at the foot of Dearborn's bed.

"Not that I trust Otto," Dearborn reflected.

"What do you think he'd do?" Benjamin asked. "Tip off the police?"

"With your blessing, I have no doubt."

"Niccoli's not joking, you know," Benjamin said. "He's even got detectives watching my place. I had to sneak out of my apartment last night."

"And you still have the gall," Dearborn declared, "to suggest that we offer ourselves up to those fools without a fight?"

"It's not the police we're supposed to be fighting, Dad . . ."

"Get on the phone and call Otto."

119

"Otto can't do anything now. It's the middle of the night."

Dearborn pointed to the telephone, and after a moment Benjamin sighed and got up.

Otto answered in the middle of the ninth ring. "Ben? What the hell is it? I'm soaking wet. I'm in the shower. I'll call you back."

"You can't call me. You don't know the number."

"Look, Ben, I didn't find that guy yet."

"What guy?"

"Hector."

Benjamin had forgotten about Hector. "Never mind. That's not why I called. Do you know a lawyer named Justin Bonnell?"

"Father or son?"

"There are two?"

"That's right."

"Both lawyers?"

"Yeah."

"Which one do you know?" Benjamin asked.

"Junior."

"Is he okay?"

"If you like broomsticks." There was a pause. Then, "What do you want now, you bastard?"

Benjamin grinned and nodded at Dearborn. "Bonnell senior is Robert Bright's lawyer. Bright supposedly signed some legal papers a few days ago. I want it verified and I want to know what the papers contain."

"Ben, have you located your father?"

"No."

"I've been talking to Mrs. Woolley. She says the police have been all over the place. They took William Rhodes down to headquarters to question him."

"And?"

"She said he came back pretty shaken. Told her the police got a couple of names out of him."

"What names?"

"A couple of people your father visited."

Benjamin nodded. There was nothing to fear there.

120

All the people Dearborn had gone to see were safely gathered at the clinic.

"Where are you?" Otto asked.

"What's the difference?"

"You want me to call you back, don't you?"

"I'll call you, Otto."

After Benjamin hung up he remained standing with his head cocked, a peculiar expression on his face.

"What are you doing?" Dearborn demanded.

"I thought I heard a receiver click. A chime in the background. There's a grandfather clock in the downstairs hall, isn't there?"

Dearborn swung his legs over the side of the bed and tried to stand up. He swore and fell back. He smacked the mattress with the palm of his hand. "Damn it, Benjamin! Don't just stand there!"

Benjamin went out into the hall. Moonlight filtered through the windows and lit the carpet with pale grids that deepened the black areas between. Only the eight rooms at the near end of the hall were occupied. He paused at the top of the stairs. The upper landing was flanked by two human-sized cactus plants growing in buckets of sand. For a moment they startled him with their lifelike appearance. Then he remembered what they were and dodged past them.

The darkness varied from medium dark under the crystal chandelier to pale on either side of the downstairs hall, where doors opened into the parlor and dining room. The corners were inky smudges, and thick blotches delineated the console tables, the occasional chairs, the front desk and switchboard, and the grandfather clock. As if to confirm what Benjamin already knew, the clock ticked off an abortive half-chime as Benjamin paused at the bottom of the stairs.

As his eyes became accustomed to the dark, he swiveled his head to examine the foyer, then walked softly to the parlor door. He fumbled around for the wall switch and clicked it on. The room was empty. He crossed to the dining room and beyond it to the game

121

room. Both rooms were empty. He returned to the employees' lounge. There was no wall switch in the room, so he crossed to a table lamp next to the couch and reached for the switch, turning his head to avoid bumping his nose on the shade.

His eyes swept across the far wall and after a shocked instant registered the fact that there was a face at the window. He stared at it, then began walking toward it. Quite suddenly, someone screamed.

Benjamin froze and turned. A figure stood in the doorway to the room. He started toward it and the figure lunged at him, ramming him in the chest with both fists. He grabbed his assailant's arms, met with only moderate resistance, and forced the arms downward.

"Stop it!" The voice was light and terrified.

"Nadine?"

"Let me go!"

Benjamin tightened his grip as her knees buckled. He swept her up, carried her to the couch, and put her down.

"Is it gone?" she asked shakily.

Benjamin nodded. "You saw him?"

"Before I saw you. I was in the hall. I looked in and saw that person looking in. Then you moved and I saw you."

"What are you doing down here?"

"My bracelet." She pushed up the sleeve of her bathrobe to show her bare wrist. "I took it off to do the dishes. I thought I left it in the kitchen. I guess I didn't. Anyway, on my way back upstairs I looked in here."

Benjamin switched on the table lamp and sat down on the arm of the couch. "I guess there's no point in going after him."

Nadine drew her bathrobe tightly around her. "You'll never find him in the dark."

"He's probably miles away by now," Benjamin conceded glumly. "Lucky my father didn't catch the scene."

"What's going on here?" a loud voice demanded from the doorway.

122

"Uh oh," Benjamin muttered.

Dearborn, in Dolly's wheelchair, bore down on them. "Well, well! Speak up!"

"It was someone at the window," Nadine offered timidly.

"Someone at the window? You mean outside?"

"That's right, Dad," Benjamin confirmed.

"What did he look like?"

Nadine shook her head. "I'm not sure."

"I couldn't see his features," Benjamin said. "He had a big head. He was pretty tall. With narrow shoulders."

"A man? A boy? What?"

"A man, I think."

"It could just as well have been a woman," Nadine remarked. "It was too dark to tell, really."

Dearborn shook his head exasperatedly. "Why didn't you go after him, Benjamin?"

"By the time I carried Nadine to the couch, it was too late."

"Why were you carrying Miss Garrett?"

"I started to faint," Nadine explained.

"You would have been perfectly all right on the floor."

"I caught her when she went down," Benjamin said. "What was I supposed to do? Drop her?"

"She's not made of glass."

"It was a reflex action, Dad. Like catching a ball."

"Going after that trespasser would have been the correct reflex action."

"It's too late now."

"My point precisely."

Nadine got up from the couch. "I'm not crazy about family arguments. Also I think I'd feel better locked in my room. Is it okay with you?"

"Want a cup of coffee, Dad?" Benjamin suggested placatingly. "It might calm us both down."

"I've had sufficient stimulation for one night, thank you. Let us check the doors and windows and go over the details of what happened. There's no use searching the grounds, but we shall keep watch for a while in case the trespasser should take it into his head to show up again. Miss Garrett, nothing to anyone about this incident. Is that clear?"

Nadine nodded. "I'd forget it myself if I could."

"I suggest you try."

Sixteen

The trespasser didn't return, and at two Benjamin and Dearborn went to bed.

Breakfast the next morning turned out to be brunch. Fannie came into the kitchen at ten-thirty, clutching her pocketbook. She was wearing a yellow-and-blue striped skirt partially unbuttoned to reveal a knee-length yellow sunsuit underneath, with a yellow visored tennis cap perched on top of her head. The others followed in quick succession. Dolly and James, puffy-eyed and pale; Stella in dungarees, work boots, and her emerald ring; Raymond Reid, pouchy and haggard but neatly dressed and sober.

Benjamin hadn't brought a razor or a change of clothes, and he loped into the kitchen with his shirt partially unbuttoned, his chinos wrinkled, and a two-day growth of beard.

Dearborn, on the other hand, was dapper and self-possessed. He wore Robert Bright's shantung suit and he waved a disapproving finger at Benjamin as he sped through the kitchen in Dolly's wheelchair. "Button your collar, Benjamin. This isn't a locker room."

Nadine was going through the mechanics of passing out napkins.

"What are you serving?" Fannie demanded as she sniffed the air.

"Juice, hot oatmeal, toast, and coffee," Nadine replied.

"Oatmeal? In the middle of August?"

Stella took the cardboard container of juice out of Nadine's hand and poured juice into the lineup of eight juice glasses. She nodded to the group to indicate that they should carry their glasses to the table. Then, with the same dispatch she brought to the feeding of her scotties, she proceeded to ladle big, sloppy spoonfuls of oatmeal from the pot on the stove into individual cereal bowls. "There," she said, satisfied that she'd done her bit. She sat down and drank her juice.

"Milk's in the pitcher, butter's in the covered dish, sugar's on the table," Nadine announced.

"How is the food situation?" James inquired. "Won't it be necessary to go to the market?"

"There's plenty of frozen food in the cellar and lots of canned goods," Nadine said. "We're low on milk and eggs, though."

"This is Wednesday," Reid informed her. "The dairy delivery is due this morning."

"Good heavens!" Dolly piped up. "Someone is coming here? We'll be seen!"

"No, we won't," James assured her. "The milkman's not coming to tea. He'll make his delivery and leave."

Nadine said, "The mailman usually comes to the front door."

"Don't buzz him in," Fannie instructed. "It's that simple."

"I've got to get the mail."

"It's all right," Benjamin said. "The mailman isn't interested in who's here."

"The fewer people who know about us, the better," Fannie insisted.

125

"Do you get a newspaper delivery?" Dearborn asked.

"No," Nadine answered. "I usually go downtown for it."

"You can do that this morning, Benjamin," Dearborn said. "I have an errand I want you to run after breakfast."

Dearborn turned to Reid. "Is there a drugstore in town?"

"Naturally."

"I assume they know you there?"

Reid nodded.

"I neglected to bring my sleeping pills. Do you think the druggist would waive the formalities if you were to ask him? I thought perhaps you could dash off a note."

"I'll have to call him first."

"I would appreciate it," Dearborn said firmly. "Rather difficult to sleep with this bad ankle."

Benjamin eyed his father curiously. His father wouldn't take any kind of pill unless it were jammed down his throat. "Dad?"

The look Dearborn shot at him was so menacing that Benjamin turned the sentence into a request for the strawberry jam.

They were all still at the table when the phone rang. Nadine went to answer it. She returned, saying, "It's for you, Ben. A Mr. Rothschild. It's the wall phone near the back stairs."

Benjamin and Dearborn stared at one another in consternation. Benjamin rose from the table and hurried out into the hall. Dearborn pressed the starter on the wheelchair and followed. "Is there another extension down here?" he called over his shoulder.

"In the infirmary," Nadine answered. "I'm pretty sure it's hooked up." She followed Dearborn down the hall. "The door's locked," she said. She reached into the neckline of her blouse and lifted out a chain with two keys dangling from it, inserted one key into the lock, and opened the door. The room was fully equipped and gleaming, with examining table, X-ray machine, and a row of immaculate white glass-fronted cabinets stocked with an impressive array of medical supplies. The single window was too high on the wall to provide much light, and Nadine switched on the electric light. She pointed to the telephone on the desk and then left the room. Dearborn picked up the receiver.

". . . don't know why I do it. Had to promise the bastard my seats for next year's hockey play-offs."

"Otto, how did you find out where I am?"

"What do you take me for? You wanted to know about Robert Bright. Your father wanted to know about Robert Bright. You're asking questions about Justin Bonnell. The only lead I had to follow was Robert Bright."

"What information did you come up with?"

"Justin says so far as he knows Bright is in Japan . . . or was in Japan up to a week ago. Bright's secretary brought in some papers from him a couple of days ago. The envelope was postmarked Tokyo."

"What are they?"

"Contracts, bills of sale, closing papers on the sale of the clinic."

"Closing papers?"

"Right. Seems like Bright sold the clinic."

"When was this?"

"A couple of weeks ago."

"Wow! Who to?"

"I don't know. It's still under wraps. Somebody who was willing to spend over a million. Nearly two million, I'd guess."

"Is it final?"

"Signed, sealed, and delivered." Otto dropped his voice. "Ben, a detective has moved into my waiting room. I can't pee without the guy looking over my shoulder. I'm being tailed all over town."

"I hope your phone's not tapped."

"I'm calling from the lobby."

"Don't tell anybody where I am. I'll stay in touch."

"Wait a minute, Ben. Have you heard from—"

"Have to go, Otto. Hang in there, buddy."

Dearborn, in the other room, broke the connection,

waited for a moment, and then picked up the phone. He dialed information. "I want the number of Dr. Walter Moltke, New York City. His office is on Park Avenue."

He waited, nodded, dialed, and waited again. Then, "Miss Wiley, Dearborn V. Pinch here. Let me speak to Dr. Moltke. Nonsense. The patient isn't going to leave. Tell Moltke to pick up the phone. No, I cannot call back. I have no intention of calling back."

A pause. "Hello? Dearborn Pinch speaking. Walter, do you remember that matter I spoke with you about last Thursday? I have succeeded in getting the sample. I am having it delivered to your niece's home today. Will she see that you receive it by tomorrow morning? I can count on that? And you will obtain the results by tomorrow afternoon? Excellent. I apologize for the mystery, Walter, but I promise you that the matter is urgent."

Benjamin left for town at eleven-thirty with Nadine's grocery list, Reid's note to the druggist, and strict instructions regarding the sealed envelope that Dearborn handed him, to be delivered to a Mrs. Hermine Kleber in Bayshore.

After Ben had gone, Dearborn informed Reid that he intended to take a look at Robert Bright's suite.

"I guess it's all right," Reid said. "Do you want me to take you up there?"

"I'll manage on my own," Dearborn said.

But Dearborn soon found that he couldn't manage on his own. As he moved toward the elevator, the wheelchair slowed down and then stopped. Dearborn started to his feet, took a few steps, growled, and fell back onto the seat. "Dolly!" he shouted.

Dolly hurried in from the main parlor. The rest of the group followed and gathered around the wheelchair.

"The battery is dead!" Dearborn said accusingly.

"I'm sorry, Dearie. I never thought to recharge it."

"Too bad, Dearie."

"Bad luck."

"You'd think there was a better system."

"Never mind the gabble!" Dearborn exploded. "Somebody get it started!"

Dolly shook her head. "It'll take hours. There's nothing to do but wait. Someone will have to push you until it's recharged."

"I'll do it," Stella volunteered.

"No, I'll do it," James insisted. "This is a job for a man."

James prevailed. He pushed the wheelchair into the elevator and conducted Dearborn to the second floor.

Robert Bright's suite was at the end of the hall. Dearborn unlocked the door and James pushed him into a large, comfortably furnished sitting room. There was a bay window facing south, with a flowered, chintz-cushioned window seat and matching drapes. Two couches flanked the fireplace. The wheels of the wheelchair made deep indentations in the thick cream-and-lime carpet.

Dearborn stopped to examine the desk. It was in perfect order: pencils in a round container, telephone pad centered in front of the telephone, ink blotter clean, letter opener in its leather pouch, desk calendar fresh and unmarked.

The bedroom was as pristine as the sitting room. The walls were wainscotted, panels and ceiling lined with blue-and-white sprigged wallpaper. The bedspread was smooth, a cerise afghan folded at the foot, the dresser top clear.

Dearborn motioned for James to push him to the closet. Inside, a row of summer suits hung in regimental order. Underneath, a dozen or so pair of shoes were lined up.

Dearborn hummed tunelessly and pointed to the bathroom. James pushed him to the door. The bathroom was large and square, with a closed door opposite the one they entered.

"Open the medicine cabinet, will you, James?"

James eased his way around the wheelchair and went into the bathroom. He threw open the mirrored cabinet over the sink. "What should I look for?"

"Toothbrush, razor, comb . . ."

"No toothbrush, but there's denture cleaner. Yes, here's a razor."

"In short," Dearborn muttered, "the only thing missing is the gentleman himself."

"That is strange, isn't it?" James frowned at the interior of the medicine cabinet. "Perhaps he has a travel kit. I imagine he's away quite often."

"Then he must have a travel wardrobe as well," Dearborn reflected, drumming his fingers on the arm of the wheelchair.

James looked at Dearborn with a startled expression. "You're implying that something may have prevented Robert from leaving. That instead of going, he disappeared. You don't think something happened to him? You don't think . . ."

"That he was murdered? No, I do not. None of the murder victims simply, as you put it, disappeared. Besides, he hasn't disappeared. He has been in contact with his secretary and with his law firm. I do not for a moment suspect him of being a hapless victim."

"Then what?"

Dearborn waved at a closed door next to the sink. "Try that door."

James turned the knob. "Locked. No key."

"Whose room is on the other side?"

"Miss Garrett's, I believe."

"All right. Turn me around, James."

James pulled the wheelchair out of the bathroom doorway and pivoted it to face the room.

"That door over there," Dearborn instructed, pointing across the room. "Wheel me over there."

James peered at the wall. "Where?"

"Next to the bed," Dearborn clucked impatiently.

James pushed the wheelchair to the far side of the bed. Dearborn reached out to grab an inconspicuous handle at one side of the wainscotted panel. "What do you call this?"

Dearborn pulled down the handle. The door opened

easily, revealing a staircase leading to another door at its base. "Would you mind taking a look down there," Dearborn commanded. "See if the downstairs door is locked."

James went down. The door at the foot of the stairs opened as easily as the one at the top. "It leads to the lawn," James reported, shutting the door and starting back up.

"A private entrance," Dearborn noted. "And unlocked."

"I suppose there are times when Robert wants to come and go undetected," James speculated. "I certainly would."

"Undetected," Dearborn murmured under his breath. "Yes, yes."

"What Dearborn? I didn't catch that."

"I didn't say anything. All right, James. I think I've seen all there is to see. Shall we rejoin the others?"

Seventeen

Benjamin came into the parlor carrying a newspaper and waving a slip of paper. "Listen, Dad, you gave me the wrong note. You gave me a receipt from the car rental."

"Did you deliver the envelope to Mrs. Kleber?"

"Yes, but I couldn't get the sleeping pills. Not without the note. I'll have to go back."

"Forget the sleeping pills. I'll do without them."

Benjamin glanced at Nadine. She was sitting on a hassock near Dearborn's chair, looking pinched and nervous. Benjamin's sense of guilt was revived whenever he looked at her. Whenever he took a really good look at any of them. His eyes drifted to Reid, who was leaning against the side of the fireplace. Reid's eyes were glazed and his face was flushed. One o'clock in the afternoon and he was already drunk. Or was he? Or, at least, was he *that* drunk? Sometimes Benjamin got the impression that Reid wanted to appear more out of it than he actually was. Benjamin felt he had to make another rational attempt to deal with the situation. "Look, I was thinking about this on the drive back. The more I think about it, the more I think we should call the police."

They pounced on him.

"No!" Fannie cried.

"Absolutely not!" James declared. "Dolly and I talked it over last night. We stand firm!"

"Even if we could convince them that Dearie is innocent," Stella broke in, "we couldn't begin to suggest who the real murderer is. How can we sift through forty years to come up with the answer? Some mornings it takes an hour for my brain to begin functioning efficiently. I can't recall the name of the delivery boy or I can't remember where I put my shoes or I forget the date."

"You seem pretty sharp to me," Benjamin argued gamely.

"I remember some things clearly," she retorted. "Others I can't recall at all."

"She's right," James agreed. "How can we be expected to come up with an answer when we don't even have a theory?"

"I don't relish the police delving into *my* past," Dolly whispered, near tears.

"That's what we've said from the start," Fannie insisted. "And that's what we'll continue to insist."

Stella turned to Dearborn. "Dearie, I'm wondering about something. How could an outsider know about the Rotten Apples?"

"*I* know about the Rotten Apples," Dearborn reminded her.

"You didn't learn about us until Toni went to you in desperation. Toni was as protective of her reputation as the rest of us. She might not have gone to you at all if you hadn't once been . . . well, you know."

Dearborn cleared his throat. "Good friends," he completed.

"Good friends," Fannie echoed.

"We were all good friends once," Dolly said wistfully.

"How true," Stella sighed. "I can remember when Toni was going through that awful divorce suit. Eddie tried to kidnap little Charlene and Fannie hid Charlene in the attic for weeks."

"Nothing to it," Fannie assured them. "Eddie was a filthy so and so. Anyway, I wasn't the only one to go out on a limb. James smuggled poor Jack Rogers onto the *Queen Mary* after Count Ambeil threatened to kill him."

"I had almost forgotten about that," James acknowledged. "I had my qualms, I admit. Did any of you ever see Caroline Ambeil's nose after the operation?"

Fannie tittered. "I understand it was worse in the summer."

"It did have a tendency to, well, spread," said James. His eyes began to tear.

Dolly clucked compassionately. "It was a genuine tragedy."

Fannie plunged her hand into the bosom of her blouse and came up holding a lace handkerchief. She snickered wickedly. "He must have been in his cups when he did it. He told me she'd never have to worry about her sinuses again." Fannie choked and dabbed at her eyes.

"And then," Stella continued, "when Arthur Howe got into difficulties—"

"What kind of difficulties?" Dearborn asked.

"Transvestite," Fannie said, lowering her handkerchief. "Picked up in Times Square wearing his wife's evening gown."

"Could have been a terrible scandal," Stella confided. "He was always so belligerent. But he called us and we all exchanged clothes and went down there."

133

"Told them it was a masquerade party," James explained. "We might all have ended up behind bars."

"I still remember what you looked like in Dolly's crepe de chine bloomers," Fannie reminisced. "And Louise. Remember Louise? She cut off some of her hair and pasted it onto her upper lip . . ." Again Fannie raised her handkerchief and tried, unsuccessfully, to suppress a rude laugh.

"Poor Louise," Dolly sighed. "Dead all these years."

"There were other instances," James mused. "When Terence Van Horne began collecting money for Spain in '37, we all chipped in generously. Every last one of us."

"And what about Bobby?" Fannie reminded him. "We got him to go straight before the police caught up with him, didn't we?"

"We chipped in then, too," declared Stella. "We contributed three thousand dollars apiece, thirty thousand dollars, so he could buy this place."

"Why, so we did," declared Fannie. "I'd forgotten. That was quite a lot of money in those days."

"It's quite a lot of money right now," Stella noted ruefully.

"I wish you'd listen to me," Benjamin interrupted again. He waved the newspaper in front of them. "It says here that the police know who killed Vernon Tree. It all but spells out my father's name. On top of that, now they've decided that Terence Van Horne was murdered—"

"The croquet mallet?" Dearborn cut in.

"Yeah. But it didn't turn out the way I thought it would."

"They think I killed Terence," Dearborn said. "They think you're protecting me."

"We're *both* missing now. What are they supposed to think?"

"Benjamin," Dearborn said, "the police have to track me down before they can arrest me. Given their general level of incompetence, that shouldn't be any too soon."

"That's the spirit!" James shouted encouragingly.

A sharp ring cut the air. Nadine got up and headed for the hall. "It's the gate," she informed them over her shoulder.

They waited, listening, while she spoke over the intercom. The conversation was brief. She returned looking worried. "It's the Smiths. Raymond, can you believe it? They came back a week early."

"And who, may I ask," Dearborn inquired, "are the Smiths?"

"The cook and the handyman," Reid answered.

"Good Lord!" Fannie wailed. "What will they think?"

"What about it?" Benjamin asked Nadine.

She looked concerned. "They'll be curious."

"We'll tell them we're visiting Robert," James declared.

"Robert's not here," Fannie reminded him.

"We'll say we're waiting for him to return."

"Can't we say it's a reunion?" Stella suggested.

Dearborn nodded. "That is exactly what we shall do. But it will call for playacting. Some verve, a little more happy camaraderie."

Dolly sighed. "I'm not very good at playacting."

James tried to rise to the occasion. " 'Come Mates, Tra-la, Lift high the glass . . .' " He faltered. "That's strange. The rest slips my mind . . ."

"How about 'Come Mates, Tra-lo, it may be our last,' " Stella supplied.

"Come, come," Dearborn said irritably, "you were snickering over one another's misfortunes five minutes ago. Surely you can put a lighter face on it if you have to."

"It might bolster your spirits, Dolly," James said gently.

"I'm for anything that might relieve the gloom," Stella said.

"You haven't commented, Fannie," Dearborn remarked. "Do you think you could bring it off?"

Fannie bridled. "You are asking *me* whether or not *I* can act?"

"So much for that," Dearborn declared. "It's settled. In front of the help we shall be revelers celebrating the golden anniversary of the . . . er . . ."

135

"RAC," Stella supplied.

"Yes, that does have a more impressive sound than the Rotten Apple Corps."

"You'd better take the golf cart down to the gate, Raymond," Nadine said. "They've got suitcases to bring up."

Reid nodded grudgingly, got up, and shuffled out of the room.

"I wish they hadn't come," Dolly murmured.

"It may be a change for the better," Fannie said. "At least the food will improve."

"They'll probably object to looking after us," Benjamin noted. "Especially since they weren't supposed to go back to work until next week."

"I'll handle that," Dearborn said. "Miss Garrett, tell them there will be a generous bonus for each of them."

"I'd better go down to the kitchen and wait for them," Nadine suggested. "The bonus will help." She followed Reid down the hall.

"Push me to the French doors," Dearborn instructed Benjamin. When they were out of earshot, Dearborn said from the side of his mouth, "Benjamin, I want you to make some subtle inquiries of Miss Garrett. I want to know if she and Reid are aware of the fact that Robert sold the clinic."

"Why don't we ask them right out?"

"Because, Benjamin, we can't ask them about the sale without informing them about the sale, and that I do not wish to do. I thought, considering your intimacy with Miss Garrett . . ."

"I'm not intimate with Nadine, Dad."

"Keep your private life to yourself. Stick to the subject. They may be facing the loss of their jobs. I want to know if they're aware of it."

"Hell, Dad, I don't like it. I'm no sneak. They're going to find out the clinic's been sold soon enough. I don't see why we just can't tell them."

"Because it may complicate an already complicated situation."

136

"Dearie?" Stella waved to Dearborn. "We've just had an idea."

"What is it?"

Benjamin pushed Dearborn's chair back across the room.

"We were just saying it might be a good idea to get together for tea. We have to have our tea anyway. And it would give the impression that we're here on pleasure rather than . . ."

"I was thinking that I might recite a few lines of poetry," James put in.

"And Fannie can play the piano," Stella suggested. "It would establish the right atmosphere, don't you agree?"

"Very constructive," Dearborn responded.

"Then shall we plan it for four o'clock, Dearie?" Stella asked.

"The logical hour," Dearborn conceded. "I suggest, in the meantime, that we maintain a discreet distance between ourselves and the new arrivals."

Eighteen

Roscoe Smith presided over the buffet table. There were fresh flowers, an array of tea sandwiches, a fruitcake, a crystal bowl filled with canned mandarin oranges, and an elaborate silver tea service. There were bread and butter sandwiches, sardine and tuna crackers with slivers of lemon, homemade biscuits, and a crock of raspberry jam.

A wedge of cheese had appeared from somewhere, along with a basket of crisp melba toast.

Smith was a tall, muscular man in his forties with a round head, mangled ears, and a sullen expression. His white jacket fit badly, his shirt cuffs were soiled, and the bow tie clipped under his Adam's apple was too tight.

"He doesn't look much like a waiter," James noted sotto voce to Dolly.

"Nevertheless," Dolly whispered back, "any waiter is an improvement over no waiter."

"Fruitcake," Stella said appreciatively. "From the smell of it I'd say it's been steeped in Napoleon brandy."

"A lot more enticing than the canned spaghetti Miss Garrett served for lunch," Dolly declared.

Fanny, her willowy figure swathed in blue-and-white lounging pajamas, took a fix on the buffet. She jabbed at the fruitcake with a rigid finger. Smith, behind the table, pulled away the platter.

Benjamin pushed Dearborn into the room and up to the buffet table.

"You are Smith?" Dearborn asked.

Smith grunted.

Dearborn signaled to Benjamin to move him closer. "You and your wife must be surprised to find us here."

Smith acknowledged the remark with another grunt.

"Mrs. Smith is in the kitchen?"

"Yeah."

"She has prepared a fine spread," Dearborn offered graciously with a nod to the table.

Smith returned Dearborn's calculating gaze expressionlessly.

"I understand that you and Mrs. Smith have been on vacation."

Smith's gaze remained unwavering and noncommittal.

"Back a week earlier than expected," Dearborn went on. "Couldn't stay away from the place, eh?"

"You want something to eat?" Smith demanded in a surly voice.

Surreptitiously Benjamin prodded Dearborn's shoulder, then announced heartily, "How about some of these bread and butter sandwiches, Dad?"

"Put a few on a plate for me. Well, Smith? What have you got to say for yourself?"

"Nothing," Smith replied insolently.

"I've got my eye on the fruitcake," James said. "Dolly, my dear, you're fond of raspberry jam."

"I'll have tea," Stella decided.

"I'd like some brandy," Fannie asserted. "Where's the liquor cabinet?"

Dearborn was losing his temper but before he could say anything, Benjamin jerked the wheelchair away from the buffet table and steered it across the room. "Dad, cool it. You're going to ruin it for everybody."

"Damned arrogant," Dearborn muttered.

"Dearie," Stella said, sidling up to Dearborn, "I've been thinking."

"What about?"

"About us. Has it occurred to you that one of us could be . . . well, responsible?"

Dearborn arranged his features into an expression of innocent surprise. "Responsible? One of you?"

"Us?" James exclaimed, joining them. "What about us?"

"I think one of us may have more to do with this situation than it seems," Stella answered calmly.

"In what way?" James asked. "Wait a minute. You don't think. . . ?" The fruitcake wobbled to the edge of James's plate and began to slide off. He set the plate on the coffee table and pulled Dolly down onto the couch next to him. "Are you suggesting, Stella, that one of us—"

"Us?" Dolly declared. "You're saying that one of us—"

Fannie, holding aloft a brandy snifter, charged into the group. "What are you talking about? What about us?"

Dolly said in a loud whisper, "Stella thinks one of us may be the one." She clutched James's hand. He put his arm around her shoulder.

Fannie's expression remained blank until she caught

on. "Us!" she exclaimed. "But it makes no sense at all! Why would one of us . . ."

Benjamin noticed that Smith was leaning across the buffet table. He raised his voice. "Did you say you were going to give a recitation, Mr. Bell?"

James looked at Benjamin blankly. Benjamin rolled his eyes and the group shifted its collective gaze to Smith. Immediately Dearborn added jovially, "Come, come, James. Let's not play coy."

James rallied to the challenge. He cleared his throat. "Er, let me see. Something rousing, I think."

"Something inspirational," Dolly urged. "Something suitable to the occasion."

James rose and folded his hands over his plump middle. " 'A fool there was and his goods he spent, even as you and I . . .' "

Dolly pulled on the hem of his jacket. "Not Rudyard Kipling, Jimmy."

James stopped and thought, then launched into " 'My heart leaps up when I behold a rainbow in the sky . . .' "

"Bobby did seem more suited to crime than the rest of us," Stella whispered behind her hand. "He took to it like the proverbial duck. He was in and out of difficulties all the time."

"That's what comes of having a butcher for a father," Fannie purred over the lip of her brandy snifter.

"Borden Bright made a million in 1917," Stella said. "Supplying jerky or horsemeat or some other unappetizing product to the troops."

"And lost a million in 1929," Fannie added.

" 'So it was when my life began . . .' " James droned on.

"What kind of difficulties?" Dearborn asked. Benjamin leaned over the back of Dearborn's chair to listen.

"You know some of it," Stella said. "The business of the oil swindle. And he forged letters. Letters under the signature of E. S. Harkness soliciting money for Great Britain back in 1930."

"How much did he make?" Benjamin asked.

"Nothing. Harkness set a bunch of private

140

bloodhounds on his trail and he was afraid to carry through."

"Ssh. Ssh," Dolly cautioned, her eyes riveted on James. "James is trying to recite."

" 'So it is now I am a man . . .' " recited James.

"Tell me more," Dearborn said.

Fannie sat down on the arm of the couch. "You know about the oil swindle. They were onto him that time, too. He has the Rotten Apples to thank for saving him from total ruin that time."

"How?" Benjamin asked.

"He had to make good or go to jail. It took everything he had. It left him penniless. We chipped in enough so he could start this place. Thirty thousand dollars."

"Pity he made such a success of it," Stella murmured. "If he'd ever decided to sell, we'd be rich."

" 'So be it when I shall grow old, or let me die . . .' " James intoned.

"How's that?" Dearborn said sharply. "What do you mean, if he ever decided to sell, we'd be rich?"

" 'So be it when I shall grow old, or let me die . . .' " James intoned.

"How's that?" Dearborn said sharply. "What do you mean, if he ever decided to sell you'd be rich?"

"We have an agreement. If he sells we share in the profits."

"What!" Dearborn exploded. "What did you say?"

Behind them Smith dropped a spoon he was polishing. It hit the sandwich platter and bounced off again onto the floor. James paused and then went on resolutely, " 'The child is father of the man . . .' "

"Benjamin," Dearborn instructed, "do something about Smith."

"What?"

"Get rid of him."

Benjamin disengaged himself from the circle and went across the room. "Look, we could use some . . ." he scanned the table, "some more fruitcake."

"You didn't eat this one yet."

141

"We'd like another."

"I'll have to go down to the cellar. Those fruitcakes are supposed to be for Christmas."

"You can serve plum pudding for Christmas."

Smith's eyes darted to Dearborn, then to the door, then to the table. He reached down, picked up the spoon, and dropped it into one of the teacups. Then he headed for the door. Benjamin rejoined the group.

Dearborn was saying to Stella, "What kind of agreement?"

"Simply that. That the group is to share in the profits if Bobby ever sells the place."

"The group? You mean the Rotten Apples?"

"Yes."

"A percentage of the profits?"

"No," James said, abandoning the recitation. "Equal shares."

Benjamin repeated incredulously, "Equal shares? You're kidding!"

"There, you see," Dolly remarked, "Stella was right when she said things slip one's mind. I don't remember it at all. Was it in writing, Stella?"

"Of course it was in writing. It *is* in writing. You must have a copy somewhere."

"I suppose so," Dolly said vaguely. "I can't imagine where."

"A fine agreement for all the good it's ever done us," James complained. "I said at the outset it should have been a ten-year loan."

"None of us dreamed we'd ever need the money," Stella said.

"You've got no gambling blood," Fannie said scathingly. "You didn't then and you don't now."

"Wasn't there a statute of limitations?" Benjamin asked.

"It's binding for our lifetimes," Stella explained. "But it can't be transferred or inherited. So unless Bobby suddenly takes it into his head to sell the place, the agreement's not worth the paper it's written on."

"And what would you say," Dearborn asked, "if I told you that Robert *has* sold the clinic?"

Stella frowned. "You aren't saying that, are you?" she asked cautiously.

"This morning I made some inquiries concerning the papers Robert had signed and mailed to Miss Garrett for forwarding to Corbett, Rubin, and Bonnell. The papers concerned the sale of the clinic. Apparently it is a fait accompli, the price being somewhere near the two-million mark."

Dolly reached out and sought James's hand. Fannie's mouth dropped open. There was a moment's silence. Fannie recovered first. "You aren't playing a practical joke on us, Dearborn?"

"No, Fannie. I'm not."

"But," she said, "do you have any idea what this means?"

"I'm beginning to."

"It means that I shall no longer be dependent on my graceless daughter or my dull son-in-law."

"That, too," Dearborn allowed.

Dolly leaned back against the couch cushions.

"Are you all right, Dolly?" James asked in alarm. "You aren't having an attack, are you?"

"I'll just close my eyes for a moment. It's all rather shocking."

Stella rose from her chair and strode to the center of the room. "Heavens! You can't possibly know! This is marvelous! I've been facing . . . taxes . . . and . . ." She stopped. "Do you know what I've just remembered? I'm the one who has the original of the agreement!"

"That's right!" Fannie exclaimed. "We drew straws to see who would hold it and you won. Where is it?"

"The original and one copy are in a sa,:e-deposit box at the First National Bank."

"I can't believe it," Dolly murmured breathlessly. She patted her breast with a fluttering hand.

"Dearborn," Fannie declared, "I have always known you to be an honest man, no matter what your other faults. I know that you would not make up a story like this."

"Very discerning of you."

"Then we are rich?"

Dearborn held up his hand. "You are forgetting something."

"What's that, Dearie?" Stella asked.

"The role Robert plays in this."

"Of course we're not overlooking it," James said. "He's the pivotal figure."

"In more ways than one," Dearborn returned.

They looked baffled. Then Stella whispered, "Oh, Lord."

"Are you trying to tell us Bobby is dead?" Fannie quavered.

"Certainly not. If he were dead we'd know it. I am trying to tell you that he is the one who sold the clinic and that he knows better than anyone else that all of you will benefit from the sale. In other words, Robert is the most likely suspect."

"But he's supposed to have been away when the murders were committed," Stella noted.

"There are a dozen suits in his closet," Dearborn cut in. "He didn't pack them. He didn't pack his toiletries either . . ."

"What about Bobby?" Dolly appealed.

"Bobby's the one, Dolly," Fannie announced theatrically. "Don't you see!"

"Oh!" Dolly stiffened.

"He has contacts all over the world, hasn't he?" Dearborn reminded them. "It wouldn't have been difficult to arrange to have his letters forwarded."

"He's here," James stated in a flat voice. "He only pretended to go on vacation."

"Of course," Fannie asserted forcefully. "There it is! That explains it! The man who tried to attack me!"

Benjamin thought back to the face peering at him through the lounge window the night before. "What does Bright look like?" he asked.

144

"We haven't seen him in ages," Stella replied.

"You've seen pictures of him, haven't you? I'm just trying to get some idea if he could have been the guy looking in the window last . . ." Benjamin stopped. "Uh oh."

"What did you say?" Fannie cried.

"Someone was looking in the window?" James demanded.

"When?" Stella asked. "When was that?"

Benjamin didn't look at Dearborn. He began to mumble something about tree branches and leaves in the wind.

"No use, Benjamin," Dearborn interrupted drily. "You might as well tell them the truth."

"What truth?" Fannie demanded.

"I saw someone at the window of the lounge last night. Late. After everyone had gone to bed."

"What did he look like?" Stella asked.

"Tall," Benjamin said. "Slender. A little stooped. With a lot of hair."

"Bobby is tall," James conceded.

"And thin," Fannie added.

"He did have a good head of hair," Stella said. "Thick. Unruly."

"Kinky," Fannie amended. "Did this person have kinky hair?"

"Yeah," Benjamin muttered. "And I'd guess kinky describes more than his haircut."

"Oh," Dolly breathed.

"My dear, are you all right?" James asked solicitously.

"Tactless though apt, Benjamin," Dearborn commented calmly. "Tactless though apt."

145

Nineteen

There was a sharp crack outside the French doors. Stella yelped and Dolly, sitting slumped against the couch cushions, started so violently that she knocked the plate out of her lap.

"What was that?" Fannie cried out. "It sounded like a shot."

"Thunder," Benjamin said.

James got to his feet. "I'll close the doors."

Fannie scurried toward the hall. "I don't like thunderstorms. I'm going to stand by an inside wall."

"My bedroom window is open," Dolly said.

"So's mine," noted Stella.

"I'll take care of the windows," Benjamin volunteered. There was another clap of thunder and a flash of lightning as he crossed the room.

"Jimmy, dear," Dolly urged, "come away from the doors."

James shut the French doors and locked them. He joined Dolly on the couch.

"This may be an opportune moment to visit the kitchen," Dearborn said. "Stella, will you push the wheelchair?"

There was a radio on the kitchen counter and it was blasting out the score from *Grease*. At the sink was Mrs. Smith, her plump backside in peach-colored slacks bouncing to the music, the colander in her hand shaking rhythmically under the running faucet.

"Mrs. Smith?"

She turned, presenting bright blue eyes, pink cheeks, full lips, and a substantial bosom.

"I'm Dearborn V. Pinch. This is Miss Gresham."

"How do you do."

"Miss Garrett explained to you who we are and what we are doing here?"

"Class reunion. She told me. I'm class of '41 myself. Phoenix High. Phoenix, Arizona."

"Obviously a vintage year," Dearborn offered gallantly.

Mrs. Smith smiled cheerfully.

"Did you and Mr. Smith have a pleasant vacation?"

"Up until yesterday," she answered.

"What happened yesterday?"

"Roscoe lost his temper."

"Ah."

"He does it every time."

"A standard pattern, is it?" Dearborn asked sympathetically.

"He's jealous," Mrs. Smith said candidly. "He doesn't like me talking to other men. You know, the green-eyed monster."

"That must make things difficult," Dearborn suggested.

"Everybody's got his faults."

"Not entirely true," Dearborn said. "Nevertheless . . ."

Mrs. Smith tapped her foot to the music. "We'll always be to . . . gether . . ."

"Tell me, how long have you and your spouse worked at the clinic?"

"Almost a year," she answered.

"And before that?"

"We managed a motel out by Orient Point. Till Roscoe lost his temper."

"At which point you abandoned the motel business?"

147

"Faster than you can say Jack Robinson."

"How did you come to this job, Mrs. Smith?"

"Through an employment agency."

"And you and your hubby are contented here?"

"Why not?" she returned breezily.

"Mr. Bright is a good employer, is he?"

"If you like working for the Howard Hughes type," she replied.

"I don't follow you."

"Mr. Bright's away a lot. We've never even seen him. The whole time we've been here we've never laid eyes on him. He comes and goes. Signs the salary checks and runs the place but keeps to himself."

The music ended and the announcer began talking about piston rings. Mrs. Smith reached across the sink and switched stations. "I'm walkin', yes indeed, and I'm talkin', yes indeed . . ." She shook her shoulders and snapped her fingers vigorously.

"He doesn't mix with the employees?" Dearborn pressed.

"Not with the guests, either. Not with anybody."

"What's going on here?" a voice growled from the doorway. It was Smith carrying a silver-foil package. "What do you want from my wife?"

"We are discussing the dinner menu," Dearborn informed him. "Aren't we, Mrs. Smith?"

"If you say so," she returned blithely.

"You were telling me that we're dining on rice and . . ."

"Beans," she supplied.

"Beans," declared Dearborn. "Yes. Rice and beans and . . ."

"Salad," Mrs. Smith filled in. "With applesauce and cinnamon. Homemade."

"Eight o'clock, then," Dearborn said. "We're looking forward to it. Rice, beans, salad, applesauce." He motioned to Stella and she rotated the wheelchair. "Oh, and Smith—skip the fruitcake. We won't be wanting it after all."

148

Smith slammed the package down on the kitchen table. The silver rectangle flattened into a thick pancake.

"Applesauce is right," Stella whispered as she wheeled Dearborn to the elevator. "And you'll end up as applesauce too if you don't steer clear of that big oaf."

Benjamin met Nadine coming out of Dearborn's room. "It's starting to rain," she said. "The windows are all open."

"I'll get the other side of the hall," Benjamin offered. He closed the windows in his and Stella's rooms while Nadine did the same for James and Dolly. Benjamin closed Reid's windows and met Nadine in front of the door to her own room. She pulled the chain out of the neckline of her blouse, selected a key, and bent down to unlock her door.

Benjamin sprinted into the room behind her. He pushed her aside and crossed to the window. Rain spattered his shirt and another gust of air blew the door shut behind them before he succeeded in shutting the window.

"Nadine, I want to ask you something. What about this trip Bright's supposed to be on?"

"Supposed to be on?" she repeated. "What do you mean?"

"Did anybody take him to the airport? You or Reid or anybody else?"

Nadine said, "Of course somebody took him to the airport."

"Who?"

She frowned. "I think it was Raymond."

"Where is he? I'd like to talk to him."

"Or was it . . . no, it wasn't Raymond. I think it was Al Kroll, the social director."

"Where's he?"

She shrugged. "Great Britain, I think. He's an Englishman. I think he's over there visiting his family. Hey, listen, what's this all about?"

149

"Did anybody else see Bright go? I mean actually get on the airplane and go?"

"What are you getting at?" Nadine burst out. "Are you trying to say you think he didn't go away? Why would you think that? Look, I've been getting letters from him from all over the Pacific."

"The letters could have been forwarded through friends."

"Oh, I'm beginning to think you're all crazy." She reached for the doorknob. Benjamin put his hand over hers to keep her from opening the door.

"Nadine, I'm sorry. We probably shouldn't have come here in the first place, but it's too late now. We're going to have to see this through."

"Or get killed in the process."

"You're not one of the targets."

"Accidents happen."

"I'm just trying to lead up to asking if you know why Bright sold the clinic."

"What are you talking about?"

Benjamin sagged. He'd done it again. "Shit."

"Who told you Mr. Bright sold the clinic?"

"My father and I have contacts at Corbett, Rubin, and Bonnell. The papers Bright asked you to forward were sales contracts." Benjamin was puzzled about something. "You delivered the papers, Nadine. Weren't you curious about them? Didn't you read them?"

"The envelope to the lawyer came as a sealed enclosure. I simply took it to town and handed it to Mr. Bonnell. Ben, are you sure about this?"

"I'm afraid so. I'm sorry."

"Not as sorry as me."

The rain drove against the windows and a clap of thunder was followed by a flash of lightning. Nadine flinched at the sound. She pulled open the door and went into the hall. "I'd better break the news to Raymond."

"What's the hurry? He'll find out soon enough."

"He might as well hear it from me."

* * *

150

The cocktail hour was livelier than they had anticipated, thanks to Smith's predinner bartending.

By the time the dinner bell rang, Stella had traced the
women's movement back to the 1928 Olympics and was
praising Sonja Henie as one of its prime movers, and
Fannie had swung into her fourth repetition of "Let's
Have Another Cup of Coffee." James and Dolly were
unable to extricate themselves from the armchair and
had to be pried loose by Benjamin.

Reid didn't show up at the dinner table. Neither did
Nadine. Benjamin noted the absences and felt another
twinge of guilt over his responsibility for upsetting them.

Fannie, the cocktail high having worn off, insisted on
sitting facing the window. Dolly and James, slightly tipsy,
shoved their chairs close together and leaned on one
another. Stella, convivial but a little vague, leaned back in
her chair and smiled pleasantly at the chandelier.

Mrs. Smith helped Mr. Smith serve the meal, a robust
Mexican dish, as promised, with beans, rice, cornbread,
and warm cinnamon applesauce. She helped Dearborn
to the biggest piece of cornbread and nudged him with
her hip while she leaned down to hold the rice platter
under his nose. Dearborn responded by clucking softly
into his wineglass while Benjamin, at the other end of the
table, deflected Smith's suspicious stare by asking for a
second helping of beans.

During the hiatus between entrée and dessert, Dearborn whipped out a small red leather notebook and
began scribbling in it, listing, crossing out, and, during
thoughtful pauses, drawing stick people with circle heads
in the margins. By the time Mrs. Smith sashayed in with
the lemon soufflé, he was in a decisive mood. He tapped
his teaspoon against his coffee cup. "I have an
announcement."

Again, with the same exquisite timing as earlier that
day, there was a roll of thunder.

"Uh, oh," Benjamin murmured. "This may tie us up
for the next forty days and forty nights."

"Very droll, Benjamin," Dearborn said coolly.

"What is it, Dearie?" Stella asked, somewhat revived. "Is it about . . ." She glanced at the Smiths.

"It is."

James and Dolly clasped one another's hands under the table.

Dearborn waited until the Smiths had finished. After they'd left the room, Fannie said, "If you're about to bring up the subject of the police, I'm leaving the table."

"Ssh." Dearborn held up his hand and waited until he heard the elevator doors close and the elevator descend to the kitchen level. Then he picked up the little red notebook and held it aloft. "I have studied the problem and examined the evidence. We are dealing with a person, seemingly normal but with one facet of his personality so exaggerated that it warps his reason. Our killer's sickness is greed. Greed of pathological enormity."

"It's true," Fannie declared. "After all, there is enough for all of us. Why would Bobby want more than his share?"

"I can understand him wanting it," James declared, "but not killing to get it."

"He's an out-and-out gangster!" Fannie remarked.

"No use analyzing him," Stella concluded. "Catching him—that's what matters."

"I agree, Stella," Dearborn said. "And catching him is just what I intend to do."

"How?" Dolly asked.

"Simple," James cried, his eyes gleaming. "By combing the house and grounds. By launching an all-out attack. 'Into the valley of death' . . . of course, one of us men will have to remain here to look after the women."

"Nonsense," Dearborn snapped. "There is nothing to be gained by chasing all over creation. There are too many places to hide."

"What have you got in mind, Dad?" Benjamin asked.

"We shall attract him to us."

"How do you expect to do that?" Dolly asked.

Dearborn tucked the notebook back into his pocket. "By laying a trap. By providing a decoy. Nothing to it."

"It's not going to be me," Fannie announced. "I don't intend to offer myself up to that lunatic."

"Dolly can't possibly do it," James objected. "She's far too delicate, and to tell you the truth, Dearborn, I'm not enthusiastic about the idea myself. Though, of course, I shall not shrink from doing my duty if it comes to that—provided that Dolly will allow it." James gave Dolly a swift glance and she patted his hand affectionately.

"I'm not afraid to act as a decoy," Stella offered. "I'll be glad to do it, Dearie."

"None of you will do it," Dearborn informed them. "The killer was able to devise and carry out a series of efficient murders. The fact that the original scheme has gone awry merely calls for a corresponding adjustment in his plan. He has nothing to fear from any of you. He knows by now that you are loath to go to the police even though you know your lives may be at stake. It is I who pose the greater threat."

"Nope," Benjamin said flatly. "Forget it. No you're not."

"Time is of the essence," Dearborn went on over Benjamin's objections. "There is every reason to believe that he will make his move soon. Therefore—"

"Damn it, Dad!"

"We shall attempt to provide him with the most conducive circumstances possible."

Twenty

"No one's interested in your choppers, James," Dearborn derided, and when Dolly attempted a "sounds like" with de Maupassant, Dearborn said irritably, "Guy doesn't rhyme with tie, it rhymes with tee."

"I'm not interested in playing charades anyway," Dolly returned. "I think it's silly."

But Dearborn insisted that they carry on, until finally James withdrew after Fannie accused him of treating *Jude the Obscure* too literally, Dolly refused to attempt *La Grande Illusion*, and Stella failed utterly to convey "I love my wife but oh you kid."

By ten no one was even trying to maintain the appearance of normalcy. A pall had fallen on the group. Dearborn was forced to accept defeat and let them retire, which they did promptly and gratefully. Benjamin wheeled Dearborn into the lounge and left him there.

Dearborn spent the time between ten and eleven-thirty absorbed in a volume he had taken from one of the bookshelves. Then at eleven, as prearranged, Benjamin rejoined him, pretending, according to Dearborn's instructions, to have happened by casually.

"Well well, Benjamin," Dearborn sang out heartily, "what are you doing still up? Come in and join me for a drink."

The lights were dim, the curtains on both windows drawn back, and Dearborn's wheelchair positioned in such a way that he could view the windows and the door without moving his head. Benjamin crossed to the liquor cabinet. "What'll you have, Dad?"

"Scotch and water," Dearborn answered loudly. "Make it a double. Why don't you have the same?"

"I believe I will," Benjamin replied genially. He poured the drinks and handed one glass to his father, then lowered himself into an armchair facing the door.

"Not there," Dearborn ordered. "Uncomfortable. Can't put up your feet. Sit on the couch, my boy."

Benjamin eyed the couch unenthusiastically. Unless he sat with his head pivoted at a 180-degree angle, he wouldn't be able to see anything but the fireplace and a small section of wall on either side. "No, it's okay, I'll just . . ."

"The couch, the couch," Dearborn declared, and Benjamin, his haunches arrested in mid-air, changed course.

"Well, Benjamin," Dearborn emoted stagily from behind Benjamin's head. "How is everything?"

Benjamin addressed himself to the andirons. "Fine, thank you, sir. How's everything with you?"

"Excellent. I'm very fit. Except for my ankle, which makes it impossible to walk or defend myself against attack, if by some remote chance that should become necessary." Dearborn hummed a few bars of "Carefully on Tiptoe Stealing" from *H.M.S. Pinafore.*

"Dad, I've got to tell you something. I talked to Nadine this afternoon."

"And?"

"She didn't know about the sale of the clinic."

"She didn't or she doesn't?"

"I spilled the beans."

Dearborn snorted.

"Sorry, Dad."

"How did she receive the information?"

"All right, I guess, considering that she's probably going to be out of a job. I'll tell you one thing—she's not happy here right now. This Rotten Apple mess has her scared."

"Why? Her life's not in danger."

Benjamin shrugged. "That's a moot point. You know, Nadine keeps her bedroom door locked? She carries her key on a chain around her neck."

"I've seen her keys," Dearborn acknowledged.

"I think we should get her out of here, Dad. She could stay somewhere else until this is over."

"Have you suggested it to her?"

"Not yet. But I will."

"She won't go," Dearborn commented.

"Want to bet?" Benjamin half-rose and turned toward Dearborn, who twirled his finger until Benjamin, with an exasperated groan, turned back to stare resignedly at the blank fireplace.

"There's nothing wrong with being fond of the ladies, Benjamin, so long as you exercise discretion."

"That's about the only thing I am exercising around here."

"Don't lose your sense of humor, Benjamin. A sense of humor is invaluable. Perhaps we should go on to a less touchy subject. Tell me, how much do you know about the Sepoy Rebellion?"

"It took place in India," said Benjamin sulkily.

"In 1857 and 1858," Dearborn informed him. "I've been reading an interesting book, *History of the Indian Mutiny*. Did you know that the British issued their Hindu soldiers cartridges coated with beef grease? Violation of Hindu law. Responsible for a lot of the subsequent trouble."

Somewhere off in the distance there was a faint roll of thunder.

"Strange way the British had of trying to exert a civilizing influence. But the British are a strange people all around. Obsessed by trivia. Prosaic people with exotic tastes. Unusual combination."

"Not so unusual," Benjamin muttered meaningfully.

"Lawrence—not of Arabia, the other one—John Lawrence was an enigmatic man . . ."

Occasionally throughout the next hour and a half omi-

156

nous rumblings punctuated Dearborn's lecture on Berhampore, Meerut, Cawnpore, Lucknow, and Delhi. By one o'clock Benjamin had fallen into a half-sleep and Dearborn's reading had taken on a monotonous quality. Outside, the wind picked up. Inside, the house was still.

"Lasted five months," droned Dearborn. "Barbaric episode. But instructive. There are lessons to be learned there."

"Right on," mumbled Benjamin.

"Preparedness and vigilance. Especially vigilance. Did you hear me, Benjamin?"

"You bet."

"I am now going to read chapter twelve . . ."

An ear-splitting crack brought Benjamin to his feet. He turned to see a flash of lightning and the first blast of wind and rain rattle against the windows. "Whew!"

But Dearborn wasn't looking at the windows. He was giving his full attention to the open doorway, his head cocked in an attitude of listening, his eyes fixed on the dim rectangle.

"What is it?" Benjamin exclaimed.

Dearborn held up his hand. "I hear something in the kitchen."

Benjamin tried to listen, but the sounds of the storm in the foreground were too loud. He began to walk toward the hall.

"Wait," Dearborn commanded. Dearborn got to his feet and stepped away from the wheelchair.

"Hey," whispered Benjamin, "since when can you walk?"

"Since this afternoon," Dearborn hissed. "Now listen to me. I want you to pretend you are talking to me. Loudly. Commence."

"The hell with that," Benjamin hissed back. "I'm better off handling this than you. You talk loudly to me."

Dearborn glared at Benjamin and then strode to the door and was gone before Benjamin could stop him.

"That's the last straw," Benjamin yelled. He started after Dearborn. Suddenly, behind him, there was the sound of breaking glass and an object sailed through the air, striking the table lamp next to the couch. Benjamin spun around just in time to see the figure at the window before it darted away.

Benjamin was ready this time. He raced to the window, threw it open, loosing a shower of broken glass, and catapulted out. He was on his feet instantly, scanning the lawn. To his left a thin white figure tore across the grass toward the blur of trees.

"Stop!" Benjamin cried.

The fugitive had a head start and Benjamin was impeded by the swelling wind that smashed against his body and sprayed rain into his eyes and nostrils. Before he reached the line of trees, the flash of white was gone, and Benjamin plunged into the trees at the point where he had seen the figure disappear, the advantage becoming his as his galloping pursuit brought him within hearing range of the rustling leaves and snapping branches ahead.

"Stop!" Benjamin shouted again. This time the runaway did stop, so abruptly that Benjamin, startled, stopped also. There was no sound other than the wind and rain. Benjamin rubbed his eyes and slicked back his wet hair. He squinted into the dimness. His eyes had become adjusted to the dark, but it was impossible to sort out the branches, leaves, and tree trunks or to identify the person camouflaged there.

A rustling sound next to Benjamin caused him to jerk his head around, but the sound was only the scramble of a small creature. Benjamin took a tentative step forward. His shoes squished as they were sucked into the muck. He paused again and waited. Then, ahead of him, there was a noise, a hair-raising bubble of laughter, an idiotic giggle that stopped Benjamin's breathing for a few seconds and made him want to turn tail.

"Stop!" he shouted again, with more bravado than conviction. He cast around for a suitable follow-up. "I'm coming in after you!"

He dashed forward. Immediately the fugitive took off,

158

charging through the bushes in a frantic twig-snapping, branch-cracking retreat that reassured Benjamin and kept him going. He gained steadily. After a dozen yards the brush gave way to a clearing, and for the first time Benjamin had a good look at the figure as it paused in the center of the clearing and half-turned before taking off again.

"Good God!" Benjamin panted. He stared incredulously. It was a man, an elderly man, tall and skinny, with a high, tangled shock of pure white hair and a grotesque smile. What's more, he was naked, his knobby white body satiny wet as a salamander's.

"Wait!" Benjamin cried out.

The old man waggled his finger at Benjamin and leaped over a tree stump. A second later he plunged into the trees on the far side of the clearing. Benjamin, recovering from the shock, initiated a wild spurt that brought him to the woods a brief moment later and carried him to within a few feet of the scrambling streaker.

"Got you!" Benjamin gasped.

But the old man's body was slippery and he slithered away with a joyous cackle. Benjamin was afraid to tackle him. The frail bones under translucent flesh looked as though they would snap as easily as the brittle twigs on the trees. Benjamin, out of breath but desperate, again closed the distance between them and dove forward to throw his arms around the old man's chest. He planted his feet and held on.

At first the old man struggled, trying to break Benjamin's grip and then attempting to loosen himself by sliding downward toward the ground. He was obviously accustomed to this kind of wrestling and was enjoying himself. He twisted his head to grin at Benjamin before kicking him neatly in the shins. He chuckled appreciatively at Benjamin's yelp of pain. They struggled for another minute or two, Benjamin swearing roundly between cries of pain. Then unexpectedly the old man relaxed and let his arms drop to his sides.

"Finally," Benjamin wheezed. He loosened his hold

cautiously and grabbed one of the old man's arms. His captive, with a docile shake of his head, turned, smiled pleasantly, moved his hand toward his crotch, with what Benjamin took to be a show of modesty, then proceeded to relieve himself against Benjamin's leg.

"E-ough! God-damn!"

The old man rolled his eyes slyly and held up his finger. Behind them, in the near distance, there were crashing sounds and Dearborn's voice demanding to know where they were.

"Here! Over this way!"

"There. To the right," Benjamin heard Nadine cry.

A moment later Dearborn and Nadine emerged from behind a clump of bushes.

"Got him, I see," Dearborn exclaimed. "Even if you did have to rip off his clothes."

Benjamin looked at Nadine. She was holding a butcher knife. "I went down to look for my bracelet again. I heard the window break—"

"Well," interrupted Dearborn, puffing heavily, "well, Miss Garrett, that's he, isn't it?"

She nodded. "Yes, of course. I told you it would be. Raymond promised me that he wouldn't leave him alone tonight, and now look what's happened!"

Twenty-One

Robert Bright was escorted back to the house wearing Benjamin's shirt like an apron with the sleeves tied in back. They found Stella, Fannie, Dolly, and James, all in their nightclothes, huddled in the kitchen doorway.

"Who is it?" Stella demanded.

"Robert Bright," Benjamin informed her.

"My heavens! *That's* Bobby?"

Dolly, with a startled look, jumped back and clutched James's arm. "What's wrong with him?"

Fannie's face registered pure horror. "That face! He's the one who chased me! And look at him! The man is starkers!" She drew her silk dressing robe around herself protectively.

"According to Miss Garrett," said Dearborn, "Robert is partial to roaming around in the buff."

Bright, with a gay wink, turned to waggle his gaunt backside at them.

"I've seen better flanks on a hack pony," Fannie declared.

"He doesn't look dangerous," James opined.

"Of course he's not dangerous," Dearborn returned shortly. "He's in his dotage. The man is senile."

Nadine crossed the room and laid the butcher knife down on the counter.

"What's that?" James asked apprehensively. "You didn't take that from Bobby, did you?"

161

"No," Nadine said quickly. "I forgot I was holding it. I was in the kitchen looking for my bracelet. Mr. Pinch startled me and I picked up the knife. Then we heard the window break and we ran outside. Ben was out on the lawn chasing Mr. Bright."

"We'd better get the old guy dried off and warmed up," Benjamin suggested.

"You're just as bedraggled as he is," Stella observed.

"And, Dearborn," Dolly said in wonderment, "you're on your feet again. How did you manage that?"

"I found myself considerably improved this afternoon, Dolly, but I thought it wiser to keep it to myself. Now, where's Reid?" Dearborn peered around the kitchen.

"We tried to rouse him," Dolly explained in a small voice, "but he is simply too intoxicated."

"I should have known better than to trust him," Nadine fretted. "He insisted that he was all right, that he wasn't too drunk to handle Mr. Bright."

"And the Smiths?"

"I don't know," Nadine said. "Their room is back of the infirmary. I guess they didn't hear anything. Shall I wake them up?"

"Dad," Benjamin intervened, "let's not turn this into a circus."

"Let them sleep," Dearborn said. "We shall manage Robert ourselves."

"Raymond's bag is in the infirmary," Nadine said. "He often gives Mr. Bright a sedative when he's giving us trouble. A hypo. Shall I go get it?"

"Do you know how to administer it?" Dearborn asked.

"Yes. I've done it before."

"Fetch it then. Benjamin, get a good grip on him." They hustled Bright to the elevator and up to the second floor. He was docile while they toweled him dry and shoveled him into his pajamas but he balked at getting into bed, grabbing the mohair afghan that was folded at the foot of his bed, throwing himself to the floor, and burying his head in its soft folds.

When Nadine relieved him of the afghan he leaped

162

up, ran into the sitting room, and repeated the performance, this time with a wide-mouthed vase. It took the combined efforts of Benjamin holding his arms and Dearborn easing the vase up and over his chin, his ears, and his ruff of hair to extricate him. Giving him the injection wasn't any easier and required the application of an arm lock. Finally, when he was sedated and tucked into bed, he closed his eyes like a contented infant and went to sleep.

Benjamin, as well as Dearborn, had to rifle Bright's closet for dry clothes. Fortunately the slacks and shirt Benjamin chose were close enough in size to be manageable. Nadine went to her room to change. Then they rejoined the group in the kitchen. The kettle was steaming and Stella had lined up seven cups containing seven tea bags and behind them a row of paper plates holding slices of pound cake covered by paper napkins.

"Take your pound cake and hand me your cups," Stella instructed. She stood next to the stove pouring boiling water into each of the proffered teacups.

"I've got this sudden urge to sing "Whistle While You Work," Benjamin murmured as he slid into a chair next to Nadine.

"Butter, anyone?" Stella asked.

"Stella, you will kindly desist," Dearborn exhorted. "I wish to talk to Miss Garrett and I do not intend to compete with an assembly line of teacups, paper plates and pound cake."

"I'm doing the best I know how, Dearie."

"We are not Scottish terriers, Stella," Dearborn said testily.

"All right." She sat down at the table, propped her chin in her hands, and waited.

"Now," Dearborn commenced, "as you tell it, Miss Garrett, you and Reid have been concealing the fact that Robert is senile and has been for some time. Am I correct?"

Nadine looked miserable. "That's right. We didn't want anyone to know that he's . . . like this . . . until . . ."

163

"Until the clinic was sold," Dearborn supplied. "Am I still correct?"

She nodded.

"Wait a minute," Benjamin broke in. "This afternoon you said you didn't know the clinic had been sold!"

Nadine returned his accusing look calmly. "This afternoon I still had hopes of protecting Mr. Bright. Tonight, when he was exposed—"

"Exposed is right!" Stella exclaimed.

"I knew that I'd have to tell the truth. And the truth is that Raymond and I have deceived you. I started to tell your father about it. Now you might as well hear it."

"I don't understand," Fannie cut in. "Why would you and Mr. Reid want to deceive anyone?"

James held up his slice of pound cake. "Deception. 'Oh, what may man within him hide, though angel on the outward side.' *Hamlet*."

"*Measure for Measure*," Dearborn corrected absentmindedly.

"We knew," Nadine said simply, "that once we let it out that Mr. Bright was . . . um . . ."

"Failing," Dearborn supplied.

"Yes, failing, it might be disastrous for the clinic. I mean the success of the clinic depended on Mr. Bright's remaining vital and er . . ."

"Functional," Dearborn said.

"Yes. He's been like this for a while. A little more than a year. He had a stroke. A slight stroke. And after that he got more and more . . . er . . ."

"Incapacitated," Dearborn said.

"You must have had to call a doctor," Stella declared. "How could you keep a thing like that quiet?"

"No," Nadine said. "We didn't call a doctor. Raymond took care of him."

"Mr. Reid? But Mr. Reid isn't a doctor."

"Stella," Dearborn remonstrated. "I am conducting this inquiry. Please stop interrupting. Go on, Miss Garrett."

"I know it must seem irresponsible. But we didn't look

at it that way. We've taken very good care of him. We've been hiding him for ages, from everyone. From the clients, from his lawyer, even from the rest of the staff."

"Ah hah!" Dearborn exclaimed. "That accounts for the fact that the Smiths have never seen him."

"Yes. But it couldn't go on forever. Lately some of the staff have begun to get suspicious. I mean, how long could we go on pretending he was away? We had to smuggle trays up to him. We had to keep him quiet. A couple of times he got loose and we caught him just in time."

"Yes, yes," Dearborn prodded. "So?"

"So we decided that once we closed the clinic for the summer, we'd try to sell the place," Nadine concluded. "And we did."

Benjamin looked at her in amazement. "You? You mean you and Raymond Reid?"

She began to tear little pieces off the edge of her napkin. She nodded.

"But why?" Benjamin asked. "Surely it wasn't your responsibility?"

"For one thing, Raymond wanted to have a say in what would happen to the clinic. He thought if it were sold to someone in the same line—health farm or beauty spa or whatever—he might be able to stay on. It wouldn't be easy for Raymond to find another job. He's been here so long and Mr. Bright put up with him, even with his drinking."

"And what was your interest in this, Miss Garrett?"

Nadine met Dearborn's gaze defiantly. "I felt sorry for Mr. Bright. I thought if we kept quiet about his condition, we could get more money for the clinic. He hasn't any family. His lawyer isn't a friend. There's no one who cares about him. I was afraid they'd make any deal they could, collect their fees, and get out. I was even afraid they might cheat him."

"Didn't you realize you were committing a crime?" Benjamin asked.

Nadine's face became flushed. "He's old. He hadn't

165

anyone to look after him. He's taken care of me, paid me well. I thought I owed it to him."

"Tell me, Miss Garrett," Dearborn inquired, "who signed the papers authorizing the sale of the clinic?"

She bit her lip, hesitated, and then said in a low voice, "Raymond did. We rerouted them through a friend of Raymond's living in Tokyo, to give the impression that Mr. Bright was away. Raymond has been signing everything for a long time, even before Mr. Bright became . . . er . . ."

"Infirm," Dearborn said.

"He's been forging Bobby's signature?" Stella said.

"Mr. Bright knew about it in the beginning. He asked Raymond to do it originally. It facilitated things when Mr. Bright was away on business trips. By now the bank, the lawyer, everybody accepts Raymond's signature as the real thing. It's the only signature they've seen for ages."

"Do you understand that you and Reid could go to jail?" Dearborn demanded.

"Of course I do. I'm not an idiot. That's why we couldn't let you know that Mr. Bright was right here all along or tell you that he's . . . you know."

"You allowed yourself to become involved in a serious felony," Dearborn remonstrated.

Nadine bristled. "I didn't think of it as being criminal. I only meant to help."

"It didn't occur to you that your misrepresentation is hardly a service to the other principals involved?"

"I didn't think about the complications. It wasn't as if I were trying to get something for myself—"

"Lay off, Dad," Benjamin interjected. "It isn't the end of the world." Benjamin gave Nadine a reassuring smile. "It'll work out. No one here's going to make waves."

"Another question, Miss Garrett," Dearborn went on. "Why did you agree to have us here? You must have known the risk you were running."

"I didn't agree," she replied promptly. "There's noth-

166

ing I wanted less. It was Raymond's idea. He thought it would be safer for Mr. Bright. He was positive he could keep Mr. Bright hidden from you."

"Miss Garrett," James ventured, "where has Bobby been? Where have you kept him? He wasn't in his room."

"Monday night Raymond improvised a place out in the shed. He lined it with gym mats, even over the windows, and he put in a cot. On Tuesday morning Mr. Bright escaped. That's when he must have chased Mrs. Tyler. Then he let himself out of the gate, and at lunchtime Raymond went after him. He found him about a quarter of a mile down the road."

"So Mr. Reid didn't have an accident with the golf cart after all," Fannie exclaimed. "I knew he didn't."

"No. He had a hard time getting Mr. Bright to come back. The bolt on the shed door was loose," Nadine continued, "and Raymond fixed it. But he didn't have much time and he didn't fix it well enough. Mr. Bright broke it last night and got out again."

"You knew it was Bright at the window last night?" Benjamin asked.

"Yes." She avoided Benjamin's eyes. "Raymond fixed the bolt again and he promised to stay with Mr. Bright tonight. He was going to give him a sedative, but he must have gotten drunk and passed out before he took care of it. You know, Mr. Pinch, Mr. Bright was loose the afternoon you came here, too. He had picked the lock on the door to his bedroom entrance. While I was talking to you, Raymond was chasing Mr. Bright."

Dearborn nodded. He remembered the sensation he'd had of someone flitting around just at the edge of his vision. "Robert's escape record is remarkable. I'm amazed at Reid's optimism, thinking we wouldn't see Robert."

"He's gotten worse the last few weeks," Nadine said. "The last couple of days were the very worst."

"Is Robert in the habit of listening in on phone conversations, Miss Garrett?" Dearborn asked.

167

She looked at Dearborn in surprise. "I don't know. Why?"

"Benjamin made a phone call last night. He was aware of a third party listening in."

"Dearie!" Stella cut in. "You didn't tell us about that!"

"That's what must have happened," Benjamin declared. "The old guy slipped into the house and started fooling around with the switchboard. When he heard me come downstairs, he ran outside."

"I must say," Stella sighed, "even though it doesn't solve our problem I'm awfully relieved to find out that it isn't Bobby."

"So am I," James concurred. "I didn't like the thought that one of us is a murderer."

"I'll say," Fannie said.

Dearborn held up a cautioning hand. "Your optimism is premature."

"Why, Dearie?" Stella inquired.

"We have merely eliminated Robert as a suspect—no one else."

Benjamin glanced sharply at Nadine to see how she was taking things. She sat very still, seemingly unruffled. But there was a stiffness in her carriage that hadn't been there a moment before. "Dad, maybe we'd better skip it for now. It's late. There's nothing we can do."

"We shall have to alter our thinking," Dearborn insisted.

"It's going to have to wait until Dolly recovers," declared James. "Look at her!"

They turned their attention to Dolly. She was slumped down on the kitchen chair with her head resting on the chairback. Her eyes were open but her lids were fluttering. "I'm all right," she whispered weakly. "Just a little unnerved."

"Since you no longer need her wheelchair, Dearborn," James said, "I think we'd better give it back to her."

"I'll get it," Benjamin volunteered. He dashed out of the kitchen.

"It's one-thirty," Stella said wearily.

"I'll never sleep," Fannie predicted.

James leaned over Dolly's semiprostrate form and whispered, "Hold on, my dear, hold on."

"We shall continue this discussion in the morning," Dearborn announced. "For once Benjamin is right. It behooves us to wait until we are better able to cope. We shall retire. Benjamin will spend the night on the couch in Robert's sitting room."

Twenty-Two

Dearborn lay in bed thinking. He had believed Robert Bright to be the murderer. It would have made sense that Robert pretend to go away and then, under cover of the alibi, eliminate the Rotten Apples. But now that Robert proved to be innocent, suspicion was thrown back onto the other Rotten Apples with the added complication that once Robert's senility became public, the sale would be invalid. The murderer wasn't going to accept that turn of events with equanimity.

Dearborn got up and dressed. He met Benjamin coming out of Robert Bright's room.

"Morning, Dad. Nadine relieved me so I could get some breakfast. You on your way down?"

"Benjamin, you look terrible."

"So would you if you had to spend the night on a five-foot-long couch."

They met James and Dolly when they got out of the elevator. Dolly, sitting in her wheelchair, was staring stonily ahead while James whispered into her ear.

"What's wrong?" Dearborn demanded.

"Wrong?" Dolly replied in an artificial voice. "Why, nothing."

"Ask Fannie," James snapped.

The wheelchair battery had been recharged. Dolly zoomed into the elevator with James behind her. James slammed the cage door and pressed the second-floor button. They disappeared by degrees, heads, shoulders, torsos, legs, and finally feet.

"What was that all about?" Benjamin wondered.

Dearborn held up his hand. They could hear Fannie's shrill voice babbling.

"Let us proceed to the parlor, Benjamin."

They entered to find Stella tucked into a corner of the couch while Fannie, all white chiffon and despair, paced up and down in front of the fireplace.

"Dearborn!" she exploded, rushing across the room, "Jimmy and Dolly knew all along that the clinic was being sold!"

Dearborn regarded her calmly. "How do you know?"

"James got it from his dentist, who is also H. Trumbell Deniker's dentist."

"H. Trumbell Deniker? The newspaper columnist? What has H. Trumbell Deniker to do with it?"

"He's a follower of Morton Yaquat, who owns Health Havens Ltd.," Stella explained from the depths of the couch.

"Ah," breathed Dearborn.

"It was Yaquat who bought the place?" Benjamin asked. "The faith healer?"

"A fact of which Dolly and James were fully aware," Fannie reiterated forcefully.

"And how did James and Dolly come to reveal this information?" Dearborn inquired.

Fannie gestured broadly. "We were sitting here talking and I told them I couldn't imagine who would pay two million dollars for this place. I mean, it's a white elephant—an enormous, drafty barn. It will take a fortune to renovate. Jimmy said, 'Morton Yaquat, that's who,' and I said, 'What do you mean?' and then, of course, they realized what they'd let slip and they tried to wriggle out of it and Dolly said, 'What do *you* mean,' and I said, 'When Jimmy said 'Morton Yaquat, that's who,' . . . and finally they owned up to it."

"I see," reflected Dearborn. "Did they tell you why they had been keeping this information secret?"

Fannie's expression was contemptuous. "Certainly. They said they were afraid you'd think they had something to do with the murders."

"Then they only pretended to have forgotten that they would benefit from the sale of the clinic."

"Of course they were pretending! And why? Because they *do* have something to do with the murders—everything!"

Behind them the elevator doors opened and almost immediately Dolly and James swept back into the room.

"Well, well," Dearborn greeted them cordially, "had second thoughts, did you?"

"Fannie," James announced gamely, "Dolly and I took the liberty of entering your bedroom a moment ago."

"You what!"

"You are apparently intent on—what is the expression—framing us for murder. Drastic measures were called for. We had suspicions of our own, just now confirmed." James held aloft a long-barreled pistol.

Fannie ran across the room and pulled the pistol out of his hand. "You went through my belongings?"

"Just your purse," said Dolly. "We thought you'd never part with it long enough for us to see what it was you've been hiding in there. And we knew you were hiding something. You've been guarding that purse as if it were made of platinum."

Dearborn held out his hand. "Give it here, Fannie."

"What for? It's a prop. It only fires blanks."

"Nevertheless," Dearborn said matter-of-factly, "it is potentially dangerous. I'll take charge of it."

Fannie, with an angry scowl at Dolly and James, held out the gun, and Dearborn took it from her.

"All the time you've been here, you've been walking around with that pistol in your pocketbook!" James accused Fannie.

"We wondered why you never let go of it," Dolly noted. "*We* wouldn't know where to get a gun if we wanted one."

"I will not demean myself by taking any further part in this foolish conversation," Fannie announced. "I'm going in to breakfast." She went to the door, head held high, chiffons flapping.

Dolly fanned herself with a limp hand. James asked, "Are you all right, my sweet?"

"I think so. A little excited, perhaps. I'll be all right in a moment."

"The waters," James said, turning to address Dearborn, "seem to be rising. I'm beginning to think I shall have to remove Dolly to higher ground."

"While you're thinking about that," Dearborn replied practically, "you might give thought to the fact that by being less than frank, you have muddied those waters considerably."

"I'm sorry, Dearborn."

"So am I, James. So am I."

"Dearie," Stella spoke up worriedly. "I don't like to think it could be one of us, but if it isn't one of us, then who's left? The only people here are Robert, you, your son, Miss Garrett, and Mr. Reid." She paused. "And the Smiths, of course."

"What about Fannie?" James suggested.

"Fannie *has* always been a little peculiar," Dolly agreed.

"Nothing is to be gained by accusing one another," Dearborn returned. "My advice is to leave the theorizing to me. I am, after all, unburdened by personal interest, prejudice, or fear."

"Do you have a plan, Dearie?" Stella asked.

"I always have a plan."

"What is it?"

"At the moment it is to go down to the kitchen and instruct Mrs. Smith in the intricacies of the three-minute egg."

172

*   *   *

"Good morning, Mrs. Smith."

"How do you like these?" She presented for inspection a tray of biscuits she had just taken out of the oven.

"Ah," Dearborn breathed in. "Something special to start off the day."

"Buttermilk biscuits," she said. She passed the tray seductively under his nose. "My ma's recipe. Would you like one?"

"I most certainly would." Dearborn slid into one of the kitchen chairs. "Where's, er—"

"Upstairs serving. I'll just put some of these onto the dumbwaiter." Deftly she transferred a dozen biscuits to a napkined basket and slipped the basket into the dumb-waiter, manipulated the pulleys, rang a bell attached to the inside of the shaft, and released the dumbwaiter door, which snapped shut. She turned back to Dearborn. "Quick as a wink."

"Yes, indeed," Dearborn responded sociably. He pointed to the chair opposite. "Care to join me, Mrs. Smith?"

She plopped down and shoved the tray across the kitchen table. "Help yourself."

Dearborn nibbled a biscuit while Mrs. Smith wiggled around in her chair, smoothed back the wisps of hair that hung over her forehead, and made some minor adjust-ments to the bodice of her dress.

"Tell me, Mrs. Smith," Dearborn said conversational-ly, "were you disturbed by the commotion last night?"

She opened her eyes very wide. "What commotion?"

"Now, now," Dearborn said, "don't feel you have to be tactful on my account. You and Mr. Smith must have been aware of the disturbance."

She made an even more strenuous effort to look inno-cent, playing with the biscuit tray and fluttering her eyelashes.

"It *was* a shocker, now wasn't it? You can be frank with me."

She struggled inwardly for a moment, then admitted

173

cheerfully, "It was a rowdydow all right." She glanced toward the dumbwaiter. "Roscoe said we shouldn't let on we saw it. We slipped into the pantry back of the kitchen and took a peek." She pointed to a swinging door with a small rectangular window at one end of the room.

Dearborn took a bite of his biscuit. "What did you see, Mrs. Smith?"

"That old gentleman in his birthday suit. Roscoe said if Mr. Bright was here he would of threw a fit."

"Roscoe was right."

"I say, what Mr. Bright don't know can't hurt him."

"Indisputable."

"Roscoe says we're not getting mixed up in any sex orgy. If anything like last night happens again we're leaving."

"Sex orgy?"

"I'm no prude. But Roscoe doesn't go in for that kind of fooling around." She threw a spirited wink at Dearborn. "He's got a mean temper. I told you about that. Especially when it comes to S. E. X."

As if on cue, the dumbwaiter bell rang. Mrs. Smith jumped up and opened the dumbwaiter door. She stuck her head inside and twisted it to peer upward. Dearborn could hear Smith's hollow voice vibrating against the metal shaft.

"He is not, Roscoe!" Mrs. Smith shouted up. "He's just eating a biscuit and talking! Come down and see for yourself!" She withdrew her head and shut the door. For a moment her placid expression was replaced by a frown. "What did I tell you?" Then it smoothed. She returned to the table. "Would you like some strawberry jam to go with the biscuits?"

Dearborn was on his feet. "No thank you. Another time."

He marched into the hall and rang for the elevator. It was somewhere in the upper reaches of the house. He heard it groan and begin moving. He glanced toward the back stairs, rattled the elevator doors gently, and then

174

paced down the hall past the infirmary door to the door of the Smiths' room and back. The elevator reached the lower level, and Dearborn opened the gates and got in. He closed the gates, pressed the button for the first floor, and waited. To his surprise the elevator, instead of rising, began to descend.

"Drat," Dearborn muttered. "Double drat." He banged on the first-floor button. "Damned antique!"

The elevator clattered to a halt at the bottom of the shaft. The basement was dark. Dearborn peered out between the bars of the elevator cage. "Anybody down here?" he called out irritably. "Who rang for the elevator?"

He reached out to renew his assault on the first-floor button, but before he connected there was a noise at the other end of the long hall outside the elevator.

"Who's there?" Dearborn called.

What sounded like a weak moan threaded out of the darkness. Dearborn opened the gates and took a tentative step down the hall. "Answer me!" he demanded. "Is someone hurt?"

There wasn't any answer. He strained his eyes toward the spot where the sound had come from. He took another step forward. Then he heard a quick, indrawn breath and reflexively bobbed to one side, out of the dim light filtering down through the elevator shaft.

The light, released, picked up the flash of steel fifteen feet in front of him. He leaped back into the elevator, slammed the gate, and pounded the first-floor button frantically. At first there was no response. Then slowly the gears meshed and the bulky old elevator rose.

Twenty-Three

"Where is everyone?" Dearborn asked. He stood next to the dining room table looking down at Benjamin.

"Mrs. Fairchild didn't feel well. She and Bell changed their minds about breakfast. Miss Gresham had a cup of coffee and went out for a walk. Sarah Bernhardt took her tray upstairs. She said there are too many windows in the dining room."

"Miss Garrett is still upstairs?"

"I guess so."

"And Reid?"

Benjamin was buttering a buttermilk biscuit and polishing off his omelet. "I haven't seen him."

"Here we are," Nadine announced as she and Reid entered the room.

"Who is with Robert?" Dearborn immediately asked.

"No one. He's asleep."

"My instructions were that he should have someone in constant attendance," Dearborn said.

"The sedative hasn't worn off. He won't wake up for another hour or two. Raymond looked in on him. He's fine."

"Sit down, Nadine." Benjamin got up to hold a chair for her.

"I would prefer that you go back up to Robert," Dearborn persisted.

"Okay, if you say so. Could I just grab a cup of coffee?"

"The man is unable to look after himself," Dearborn pointed out. "He's a victim of dementia."

"OMS," Reid contradicted.

"OMS? What's OMS?"

"Organic mental syndrome. Senility."

"Let's not quibble over labels, Reid. The point is that the man is helpless. Incidentally, has Miss Garrett talked to you?"

"Yes," Reid answered shortly. He crossed to the sideboard and helped himself to coffee.

"The cat's out of the bag, Reid."

"So I understand."

"You not only deceived us regarding Robert's physical deterioration but also about the fraudulent sale of the clinic."

"What do you propose to do about it?"

"At the moment," Dearborn replied, "I am more concerned with the consequences than with the act itself. But I wish to go on record as saying that I am amazed by what you and Miss Garrett did. Amazed and perturbed."

"We didn't do it for ourselves."

"I know all about your so-called altruistic impulses. You and Miss Garrett are either remarkably naive or totally unscrupulous, and the results of your thoughtless conniving have been catastrophic."

"Wait a minute, Dad," Benjamin cut in.

"You are not even penitent," continued Dearborn. "For shame. Perhaps Miss Garrett might be excused on the grounds of youth and inexperience, but not you, Reid."

Reid carried his coffee to a place at the end of the table and sat down with it. "Think what you want to think," he told Dearborn. "My conscience is clear."

"You have a strange set of values," Dearborn continued. "Mark my words, the authorities are not going to be any more tolerant than I. However, present circumstances force us to postpone the day of reckoning."

177

Nadine and Reid exchanged pained glances.

"Miss Garrett," Dearborn asked, "how many entrances are there to the basement?"

"There's the elevator and one of those wooden double-door contraptions that leads down from the yard."

"Are those doors locked?"

"I don't know." She looked inquiringly at Raymond. "Are they, Raymond?"

"I think they're open," Raymond muttered. "I was in the cellar looking for Mr. Bright yesterday. I don't remember locking them."

"Why, Dad?" Benjamin asked. "What's all the interest in the basement?"

"Nothing. Nothing at all." Dearborn went to the sideboard and picked up the lid to the silver chafing dish. "An egg pancake," he mumbled, peering inside. "Call it what you like." He replaced the lid and turned to the coffee urn. He poured half a cup of coffee, filled the cup with cream, added four heaping teaspoonsful of sugar, and carried the cup to the table.

"I thought you were going to ask Mrs. Smith to boil you a couple of eggs, Dad?"

"I changed my mind. Reid, I've decided to organize some outdoor activities. Take all their minds off their problems, keep them outside for a couple of hours."

"That should go over big," Benjamin said skeptically.

Dearborn ignored him. "You're the health director, Reid. What do you suggest?"

"A walk," Reid replied indifferently.

"Uninspired."

"Those people aren't in any shape for outdoor sports," Benjamin objected. "And they're not going to cooperate, either."

"Miss Garrett? Any ideas? Some kind of team activity. Something they can all participate in."

"Can you see Mrs. Fairchild playing badminton?" Benjamin exclaimed. "Or Mr. Bell doing calisthenics? I'm not sure you'll even be able to get Miss Tyler outside, much less involved in team sports."

"You're underestimating Fannie's competitive spirit," Dearborn said.

"How about shuffleboard?" Nadine suggested. "We've got four shuffleboard courts on the north terrace."

"Excellent, Miss Garrett. Excellent. Reid, you will supervise the games. Miss Garrett, I'm sorry to exclude you from the activities, but you will have to remain with Robert. As a matter of fact, it will expedite matters if you will take a tray and go up now. Benjamin and I will relieve you within the hour."

Nadine got up from the table. "You win. I'll ask Mrs. Smith to send something up on the dumbwaiter." She left the room and they listened to her heels click down the hall.

"Smith will serve lunch on the terrace," Dearborn said. "Luncheon al fresco. It will go a long way toward improving morale. All right, Benjamin. Let's round up the troops."

"Benjamin and I have matters to attend to," Dearborn informed the group. "We'll rejoin you presently."

"You mean you're not going to participate?" Stella demanded, squinting at him through a pair of round blue-green sunglasses. "You got us out here to play this silly game and you're not even going to participate?"

"Neither am I," Dolly announced from her wheelchair. She sat on the sidelines, palely resolute, jabbing a needle in and out of her patchwork quilt.

The ground was soggy. But the sun, weak as it was, had dried the broad cement terrace. Smith had carried out the equipment and half a dozen striped canvas chairs and arranged them in a row along one side of the shuffleboard court.

"Dolly," Dearborn remonstrated, "James needs the diversion. And you need the exercise. If you persist in this hypochondria, your legs will atrophy and you'll spend the remainder of your life sitting down."

"Oh, Dearie, please . . ."

"If Dolly prefers to watch, she may," James declared

179

bravely. "Don't bully us, Dearborn! We're not children, you know!"

"*Someone's* got to play," Fannie stated flatly. Fannie had exchanged her chiffon morning dress for a pair of peach-colored jodhpurs and matching boots. "It seems to me it might be interesting to bet on the point spread. I've calculated the odds—"

"We are not going to bet large sums of money," Stella interrupted. "In the first place, no one has any appreciable amount to lose. At least I—"

"A dime a point," James suggested.

"No!" Fannie shot back. "A dollar a point."

"I don't remember how to play," Dolly said petulantly. "I haven't played since 1934 when I made the maiden crossing on the *Normandie*."

"Reid will go over the rules and keep score," Dearborn cut in. "You can choose teams—"

"No teams," Fannie stated firmly. "It's every man for himself."

"That's not fair," James objected. "Dolly isn't very strong—"

"I'm not even going to play," Dolly reminded them.

"I'm not up to snuff myself," Stella put in. "Not after what happened last night."

"Hells bells!" Fannie cried out exasperatedly. "This isn't the NHL! It doesn't take any strength to push a puck across six feet of cement!"

Dearborn nudged Benjamin and they slipped around the corner of the house.

"Okay, Dad, now how about leveling with me. What's all this shuffleboard business about?"

"I want you to take Robert Bright away from here. Now. While everyone is occupied and won't notice. A surreptitious retreat. An escape, if you will."

"Why?"

"Everyone knows now that Robert is mentally incompetent."

"So?"

"And that the sale of the clinic was fraudulently accomplished."

"So?"

"Benjamin, hasn't it yet occurred to you that the murderer has no choice but to eliminate Robert?"

"I don't agree with you. Too many people already know Bright's alive."

"Let me try it another way. Are you ready to turn Miss Garrett and Reid over to the police?"

"Hell, no. So far as I'm concerned, they're not criminals. They thought they were doing the right thing."

"Exactly. Well, I can assure you that neither Miss Garrett nor Reid will confess voluntarily to being criminals. And none of the remaining principals will risk a share in the profits by coming forward with the truth. The murderer knows it, too. Therefore he'll be perfectly safe in getting rid of Robert. You're to spirit Robert away before that happens."

"Spirit him away? How am I supposed to do that? Carry him off in a laundry bag? Where am I supposed to spirit him away to? They're watching my apartment. I can't check into a motel with him. I might as well check in with a kangaroo. Besides, there's something else. You're in as much danger as he is. You said so yourself."

"I can take care of myself."

"Maybe so. But I'm not taking any chances. You're as much of a fly in the ointment as Bright. I'd say it's a toss-up who's going to get it first."

"Nonsense."

"You're not safe, Dad."

"We shall discuss my safety later. Now let's attend to Robert."

"It's a waste of time."

"Are you refusing to go with me?"

"I'll go *with* you. The point is that I won't go *without* you."

"Wait a moment." Dearborn hurried over to the horizontal doors leading down to the cellar. He pulled up on

181

the handles. The doors opened. "Unlocked," he declared. "But fortunately there's an outside bolt." He threw the bolt and tested the doors. "There, that's better," he said, satisfied.

"What's better about it?" Benjamin remarked. "It may keep somebody in, but it sure as hell isn't going to keep anybody out."

"Just a precaution, Benjamin. Just a precaution."

But precautions where Robert Bright was concerned were useless.

As Dearborn and Benjamin stepped out of the elevator into the upstairs hallway, the door to Bright's room was thrown open and Nadine burst out.

"What's the matter?" Benjamin cried.

"Mr. Bright," she answered in a frightened voice.

"What about him?" Dearborn demanded.

"He's—he's—"

"He's what?"

"I thought he was sleeping, but when I went to check on him just now I saw that he's . . . dead."

Twenty-Four

Robert Bright lay on his bed, his head resting on the pillow, the cerise afghan covering his legs. Except for his eyes staring sightlessly at the ceiling, he looked asleep.

Nadine joined Benjamin and Dearborn at the bedside. "It must have been a stroke."

Benjamin studied Bright's face. "His face is blue."

"What does that mean?"

"Don't ask me." Benjamin bent over the bed and made a gingerly inspection of the body. "Look, Dad. No signs of *rigor mortis*. The body is still warm."

"What does that mean?" Nadine asked again.

"Only that he hasn't been dead long."

"Of course he hasn't. He was all right when I gave him breakfast."

"Which was?" Dearborn asked.

"At about eight." She prodded Benjamin. "You remember. I came in at quarter to eight to relieve you. He was fine then."

Benjamin nodded.

Nadine pointed to a call box on the wall near the bedroom door. "I called down to Mrs. Smith and she sent a tray up on the dumbwaiter. Cereal, toast, juice, a cup of tea. I fed Mr. Bright. Raymond came in at about eight-fifteen. Raymond saw him, too."

"Is that Robert's tray?" Dearborn asked, pointing to a tray on top of the bureau.

"No, that's mine. The one Mrs. Smith sent up. I took Mr. Bright's tray to the kitchen when Raymond and I went down earlier."

"Are you certain, Miss Garrett, that when you and Reid left the room Robert was sleeping and not already . . . um . . ."

"He was snoring," she replied. "Ask Raymond."

"We're going to have to call an ambulance," Benjamin said.

"No," Dearborn cut in. "Not before we know how he died."

"How are we supposed to figure that out? We're not doctors."

"Reid will have an opinion."

"Reid's no doctor either."

"Old people die with depressing regularity. Reid will have at least a rudimentary knowledge of the phenomenon."

"He's not a coroner."

"A coroner?" Nadine exclaimed. "Why would we need a coroner?"

"The question is a simple one," Dearborn said. "I merely want to find out whether or not Robert could have been smothered."

"Oh," Nadine said in a soft voice.

"Miss Garrett, will you call Reid, please? Say nothing to the others. The less said the better. Tell Reid that Bright is calling for him. You'd better stay downstairs. Keep the group occupied. Think you can handle that?"

Nadine wiped her hands on the sides of her slacks and took a deep breath. "I'm not feeling so well. But I'll try."

"Nadine asked me to come up," Reid said, looking toward the bed. "She told me Mr. Bright wanted me. He asleep again?"

"Mr. Bright is dead," Dearborn informed him.

"Dead?"

"Dead. Deceased. Departed. Gone to his glory."

Reid stared at Dearborn blankly. When the words finally registered, he hurried to the bed and leaned over it. "How? When?"

"See for yourself."

Reid lifted Bright's eyelids and put his ear to Bright's chest. He straightened up. Then, abruptly, he placed one hand on Bright's chest and began pounding on it with his other hand.

"Waste of time, Reid," Dearborn remarked.

Reid sank into a chair next to the bed. "I thought it was over," he said in an agonized voice.

"You don't think he died of natural causes either," Dearborn remarked.

Reid shook his head and rubbed his hands over his face.

"It couldn't have been his heart?" Benjamin asked.

"No. There was nothing wrong with his heart."

"I took a good look at him before you came up," Benjamin said. "He doesn't have any wounds on him. A

184

couple of bruises from the wrestling match last night. That's all."

"His face is blue," Dearborn pointed out. "What does that signify?"

"Oxygen deprivation," Reid answered dully.

"Meaning what?"

Reid was silent. He sat with his head in his hands.

"Suffocation?" Dearborn prompted.

Reid didn't answer.

"Speak up, Reid."

"He's lying on his back."

"My question stands."

"If someone held a pillow over his face..." Reid raised his head but didn't finish the sentence.

"We'd better call somebody," Benjamin said. "An ambulance. The local hospital."

"They're not going to sign the death certificate without an autopsy," Dearborn said. "We shall all be behind bars before the day's over."

"My God," Reid whispered. He reached out and pulled the afghan over Bright's face. His hands were trembling.

"We can't bury him in the garden," Benjamin declared. "What do you suggest we do with him?"

"Reid," Dearborn asked, "is there a cold-storage room in the basement?"

"Why?" Reid responded.

"Answer the question."

"Yes. The room where we keep the freezer chests."

"Oh, hey, now wait a minute, Dad!"

"The murderer knows there's no turning back," Dearborn stated firmly. "He intends to dispatch every person who stands between him and his goal. It is imperative that we stop him."

"The police will have to stop him."

"It is I whom the police will arrest. And even if I were able to talk my way out of the situation, I would not yet be able to present them with an alternative suspect. I admit that poor old Robert here was something of a red herring, but now that he's out of the way I have a much clearer picture of the road ahead."

"Out of the way?" Reid broke in. "That's the way you talk about him?"

"I doubt that it makes much difference to Robert."

"I can't go along with it," Benjamin objected. "It's no good, Dad. It's gone too far."

"Think of the consequences," Dearborn argued. "To you. To me. To the people down there. To Reid . . ." He eyed Benjamin shrewdly. "And to Miss Garrett . . ."

"It's going to come to it in the end," Benjamin argued. "The longer we delay it, the harder it's going to be."

"Twenty-four hours more won't matter."

"Except to the next victim."

"There won't be a next victim, Benjamin. I intend to see to that."

Benjamin turned to Reid. "Aren't you going to back me up? Don't you see the lunacy in it?"

Reid had found his flask and unscrewed the cover. He closed his eyes and drank deeply before answering. "I don't know. Either way I lose."

"Reid," Dearborn said, "the only tactic open to you is delay."

"Not much of a prospect," Reid said bitterly.

"Better than none. As for you, Benjamin, if I can't call upon your common sense, then I insist upon your recognizing your filial responsibility."

"Shit."

"Now, I suggest we get Robert into the elevator and down into the cellar immediately while he's still somewhat . . . pliable. After we've packed him away we'll have a quiet word with Miss Garrett. No reason to say anything about this to the others. It will only create panic."

"What about the Smiths?" Benjamin asked. "They go down to the storage room a couple of times a day."

"Well?" Dearborn demanded of Reid.

"The freezer units have locks," Reid said.

"Good enough," Dearborn declared. "It will work out

186

splendidly. Now, Reid, if you and Benjamin will gather up poor old Robert, I shall ring for the elevator."

"If the sale of the clinic is invalid," James said at dinner, "it means that we no longer have anything to be afraid of. We can go home tomorrow and forget it ever happened."

"Yes," Dolly agreed, "it was such a relief when James realized that and pointed it out to me. I don't know why *you* didn't point it out to us yourself, Dearie. We were so caught up in this awful situation that we weren't thinking clearly."

"I don't see how you can forget it ever happened," Stella remarked. "Four people are dead."

"We can't bring them back," James responded.

"You're such fools!" Fannie declared. "If the sale doesn't go through, we won't collect our share of the money—"

"I would have expected you to say that," James accused.

"What good will money do us if we're dead?" Dolly reasoned.

"We're not dead yet," Stella put in mildly. "And the clinic will be sold anyway, eventually. "I think Fannie's got a good point."

"I'm not interested in eventualities," James shot back. "For the moment we're safe and that's all that matters." He put down his dessert fork and took Dolly's hand.

"We've been plucked from the jaws of death," she sighed. "I can't help feeling as if it's a miracle. It reminds me—"

"The only miracle," Fannie retorted, "is that you actually think nothing will happen to us now. I suppose you think that madman, whoever he is, will simply burrow back into the woodwork and disappear?"

"Won't he?" Dolly asked supplicatingly.

Fannie rose from her place at the table. She was wearing a man-tailored red moiré evening suit, and when she threw out her arms, the effect was stunning. "Can't you

187

try to understand! He hasn't gotten what he wants! We know more than he wants us to know! He'll go after us one by one!"

Stella said, "I agree with Fannie. In fact, I'll go one step further—I think logically he'll begin by trying to do away with Bobby." Stella looked toward the head of the table at Dearborn, who was holding his wineglass in both hands, leaning back in his chair, and studying them through half-closed eyes. "I notice," Stella went on, "that you're being very careful not to let anyone near his room, Dearie. Miss Garrett was up there most of the morning, Reid all afternoon. Now Benjamin . . ."

Nadine and Reid, at the foot of the table, exchanged wary glances.

"Not at all," Dearborn answered. "It's simply that I don't want to spend another night chasing Robert through the shrubbery."

"You see," Dolly remonstrated, "even Dearie has stopped being concerned, haven't you Dearie?"

"There is still the question of a murderer on the loose," Dearborn lectured, "and the question of where our responsibilities lie."

"Our responsibilities don't include revealing our private affairs to the police," James stated flatly.

"Once we have the guilty party in hand," Dearborn said, "no one will be interested in the details of your lives. Except, of course, for the part that involves lending Robert the money to start the clinic."

"So long as we stay here," Dolly said timidly, "we're in the position of hobnobbing with a killer." Her eyes were drawn to Fannie.

"Don't look at me!" Fannie bawled. "I had nothing to do with any of this!"

Stella got up from the table. "We can't leave tonight anyway. If you don't mind I'm going into the parlor and have a glass of brandy." She put her napkin on the table and left the room.

"Brandy sounds good to me," Fannie announced.

"Running away!" Dearborn announced disapprovingly. "Afraid to face it!"

"You're trying to make us look like rats deserting a sinking ship," James declared.

"As usual," Dearborn returned, "your simile lacks originality."

"Well, we're not staying," Dolly insisted. She got up from the table and transferred to the wheelchair. "We don't care what we're compared to. We've had quite enough of this place." She steered for the door.

Nadine had said little during dinner. Now she suddenly spoke up. "I never thought I'd want them to stay, but . . ."

James stopped short in his flight after Dolly. "*You* want us to stay? Why?"

"Miss Garrett's concern is understandable," Dearborn returned. "She and Reid will be facing criminal charges. It would be irresponsible to leave before we have at least discussed the best way to deal with that situation."

"Oh." Dolly halted just outside the dining room doors. She turned the wheelchair around. "I wasn't thinking about her."

"Dearie?"

Stella was back, standing on the periphery of the group, her arms filled with Dolly's patchwork quilt.

"What is it, Stella?"

"Look at this." She held out Dolly's patchwork quilt. "Here. This square here. The one on the end."

"What is it?" Dolly asked. "What are you doing with my quilt?"

Dearborn squinted at the cloth Stella was pointing to. "What is it?"

"Don't you recognize it? It's the same as the piece of cloth I found on the floor in my living room."

"What?" Dearborn picked up a corner of the quilt and examined the square of fabric, then reached into his breast pocket and pulled out the piece of cloth Stella had given him the week before and that he'd carefully transferred from one suit to the next. He held it next to the six-inch square of yellow-and-red plaid sewn into the quilt. "Where did you get this?" he demanded of Dolly.

"Why . . . why . . . I . . ." She fluttered her hands in confusion. "There's a utility closet in the hall at the top of the back stairs. I got it out of a ragbag in the closet. Why? What's wrong?"

"Someone trespassed into Stella's house—"

"We know about that," James broke in impatiently.

"The dogs attacked him," Stella explained. "They ripped away a piece of cloth. A piece of cloth exactly like this."

"There!" Fannie boomed. "There! You see! What more do you want!" She pointed at James and Dolly. "And *they* were accusing *me*!"

Dearborn examined the fabric. The two pieces placed together formed a rectangle roughly six inches by nine inches, clearly showing the plaid pattern in one continued in the other. "Dolly, can you tell us what this comes from? I assume you didn't dip into the ragbag and come up with a perfect square."

Dolly sought James's hand. "I'm not sure. It looked like a shirt. Part of a shirt. There were a couple of buttonholes and a collar."

"What did you do with the pieces you cut off?"

"I shredded them with my scissors and stuffed them into the quilt."

Dearborn turned to Nadine. "Do you recognize the fabric, Miss Garrett?"

Nadine shook her head. "I don't remember ever seeing it before."

"Dolly," Dearborn asked, "did you notice if there were any more pieces of the same fabric in the ragbag? If somebody ripped up a shirt, for instance, they would have put all the pieces in the bag."

"I don't recall," Dolly answered. "I picked out this piece and a bit of blue-and-white gingham, and a piece of pink flannel, and a piece of yellow, sprigged muslin."

"Dearie," Stella asked, "shall I go and get the ragbag?"

190

"If you don't mind."

She piled the quilt onto the sideboard and hurried out into the hall. Reid got up from the table and walked to the door.

"Where are you going, Reid?"

"I left something in the lounge."

Dearborn saw Reid pat his hip pocket and knew immediately what the something was. "Wait a minute." He held out the scrap of cloth and pointed to the larger patch in Dolly's quilt. "You're part of this, too. Have you ever seen this fabric before?"

Reid took the cloth out of Dearborn's hand, looked at it, shook his head, and handed it back.

"Who would have put those remnants into the rag-bag?" James asked.

"That's simple," Fannie said. "The murderer, of course. Deliberately. As a—what do you call it—a plant. Before he knew that Bobby was senile. To make it look like Bobby was the guilty one."

"That's a facile answer," James asserted vindictively. "Almost too facile to have been spur-of-the-moment."

"I have an explanation even more facile," Fannie returned. "Maybe there was never a piece of cloth like this in the ragbag."

"You're making snide accusations again!" James warned.

Dearborn glared at them. "It is enough that I am trying to unscramble this unsavory puzzle without having to act as arbitrator to your internecine squabbles!"

They fell silent. James sat down again and Fannie tapped her long fingernails against the edge of her plate. It sounded, in the quiet room, like the clicking of a metronome.

After a few minutes Stella came back into the room holding a large cloth drawstring bag. "Is this it?"

Dolly nodded.

"Let's have a look at it," Dearborn commanded.

Stella turned the bag over and dumped the contents out onto the table. She spread out the pieces of fabric, then picked up each scrap and held it out for Dearborn's inspection. "Nothing like it."

"Surprise, surprise," Fannie murmured sarcastically.

"The matching pieces could have been removed," Dearborn commented.

"When?" Stella asked.

"Sometime between last night and this morning."

"Or between last night and this moment," Dolly suddenly piped up in a brave voice.

"This moment?" Stella repeated curiously.

"I'm sorry, Stella. But I do think we must point out all the possibilities. Especially since there is so much venom directed toward Jimmy and me. *You* could have removed the rest of the fabric just now when you left the room."

"And done what with it?" Stella demanded. She held out her arms and slowly rotated. Her thin bony frame in skintight dungarees and jersey shirt couldn't have concealed a handkerchief.

"Well, you could have . . . flushed it down the toilet."

"I'd have to go through the dining room to get to the first floor rest room. I can't make myself invisible." Stella picked up the scraps of fabric and began replacing them in the ragbag.

Dolly fanned herself with her hand. "Remember, you're the one with the original copy of the agreement, Stella. You probably had more cause to realize the possibilities than we did. We didn't even remember there *was* an agreement."

"Don't be silly. I told you I had forgotten all about the agreement."

"You poisoned a dog at the Westminster Dog Show," Dolly reminded her.

"And you took an ice pick to Barbara Sharp . . ."

"Ah," Dearborn noted. "Barbara Sharp. I thought it might have been Barbara Sharp. Cheap piece of baggage, for all her money. Can't say I'm surprised, Dolly."

Dolly turned. "You're not listening to me! You're not taking anything I say seriously!"

"How can we?" Fannie demanded. "You're trying too

hard. It only makes you and James look all the more guilty."

"How dare you!" Dolly returned shrilly. "How dare you!" She stood up, stepped away from her wheelchair, gave a choked cry, and then suddenly, without warning, pitched forward.

Twenty-Five

Dolly fell against James, who tried to catch her and missed. She landed face down on the carpet. Instantly Reid was on his knees beside her. He turned her over, lifted her eyelids, loosened the collar of her dress, and began rubbing her hands.

"Dolly!" James cried in anguish. He dashed forward and threw himself down beside her. He took her face in his hands. "Dolly, Dolly, open your eyes!" The others crowded around.

Reid looked up. "Nadine, get the medical bag out of the infirmary."

Nadine ran out of the room.

"Mr. Pinch," Reid said to Dearborn, "help me lift her."

Dearborn stooped and assisted Reid in pulling Dolly up into the wheelchair. Her face was white, and she was breathing with difficulty.

"What is it, James?" Dearborn asked. "What's wrong with her? Does she often faint like this?"

"Ménière's disease," James said shortly.

"What disease?" Dearborn repeated.

"Ménière's."

"Sounds like a butter sauce," Fannie declared.

"Sometimes the attacks are severe," James said. "Sometimes not."

"Does she carry medication?" Reid cut in. "Diamox, Diuril, Benadryl?"

"I'm not sure whether or not she packed her medicine," James answered. "I'll go see."

"Never mind. I've got some Atropine. That'll do the trick." Reid addressed himself to James. "The usual symptoms? Vertigo and tinnitus?"

"Yes," replied James. "If the attack is severe."

"What is Ménière's disease?" Stella asked in bewilderment.

"It has to do with her hearing and her sense of balance," James answered.

"Faulty function of the inner ear," Reid supplied.

Everyone hovered over the wheelchair staring down at Dolly, who opened her eyes once and then, with a sick moan, closed them again.

Nadine returned quickly with the medical bag. Reid dug around inside and pulled out a hypodermic syringe and a small bottle. Skillfully he prepared the syringe, rolled up Dolly's sleeve, and injected the Atropine. Almost immediately Dolly's body relaxed, and after a few moments she opened her eyes.

"Better?" Reid asked.

"Everything has stopped spinning," she answered weakly.

"You'll be all right now. Rest for a couple of minutes."

James, whose face had been as white as Dolly's, began to get his color back, too. He sank heavily to the floor, slipped off Dolly's shoes, and began massaging her feet. The others stood around helplessly until Reid pronounced Dolly well enough to be moved to the parlor.

"James," Dearborn said, "I'd like to speak with you in private."

James got up and followed Dearborn to one corner of the large dining room.

"James, have you been locking your bedroom door?"

194

"Not until today," James answered. "It's locked now. Why?"

"Dolly's room, too?"

"Yes." James frowned. "Why, Dearborn?"

"I think caution is advisable."

"What's that?" Stella came over to join them. "Are you asking if our bedroom doors are locked?"

"That's right."

"Mine certainly is. And I saw Fannie lock hers before we came down to dinner. Fannie said, er . . ." Stella peeked at James self-consciously. "She was still upset that James and Dolly had gone into her room this morning."

"Good."

"Then Fannie and I are right. We're not out of the woods at all, are we?"

"I'm afraid not."

"What is it?" Dolly called out faintly. "Is something wrong?"

They rejoined Dolly. James managed an innocuous smile. "Dearborn wants me to watch that you don't over-exert, Dolly."

"She already has overexerted," Fannie noted snidely.

"What do you mean by that?" James demanded.

"Dolly's performance of a few minutes ago."

"That's unfair," Dolly murmured weakly.

"You *are* wringing the last bit of drama out of it, aren't you?"

"We know you're not fond of being upstaged," James returned, "but do try to have a little compassion, Fannie."

"That will be enough," Dearborn cut in firmly. "Miss Garrett, I wonder if you would go upstairs and send Benjamin down so he can have his dinner."

Nadine glanced uneasily at Reid, who was replacing the hypodermic equipment in the medical bag. "Raymond, are you going to stay down here?"

Raymond didn't answer.

"You shouldn't really . . ." Nadine hesitated, then plunged ahead. "Don't you think you should have a good strong cup of coffee and go up to bed?"

Raymond answered without looking at her. "I'm going into the lounge and have a drink."

"Mrs. Fairchild may need you again later."

"I am sober, Nadine," Reid replied in a cold voice, "if that's what's worrying you."

Nadine made a helpless gesture.

Reid snapped the bag shut and thrust it under his arm. He glanced at Nadine, pushed past her, and left the room. They heard him go into the employee's lounge and shut the door.

"Should I follow him?" Nadine asked.

"No," Dearborn said. "I doubt that it would do any good. You might as well go upstairs."

Dearborn waited until the others had left the dining room. Then he gathered up the quilt, carried it to the back stairs, and started down to the kitchen. Halfway down he heard Smith's complaining voice saying something about a "dirty-minded old coot."

"Talking about Bright, no doubt," Dearborn concluded. "No use expecting him to cooperate while he's in that frame of mind." Dearborn checked himself, reversed direction, and carried the quilt upstairs to his bedroom. He closed the door, went into the bathroom, and returned with the shower curtain, in which he wrapped the quilt and the piece of torn fabric he'd been carrying. Then he went across the room and opened the window. The chimney was within arm's reach. The angle where the chimney and roof met formed a snug niche where Dearborn jammed the bundle. That accomplished, he left his room, locked the door, and started back down the hall. He paused by Bright's door to listen. Inside he heard Benjamin saying, "Wait a minute, Nadine. Let me get this straight. You say my father was carrying a matching piece of cloth in his pocket?"

"Saves me the trouble," Dearborn muttered as he started down the back stairs.

Dearborn found Mrs. Smith and her husband sitting at the kitchen table. Smith had taken off his white jacket

196

and rolled up his shirtsleeves. His biceps, noted Dearborn, were impressive.

"Speak of the devil," Smith mumbled.

Mrs. Smith smiled receptively. "Hi, Mr. Pinch. Can we help you?"

"There will be one more for dinner," Dearborn informed them.

"Dinner's over," Smith returned rudely.

Dearborn folded his arms and planted his feet. "I shall decide when dinner is over."

"Now, Roscoe," Mrs. Smith admonished, "there's plenty of food. I'll heat up the rolls."

"I'm not waiting on anybody else," Smith declared.

"I'll serve," Mrs. Smith immediately offered.

"Listen," Smith burst out, "I was down in the basement before. Somebody took all the frozen vegetables out of the freezer and piled them on the floor. They're so soggy they're dripping water all over the cement. Whose bright idea was that? And the freezer's locked. Who locked the freezer?"

"You will have to speak with Miss Garrett or Mr. Reid about that."

"If Mr. Bright knew about it, he'd blow his stack." Smith suddenly banged on the table with one massive fist. "I don't like what's going on around here! I don't believe Bright asked you here. I don't believe he even knows who you are. There's that funny business last night. Now there's the business with the freezer. Meantime you're sneaking around making goo-goo eyes at my wife . . ."

"Goo-goo?" Dearborn repeated.

"Roscoe," Mrs. Smith scolded, "Mr. Pinch isn't making goo-goo eyes at me."

Dearborn's self-control trickled away. He fixed Smith with a withering look. "Gardener, handyman, waiter, whatever it is you purport to do—none of them entitles you to behave in this surly manner!"

"Behave? Who are you to talk about behaving!" Smith

retorted pugnaciously, pointing his fork at Dearborn. "You better know that nobody fools around with my wife!"

"Mr. Pinch is innocent," Mrs. Smith objected mildly. "Aren't you, Mr. Pinch."

"The point at issue is your husband's insolence," Dearborn returned. "It is inappropriate and inexcusable." Dearborn puffed out his chest.

"Dad, I want to talk to you," Benjamin announced, loping into the room. "Nadine's just been saying—" Benjamin stopped short and peered at Smith over Dearborn's shoulder. "Trouble?"

"A misunderstanding." Dearborn addressed Smith. "Do you wish to continue this pointless exchange?"

Mrs. Smith answered. "No, he doesn't. He wants to eat his cauliflower. Isn't that right, Roscoe? Mr. Pinch, I'll bring supper up to the dining room." She stepped behind her husband to wink encouragingly at Dearborn.

Smith, with a scowl, dropped back into his chair.

Dearborn confirmed what Nadine had told Benjamin, then excused himself and went upstairs before Benjamin's warnings and dire predictions could turn into another argument.

The hall was deserted. Dearborn listened at each door. No one had come upstairs except Nadine, who was sitting in Robert Bright's suite. He could hear the creaking of the armchair as she shifted her body. Dearborn went into his own room and began going through the empty dresser drawers and poking through the desk. The night table held a Bible, a broken penknife, a spool of brown thread, an airlines emergency instruction card, and a pocket mirror. "Ah," he breathed happily, choosing the plastic airlines card and discarding the rest.

Tiptoeing into the hall, he approached one of the bedrooms and carefully inserted the card into the crack of the door above the lock. After a moment's manipulation the door opened and he went in. The room was dark. He flipped the wall switch. It lighted a table lamp next to the bed. He gazed around the room. "Just as I thought," he whispered.

He crossed to one of the two dressers in the room and quickly went through the drawers, sliding them open and closing them with stealthy efficiency. He did the same with the second dresser and with the desk. He examined the double bed hurriedly, slipping his hands under the mattress on all sides and kneeling to peer underneath. "What's this?" he said finally, straining his eyes to see into the dimness under the bed frame. He reached under and pulled out a leather case. The case was locked, but two small keys dangled from a chain on the handle. Dearborn stood up, put the case on the bed, and unlocked it. He lifted the lid and looked at the contents. He picked out one, then another of the items inside and inspected them.

"Just what I thought," he whispered again.

He lifted up a diamond wristwatch and held it to the light. Then he squinted at the inscription on the reverse side of the watch case. It read "AO from AO, 1946."

"Poor Toni," he thought, "you deserved better than this."

With a deep sigh he replaced the contents and put the case back where he'd found it. Then he tiptoed to the door, listened for a moment, then let himself out, turning off the light, shutting the door, and creeping silently back to his own room.

Now only one fact needed to be confirmed. The last bit of evidence. The missing link.

"The final nail in the coffin," he told himself in a wry, sorrowful whisper.

Twenty-Six

Stella tracked Dearborn down in the dining room, where he had rejoined Benjamin for a second cup of coffee. "Dearie, Fannie intends to fly the coop! She's been carrying on dreadfully. So have James and Dolly. Now James and Dolly have gone upstairs and she's calling a cab."

"What's it about?"

"The same thing," Stella replied. "They're all three behaving like children, making accusations and calling one another names."

Dearborn put down his coffee cup. "Where is Fannie?"

"I left her in the parlor."

Dearborn, with Stella and Benjamin following, hustled out of the dining room, across the front hall, and into the parlor. Fannie was gone.

"She couldn't have gotten far," Stella declared. "She was here a minute ago."

The elevator mechanism began grinding. The ropes squeaked and the elevator descended. It ground to a halt and Dolly and James emerged, James carrying an attaché case under one arm and a suitcase in either hand, Dolly with her makeup case in her lap.

"Where are *you* going?" Stella challenged.

"We've had quite enough," Dolly announced. "We are going home."

"Nothing of the kind!" Dearborn objected.

"Don't try to stop us," James warned. "We've decided that the best place for us is back in the city."

Dearborn was irate. "Don't behave like nincompoops! No one is leaving here!"

"Fannie has already left," Stella reminded him.

Dearborn whirled toward the door. "Benjamin," he ordered, "go after her!"

Benjamin went to the door, opened it, and dashed out without bothering to close it.

"What's the matter with you!" Dearborn demanded. "Can't you see how foolish you're being?"

"It's ridiculous," Stella agreed. "It started out tamely enough. We were all making an effort to be pleasant. Fannie and James were discussing Lily Langtry—"

"Fannie was discussing Lily Langtry," James amended. "I merely corrected a misapprehension of Fannie's concerning Lily Langry."

"They got into an argument about when she died," Stella explained.

"James has an excellent memory for dates," Dolly cut in.

"Fannie was saying 1927," Stella went on. "And James contradicted her and said 1929 . . ."

"It just so happens I wrote a poem commemorating her death," James said. " 'The garden in profusion blooms, less one lily . . .' "

"It got rather heated," Stella went on, talking over James's recitation. "James claimed that 1927 was when Lizzie Borden died, which is what he thought Fannie must have had in mind. And of course then Fannie wanted to know why he thought she would have such a fact in mind and accused him of baiting her . . ."

"I knew that Fannie had once played the part," James claimed defensively. "A play called *Forty Whacks* as I recall."

"Who cares!" Dearborn interrupted. "What difference does it make!"

"James merely remarked," Dolly picked up, "that Fannie has a natural affinity for the bizarre. There's nothing wrong about that, is there? After all, Fannie does have a taste for the grotesque. And Lizzie Borden *was* grotesque. No one would argue that."

"She *was* a murderer," Stella commented. "Or at least most people think she was. Which puts a less innocent complexion on James's remark."

"Nevertheless, there was no need for Fannie to turn ugly," James declared.

"Enough!" Dearborn interjected.

"She said," Stella went on, "that she was certain Dolly sewed that patch into her quilt as a memento of the crimes."

"The woman is a ghoul!" Dolly exclaimed.

"And a sadist," James concurred. "Which only goes to suggest that she, and she alone, is responsible for those terrible murders."

"Not one more word!" Dearborn commanded. "What matters is that the woman is gone."

"To the trotters," Stella added.

"She's gone where?"

"When James and Dolly left in a huff, Fannie said she wasn't going to sit around twiddling her thumbs for another evening and that if everyone was deserting her she was going to call a cab and go to Roosevelt Raceway."

"You should have told me that in the first place!"

Benjamin stumbled back up the front stoop and through the open door. "Gone," he panted. "I heard the cab drive off. I couldn't get there in time."

"Benjamin," Dearborn instructed, "get your car out of the garage. We cannot leave that foolish woman to her own resorts. Who knows what she might say or do."

"Hell, Dad, the woman lives in Englewood, New Jersey. It'll take us two and a half hours to drive there. Suppose somebody recognizes my car?"

"We're not going to New Jersey."

"Where are we going?"

"Roosevelt Raceway."

"Where? Why?"

"Dolly and I are leaving," James interrupted grimly.

"No, you are not leaving," Dearborn said firmly, turning his attention back to James and Dolly. "It would not be in your best interests. If you persist in your determination to leave, I shall be forced to do what I had hoped to avoid."

"What's that?" Stella asked anxiously.

"Call the police," Dearborn answered.

"Now you're finally making some sense," Benjamin declared.

"You can't do that!" James objected.

Dolly leaned her head against the back of her wheelchair and closed her eyes.

"It isn't what I want to do. It will complicate an already complicated situation." Dearborn pursed his lips. "Especially since there is something I haven't told you."

"What's that?" asked James.

Dearborn began to hum. He exchanged meaningful looks with Benjamin. "Robert has . . ." Dearborn gazed into space. "Robert has . . . er . . . expired."

"Expired!" they chorused.

"Under mysterious circumstances," Dearborn added calmly. "I believe that is the appropriate expression."

"Bobby's dead!" Stella shrilled. "When did it happen? How? It wasn't—he wasn't—"

"Sometime this morning. Suffocation seems likely."

"Suffocation!" they chorused.

"Of course, it's by no means official. But if it should turn out to be murder, then you can see how much more difficult the situation becomes."

"You've no right to ask them to take any more chances," Benjamin insisted. "It's one thing when they wanted to stay, but you can't ask them to stay if they want to go."

"There is no element of chance involved. I am prepared to bring the evidence—conclusive evidence as to the murderer's identity—to light by tomorrow evening.

At which time it will be safe to call in the authorities. In the meantime, I think that James, Dolly, and Stella will agree that it is necessary to remain here."

"Are you sure about what you're saying?" James asked dubiously.

"Positive."

"What about Fannie?" James asked. "How will you get her to come back?"

"By telling her what I have just told you."

"And if she's the murderess?" Dolly declared.

"Her refusal to return," Dearborn stated matter-of-factly, "would be tantamount to a confession, would it not?"

The three paused to regard Dearborn with somber, frightened faces.

"So you see, there is no question of her not coming back."

"How could Bobby have been killed?" Dolly asked in a small voice. "I thought Miss Garrett, Mr. Reid, your son, were watching him?"

"There was, unfortunately, a brief time when he was alone," Dearborn replied.

"Who found the body?" James asked.

"Miss Garrett."

"But she didn't say anything to us."

"Miss Garrett, Reid, Benjamin, and I were part of a conspiracy to protect you from unnecessary stress."

"Where's the body?" James demanded. "Still in his bed?"

"He's in the basement," Benjamin answered. "Locked in a freezer."

"Oh . . ." Dolly closed her eyes.

"Benjamin," Dearborn remarked severely, "are you still here? Didn't I tell you to get the car?"

"A freezer?" Stella declared. "Among the frozen foods?"

"He has an entire freezer to himself," Dearborn said reassuringly.

204

"James, dear," Dolly said weakly, "I think I'd like to go back upstairs."

"I don't see her, do you?" Benjamin asked as he peered at the faces in the clubhouse.

"I see her," Dearborn replied. He was looking out toward the grandstands. "She's down there talking to that fellow in the beret."

Benjamin studied the spot near the rail. Sure enough, Fannie, striking in her red moiré evening suit, was there engaged in conversation with a small gentleman in green checked slacks and a matching beret.

"Looks like a tout," Benjamin muttered.

"Unquestionably," Dearborn concurred.

"Let's go get her," said Benjamin.

"That may be more difficult than we anticipated."

"How come?"

Dearborn pointed to a pair of men standing a few feet to one side of Fannie. "Look who's just arrived."

"Where?"

"There, next to Fannie. That swarthy fellow with the eyeglasses and the baggy suit."

Benjamin looked. "That one there? Who is he?"

"You don't recognize him?" Dearborn asked. "It's that imbecile of a police lieutenant."

"Niccoli?"

"He's got that moron assistant of his with him," Dearborn noted. "What's his name? Barnovich?"

Benjamin leaned out to take a better look. "You're right, Dad. Of all the breaks. The son of a bitch had to pick tonight to go to the track."

Dearborn glanced around him. They were in the upper section of the clubhouse. A stairway led down and out to the grandstands. It would be simple enough to get to Fannie, but not so simple to ease past Niccoli.

"I shall distract Niccoli while you take whatever steps are necessary to deal with Fannie," Dearborn instructed.

"Distract Niccoli? He'll have you in handcuffs before you can count to five."

"You have a better idea?"

"Yes, as a matter of fact. How about paging him? When he and Stefanich go to see who wants them, we grab Mrs. Tyler and run."

"We can't snatch her up like a bag of groceries," Dearborn objected. "Knowing Fannie, she will be loath to leave. May even create a scene. It will take some diplomacy. She may behave better with you, Benjamin."

"And while I'm reasoning with her, what are you going to be doing? Running under Niccoli's nose shouting oley, oley, home free?"

"Don't be disrespectful."

"I say we try paging him."

Dearborn sighed. "If you insist. But I warn you, it won't work."

There were three minutes remaining before the third race. Spectators were eddying around Dearborn and Benjamin as they moved through the crush back toward the betting counters. Dearborn took up a position near a clubhouse window while Benjamin went to the clubhouse office. Before Benjamin got through the bell sounded and the race commenced. Dearborn saw Niccoli and Stefanich move down to the stand at the rail directly behind Fannie. Dearborn waited until the race was over. Then, in the postrace lull, he heard a voice crackle over the loudspeaker. "Police Lieutenant Niccoli. Report to the clubhouse office. Police Lieutenant Niccoli."

Niccoli looked up. He spoke a few words to Stefanich and walked away, skirting the edge of the crowd and disappearing through one of the exits.

"Okay?" Benjamin asked anxiously, walking up to Dearborn. "Did he fall for it?"

"He did," Dearborn replied. "But Barnovich did not."

Benjamin looked over Dearborn's shoulder. "Shit."

"Never let it be said that you weren't warned."

"Wait a minute," Benjamin said. "She'll be going to the betting windows. Maybe we can grab her there."

"I don't recommend creating a commotion at the betting windows," Dearborn countered. "Niccoli isn't the only law enforcement agent on the premises."

"Then we'll have to hope they get far enough away from her so we have time to get to her."

"Precisely," Dearborn said. "Which brings us full circle to the point where I provide the distraction and you move in to reason with the woman."

"What are you going to do?"

"Leave it to me, Benjamin. When the coast is clear, you move in on Fannie."

Dearborn walked away and was swallowed up in the crowd. Before he emerged from the clubhouse, Benjamin saw Niccoli rejoin Stefanich and shake his head in bewilderment, then look around him curiously, his professional instincts aroused. Benjamin was aware of a peculiar sensation, a sense of disengagement. The situation was impossible for him to assimilate. The improbability of it stunned him. He glanced at the tote board. Four minutes to post time. What insanity was his father planning?

Fannie had been consulting her program and jotting notes in the margin. Now she walked away from the rail, heading for the betting windows at the back of the grandstand. A moment later Stefanich moved away from the rail and began walking in the same direction. For the first time a startling notion occurred to Benjamin. Was it possible that Niccoli and Stefanich were following Fannie?

Something clicked into place. Otto had said the police questioned William Rhodes, that Rhodes told them the names of the people Dearborn had visited during the last week. One of them was Fannie Tyler. The police must have checked. And if they'd checked, then they knew all about her—that she was an old friend of Dearborn's, that she had disappeared about the same time as Dearborn, that there was a connection between her, Dearborn, and the others whom Dearborn had visited. More—that she was an inveterate gambler with a fondness for harness racing.

"Christ," Benjamin muttered. His indifference evaporated. He started toward the stairs. There wasn't any way his father could separate the policemen from Fannie Tyler.

Twenty-Seven

Benjamin spotted Dearborn hovering at the edge of the crowd. About twenty feet away, Niccoli had just stepped away from the two-dollar ticket window. Dearborn was watching Niccoli from behind a pillar, unaware that Fannie, with Stefanich behind, was walking toward him. Benjamin watched apprehensively. Fannie passed a couple of feet to Dearborn's right, forcing passage to a place on the end of one of the betting lines. She didn't look up from her program and Stefanich kept his eyes on her back. Neither of them noticed Dearborn. But Dearborn finally spotted them. Benjamin saw him pull his head in back of the pillar and then poke it out again cautiously.

Benjamin started across the floor. He dodged through the crowd, hunching his shoulders and taking care to keep his head down. Before he reached Dearborn there was a scuffle and a woman forced her way through the crush of bodies. She was flailing her arms and yelling

"Rape!" at the top of her lungs. For thirty seconds the center of the floor was a maelstrom of moving, shouting, bumping bodies.

It took Benjamin a moment to realize that this was the diversionary tactic his father had promised. But he understood it when Dearborn slithered out from among a clump of bewildered bystanders and lit out across the floor, bolting past Niccoli at full speed.

Niccoli sprang forward, dropping the ticket he was holding in an attempt to grab Dearborn by the coat tail. He missed.

"Rape!" the woman cried again. "Rape! Rape!"

Stefanich ran forward to join Niccoli, who pointed toward Dearborn's retreating back, and together they lit out after him, cutting through the thick knot of people pushing in the opposite direction. A few seconds later a couple of track guards materialized and joined the chase. Benjamin, who was taller than most of the people surrounding him, stretched out his neck and stood on tiptoe to catch a last glimpse of his father clattering out one of the exits leading to the stands.

Dearborn didn't stand a chance once Niccoli broke through the crowds. Benjamin was sure of it. His inclination was to join the chase but a lifetime of resigned compliance sent him, instead, threading his way through the body of people that separated him and Fannie Tyler.

"He tried to drag me behind the soda machine!" the woman was shouting. She was a heavyset woman with a pitted complexion and a slight moustache. "An old geezer!" she brayed. "A maniac!"

Benjamin moved up behind Fannie, who was at the edge of the circle. "Mrs. Tyler?" He put his hand on her arm.

"He asked me if I'd like to be ravaged! I thought the old goat was asking if I wanted a beverage. What do I know from ravage!"

Fannie looked up in surprise. "Benjamin? What are you doing here?"

"Could you come with me? I've got to talk to you."

"I'm on a winning streak. I've got ten dollars on the fourth race."

"Look. Miss Gresham told us you were here. Something's happened. In fact, a few things have happened."

"What?"

"Would you come out of this crowd so we can talk?"

Fannie said adamantly, "I'll return to the clinic later."

"Look. It's about—it's serious. There's been another—another death."

Fannie's huge eyes were suddenly fixed on him with horror. "Stella?"

"Not Miss Gresham. Look, let's get out of here. I'll tell you about it on the way to the parking lot."

There were no more objections. She followed Benjamin toward the stairs.

Behind them the woman went on indignantly bellowing. "He burst open the safety pin on my bra! Just took ahold of me around my bust and began dragging me behind the soda machine! That one. Over by the men's room. I tell you, the old fart's seventy if he's a day! He had ahold of me! Right around my bust!"

From where Benjamin and Fannie stood behind the cream-colored Ferrari in the parking lot, they could see most of the action in front of the main entrance. The lot was dim, especially in the far corner where Benjamin had parked. But there were spotlights on the main building. Four police cars had pulled up a few minutes before and discharged a battery of policemen, some of whom took up positions outside the exits while the rest dashed inside.

"They'll start searching the parking lot soon," Benjamin said. "We're going to have to get out of here."

"And leave Dearie?" Fannie asked.

"I'll take you back to the clinic. Then I'll see what I can do to help my father. He's in for it now," Benjamin predicted gloomily. "I told him this idea of his was nuts. This time he's got himself into something I can't get him out of so easily. Murder, extortion . . ."

"Attempted rape," Fannie added. "That will certainly upset him."

"Uh oh," Benjamin murmured.

A handful of policemen charged out of the building and converged at the main entrance. Benjamin and Fannie were too far away to hear what they were shouting, but a couple of them had drawn guns. One of them, a race-track guard, seemed to be hurt. His cap was askew, his jacket unbuttoned, and he was pressing his hand against his shoulder. He barked out instructions and raised his arm painfully to point to the far end of the building. Four of the policemen ran in the direction he was pointing. He issued a few more orders to the men nearest him. The words were unintelligible, but the import was clear. Three of the remaining police, along with the wounded guard, began to fan out into the parking lot.

"That's it," Benjamin announced. "We've got to get out of here. Get into the car, Mrs. Tyler."

"If they're searching the parking lot," Fannie declared in a frightened but resolute voice, "then Dearie must have gotten out somehow."

"We've been standing here watching for the past fifteen minutes. We would have seen him if he'd gotten out."

"There may be another exit around the corner of the building. You saw the guard point that way."

"Duck," Benjamin commanded. "Don't let them see us. You stand out like a fire engine in that suit."

Fannie crouched in the space between Benjamin's car and the car parked beside it. The police had entered the parking lot. All but the guard were carrying weapons. They were still a distance away from Benjamin and Fannie, but they were advancing.

"I was once on safari," Fannie murmured in a tight voice. "The natives beat the bushes in exactly the same way."

"Mrs. Tyler," Benjamin hissed, "I'm going to open the car door. You slip inside. You'd better lie on the seat."

Fannie's composure began to crumble. "Yes, all right."

Benjamin popped his head up over the car hood just in time to spot Niccoli and Stefanich careening out of the building entrance. Niccoli was waving his arms and gesturing wildly. One of the remaining policemen guarding the entrance pointed toward the parking lot. Niccoli began running toward the lot. He was holding his gun with the barrel pointing upward. In the light from the parking-lot sign, it looked huge and deadly.

"Damn. I think Niccoli's spotted us," Benjamin declared. Sure enough, Niccoli shouted something at the guard and the guard changed direction and began sprinting toward them. He was closer than Niccoli. Benjamin would never get the car backed out and turned around before he got there.

"Get in!" Benjamin shouted.

Fannie scrambled for the door, dropping her program and issuing sharp, desperate screams as she fumbled with the door handle, finally managing to pull it open and diving inside. Benjamin was already behind the wheel. He started the engine just as the guard reached the car.

"Shut the door!" Benjamin shouted to Fannie. "Shut the door!" He threw the car into gear and lurched backward. The guard grabbed the door as Fannie struggled with it and thrust himself inside.

Fannie screamed and began beating him with her fists. Niccoli, twenty yards away, roared at Benjamin to halt, then aimed his gun at the car.

"Get out!" Fannie screeched at the guard. She pushed against him as he piled into the back seat on top of her. "Get out of here!"

"Stop hammering at me, Fannie! Take your fist out of my eye!"

"Dearie!" Fannie shrieked. She switched from pushing to pulling, taking hold of Dearborn's shirt front and tugging at him until he fell across her lap, then reaching out to hold onto the door as Benjamin skidded into a wild turn and headed for the exit.

A shot rang out. It hit the trunk with a loud crack.

"He's trying to kill us!" Fannie bawled.

"No he's not. He's aiming for the tires."

Niccoli fired again. The bullet pinged against the rear bumper. Benjamin skidded through the exit gate at sixty miles an hour and teetered on two wheels as he turned onto the highway.

"That tears it," Benjamin said disconsolately. "Now we're in for it. You've really blown it this time, Dad."

"Nonsense. There's no reason for pessimism, Benjamin. In another few hours it will all be over."

They were parked in the garage behind the grounds of the clinic. Benjamin had driven in a minute before, and the three of them were sitting in the dark fighting to regain their composure. The ride back to the clinic had taken twenty hair-raising minutes. It was the first time Benjamin felt that the Ferrari had justified the price he'd paid for it.

"How's your shoulder, Dearie?" Fannie asked.

"Satisfactory. The puncture has sealed itself."

"You would have been killed if it had been a few inches lower," Fannie declared. "What kind of woman is held together by safety pins? You shouldn't have embraced her."

"Not 'embrace,' " Dearborn corrected. "I did not embrace her."

"Well, hugged her, then."

"I thought I'd been shot," Dearborn mused, "until I reached in and felt the wound."

"It's only a matter of time before Niccoli tracks us down," Benjamin interrupted. "He's hot on the trail and he's no dope. He knew enough to stake out the racetrack. He saw that we didn't head back to the city just now. He's gotten information out of Mrs. Woolley and Rhodes. Probably even out of Otto. He'll find his way to the clinic next."

"I don't need much time, Benjamin. Just a few more hours."

"Dad, come on. You're just kidding yourself."

"Nonsense!" Dearborn declared.

"You shouldn't have bashed that guard over the head!"

"A light tap, Benjamin. Just a light tap with an empty soda bottle. Enough to stun him."

"I hope, for your sake, that's true. All you accomplished with that maneuver was to convince Niccoli that he's after the right man."

"It was a question of seizing the opportunity. The guard paused by the refuse container. Attention was elsewhere. I lifted the lid to survey the situation. And . . ."

"Whack!" Fannie supplied. "Whack! Whack!"

"Go easy on these whacks, Fannie," Dearborn cautioned. "I only struck him once."

"I can't even remember how I got myself roped into this expedition," Benjamin said glumly. "What happened to the happy-go-lucky guy I used to be? Now I don't know if I should call Niccoli and beg for mercy or contact F. Lee Bailey."

"Look at it this way," Dearborn said philosophically. "Last week you were a has-been. This week you're back in the limelight."

"Next week jail," Benjamin concluded morosely.

Once undressed and in bed, Dearborn lay awake savoring the events of the past few hours. He was exhilarated by his adventure. Still capable of outwitting the nitwits and rattlebrains. It had been a heady experience. And there was more to come. He knew who the murderer was. As soon as he had the last bit of crucial evidence in hand, he would turn the murderer over to the police. It was going to be a triumph.

Twenty-Eight

"How come you're asking me? You could do it yourself."

"I am not going to discuss the complexities of my problem. I have chosen you because you have the requisite qualifications."

"Which is what?"

"A thick skin and a fundamental disregard for the law."

"Thanks a lot."

"You will be well compensated."

"How much?"

"Twenty dollars now. Another twenty after the information is obtained."

"Fifty at both ends."

"Thirty."

"Forty-five."

"Forty."

"Sold. But I got to get somebody to mind the store and I got to give him something."

"I shall take care of it, Hector. Let's say another ten."

"Twenty."

"Fifteen," Dearborn stated flatly.

"Okay."

"This is what I require, Hector. Do you have a pencil? I want you to write this down." Dearborn could hear Hector scratching down the instructions as he gave them.

"Got it," Hector said finally.

"Call me back as soon as you can. No later than this evening."

"I'll try."

"Trying is not good enough."

Hector sighed. "Okay, okay, will do."

Benjamin met Nadine in the hall outside his father's room. "You look beat."

"I'm afraid I didn't sleep too well last night. Nerves, I guess."

"You're not the only one."

She smiled bleakly. "Miss Gresham told me where you'd gone last night. She came upstairs and said I didn't have to pretend I was sitting with Mr. Bright any longer. Did you find Mrs. Tyler?"

"We found her. But the New York Police Department found her, too. It took a little doing to get her out of there."

"What happened? Do the police know you're here, then?"

"Not yet. But I guess it's only a matter of time. Come on. I'll fill you in on the way downstairs." They walked toward the elevator. Benjamin hesitated in front of Dearborn's door. "I wonder if I should get him up."

"He is up," Nadine informed Benjamin. "But I don't think he'd appreciate your disturbing him."

"Why not?"

"He's not alone."

Benjamin looked at her curiously. She nodded.

"Come on, now. You're kidding."

"I couldn't help overhearing. I was the only one in the hall."

"Who is it? Miss Gresham?"

Nadine shook her head. "Guess again."

"Not Mrs. . . ."

Nadine nodded.

Benjamin paled. He walked over to his father's door and pounded on it. "Dad?"

216

There was a pause. Then Dearborn asked, "Who's there?"

"Dad, come out of there! Right now!"

The door opened promptly. Dearborn, wearing a shantung suit and one of Robert Bright's silk ties, confronted Benjamin. Behind him, smiling genially, was Mrs. Smith.

"Dad, for pity's sake . . ."

"Mr. Pinch wanted my opinion about something," Mrs. Smith offered cheerfully.

"I'll bet."

Mrs. Smith, dripping loose hairpins, bounced out of the room and headed for the back stairs.

"Thank you, Mrs. Smith," Dearborn called after her. "I appreciate your coming up."

"Any time," she sang out gaily.

"Benjamin," Dearborn asked sternly, "is there something you wish?"

"Yes. I wish you to come down to breakfast." Benjamin got a grip on Dearborn's arm and propelled him firmly out of the doorway into the hall. "How would you like it if Mr. Smith caught her coming out of there?"

Dearborn jerked his arm away from Benjamin. "Damn it, don't paw me. And don't startle me like that again. You've rattled me with that infantile shouting."

Smith was in the dining room, sullenly removing dirty dishes from the table. Stella was finishing a cup of coffee. Fannie, wearing purple coveralls and a red bandana, was sitting opposite her. James and Dolly hadn't come downstairs. Neither had Reid.

"Oh Dearie," Stella greeted him. "Here you are. Good morning, Miss Garrett. Good morning, Benjamin. Dearie, Fannie's just told me what happened last night. I'm aghast. How do you feel? How's your shoulder? Are you all right?"

"You see me standing here in one piece, don't you?"

Stella glanced at Smith. "The person you had the little run-in with—do you think he'll find us here?"

217

Dearborn sat down at the head of the table and tucked his napkin into his collar. Benjamin sat on his left, Nadine on his right. "Smith, I shall have a soft-boiled egg. Three minutes exactly. In an egg cup. A glass of juice. I suppose it can't be fresh. You might have Mrs. Smith squeeze a few drops of lemon juice into it. Tea, toast. Brown, not scorched. And raspberry jam."

"There's oatmeal and coffee," Smith advised. "The toast's right in front of you. No juice. The juice containers got soggy sitting on the basement floor."

Dearborn tapped his fingers on the tabletop. "Now look here, Smith . . ."

Benjamin gave him a gentle kick under the table and pushed the plate of toast in front of him. Dearborn, humming furiously, satisfied himself with an imperious gesture toward the coffee urn on the sideboard.

Nadine unfolded her napkin. "Mr. Pinch, suppose that person *does* come here."

"Nonsense. Put it out of your mind."

"Just the same," Benjamin suggested, "everybody had better stay indoors."

"I was going for a walk after breakfast," Stella said disappointedly. "I'm beginning to feel claustrophobic."

"Maybe you could get up a bridge game or watch some television," Benjamin suggested.

"I don't watch television," Stella said. "It has done more to denigrate the image of women than any other art form."

"Poker might not be a bad idea," Fannie reflected. "It might pass the time. Nothing cutthroat. Maybe a few pennies to make it interesting. I'm going to see how many decks of cards I can find." She got up from the table.

"I might as well go with you," Stella said. "Just to make sure you don't mark the deck."

"Make no mistake, Benjamin," Dearborn said after they'd left the room, "they're putting up a brave show."

"I agree, Dad. But I don't think you should lead them to expect miracles."

"The case is as good as solved."

Benjamin shook his head. "You're in a pretty rough position. I can't see it getting any better."

Dearborn cast a nervous eye on Smith, who was loading dishes onto a tray. "Smith," he instructed, "bring me some more toast. And so long as you're making the trip anyway, bring up that raspberry jam I asked for."

Smith grunted unpleasantly, picked up the loaded tray, and left the room.

"When it comes down to it," Benjamin went on, "I guess the group'll come through. They'll go to bat for you. But still, it's one hell of a mess."

"Miss Garrett," Dearborn said suddenly, "what do you think? Do you think I should turn myself in? Are you and Reid prepared to take responsibility for the part you've played in this debacle?"

Nadine looked down at her plate and didn't answer.

"Well? Are you ready to face the authorities?"

"It isn't up to me," Nadine answered stiffly.

"Hell, Dad," Benjamin declared. "Don't put her on the spot. That's dirty pool. Listen, Nadine, nobody wants you or Reid to go to jail. Whatever else happens, we'll figure out some way to get you both out of this."

Nadine pushed away her plate and stood up. "I appreciate your saying that, but I'm afraid it isn't going to be that easy. Will you excuse me?" She put down her napkin and, without looking at either of them, left the room.

"Now look what you've done," Benjamin said angrily. "That wasn't fair and you know it. If you've got nothing to offer, why torture her?"

"Benjamin, given a few more hours, I shall untangle this situation and clear the way for a just resolution of everyone's individual predicament. Including Miss Garrett's."

"What's that mean, exactly?"

"That by tonight it will be over."

"It better be," Benjamin declared heatedly. "Because I'm giving you a deadline. And I'm not kidding about it, either. At midnight I take over. From then on you do what *I* say." He got up from the table. "I'm going to find Nadine and apologize."

"All right, my boy. You do that. Would·you mind pouring me a second cup of coffee on your way out?"

Benjamin caught up with Nadine at the elevator. "Where are you going?"

"I'm going to bring up some chianti for lunch."

Benjamin got into the elevator with her. "Look. I want to apologize. I'm giving my father until the end of the day to come up with something. Then I'm going to call the police. But I want you to know that I'm going to see that you don't go to jail. I don't know how. But I've got friends. I know a good lawyer . . ."

"Please," she said, holding up her hand. "Please, don't worry about me. I'm not your responsibility."

"I'm making you my responsibility. But I have to tell you. The longer we delay facing up to the police, the more chance there is that something else could go wrong. You know what I mean, don't you?"

Nadine pushed the button for the basement. "Yes, I do."

"The old man's in danger. Physical danger, I mean. He keeps implying he knows things nobody else knows and bragging about how he's going to bring in the killer. Damn it, I'm scared to leave him alone for more than five minutes at a time. From now on I'm sticking to him like glue."

"I don't think he'll like that."

"Who cares? I'm not letting anyone get within three feet of him until this is over."

"I appreciate how you feel."

The elevator clanked to a stop. Nadine pushed open the door, reached out for the light cord, and tugged on it. The pale light did little more than deepen the shadows. "Wait here," Nadine said. "You don't know your way around and it'll only take a minute."

She disappeared through the archway at the end of the hall and Benjamin heard her unlocking the door to the

220

wine cellar. A moment later she cried out "Damn!" in an exasperated voice.

"Something wrong?"

"Light's out again. Well, it doesn't matter. The chianti's stacked near the door."

Benjamin was distracted. His father was in danger. The possibilities for disaster loomed large in Benjamin's mind. He promised himself this would be the last time he'd let his father drag him into his adventures. Up until now Dearborn's escapades had been relatively innocuous, but murder—it was more than Benjamin could cope with . . .

There was a sudden, sharp crack and the sound of breaking glass. "Nadine?"

She didn't answer.

He rushed down the hall. Behind him the cage door banged shut. He peered into the darkness. The room was perhaps twenty-five feet deep, and there were rows of wine racks reaching from floor to ceiling. Aside from the dim arc of light at the door and the murkiness directly down the center aisle, the room was pitch black. Benjamin started down the center row of wine racks. "Nadine?"

He brushed against the wine racks on his right. Three-quarters of the way down the aisle he felt one of the wine bottles slip forward and graze his shoulder. Instinctively he threw his shoulder against the rack to steady it. A second later there was a sharp blow to his left shoulder as something hurtled down and crashed to the floor. At the same instant he heard Nadine cry out and he leaped forward, away from the flying shards and the deluge of sweet, sticky wine that gushed geyserlike in all directions.

He almost fell over Nadine, who was huddled against the back wall at the end of the aisle. He dropped to his knees next to her. "You okay?"

"What's that?" she whispered.

Out in the hall the elevator creaked and groaned and began moving.

"Someone must have rung for the elevator."

221

Nadine took a deep breath. "I was getting the wine. I heard a bottle break." She pointed to a row of racks several aisles over. "I went to see what had happened. Then you ran in and before I could say anything something crashed. I began to run back but I was so frightened, I . . . I guess my knees went out from under me."

"But you're okay? Not hurt?"

"I'm fine. What about you?"

"I smell like a Bowery bum, but the damned thing missed me."

"What missed you?"

"Come here and look." Benjamin helped her to her feet and led her back to the shattered container and spilled wine. "It's some kind of cask."

"A tinaja," Nadine said. "Mr. Bright has a half-dozen of them. Look." She pointed above. Five squat earthenware pots sat on the topmost shelf. Between two of them was an empty space. "They hold Cortez Montilla Fino. It's a Spanish wine. They ferment in giant, open casks and then they're bottled into these smaller replicas."

"If that thing had hit me it would have killed me," Benjamin said, rubbing his arm.

"How could it have happened?"

Benjamin pointed to a heavy stick with a clamp on the end. It was lying on one of the shelves. "Someone could have been poking around for something with one of these sometime or another and partially dislodged a cask. When I pushed against the racks I could have dislodged it even more. Enough to tip it over."

"It sounds reasonable."

Benjamin was relieved that she'd bought it. No use telling her what he really thought. What he really thought made his own knees feel like rubber.

Benjamin turned his head. The elevator announced itself again with creaks and groans. "Come on," Benjamin said.

They walked out of the wine cellar into the dim hall. Reid was stepping out of the elevator. "Smith told me he saw you go by the kitchen," Reid said. "You'd better come upstairs. We've got callers."

"We do?" Nadine said in surprise. "Who?"

"Lieutenant Niccoli, New York City police. Down at the front gate."

Twenty-Nine

There was a scramble to get rid of the remaining breakfast dishes and get upstairs and out of sight. It was decided that Reid should stay out of sight, too. His speech was slurred, his reflexes slow, and Dearborn was afraid he'd make a bad show of it.

Nadine was instructed to keep in mind that she didn't know, had never met, and could in no way recall Benjamin, Dearborn, or the others and that she should stick close to the truth otherwise when Niccoli questioned her.

It took Niccoli five minutes to cover the distance between the gate and the house. He marched across the lawn trailed by three policemen. Before coming in he issued brief orders to his men. One started around the house to the back, the second took up a position at the foot of the front steps. The third, Stefanich, followed Niccoli to the front door.

Nadine greeted them coolly. She led them into the parlor. Dearborn was tucked behind the half-open door of the employees' lounge and Benjamin skulked on the back stairs.

"What's this all about?" Nadine inquired.

Niccoli didn't waste any time. "Do you know a man named Dearborn Pinch?"

"No," Nadine answered. "Should I?"

"That's what I'm asking you. What about Benjamin Pinch? You ever met him?"

Nadine regarded him with mild curiosity. "I don't know any Pinches," she replied.

"Fannie Tyler?"

Nadine shook her head.

"Stella Gresham?"

"Why would you think I'd know these people?"

"Dolly, um, er . . . Stefanich?" Niccoli snapped his fingers at Stefanich.

"Dolly Fairchild," Stefanich supplied.

"That's right. Dolly Fairchild? James Bell?"

"Sorry," Nadine answered imperturbably.

"Where's Bright?" Niccoli asked.

"He's not here. He's away on a trip."

"You expect him back soon?"

"In a few weeks. Why?"

Niccoli strolled around the parlor, picking up ashtrays and glancing out windows. "How many people you got here?"

"Now or usually?"

"Now."

"I'm here. The health director, the cook, and the handyman."

"What's your job?"

"I'm Mr. Bright's secretary."

"I'd like to talk with the health director."

"Mr. Reid is upstairs. I don't think he'll be able to tell you any more than I."

"I didn't get your name, Miss."

"Miss Garrett."

"Miss Garrett, I'd like to decide that for myself, if you don't mind."

"All right." Nadine went into the hall to the switchboard. She rang Reid's room. "Raymond? You'll have to come down. The lieutenant wants to talk to you." She

224

paused. "I know. You'll have to come down, after all."
She hung up and returned to the parlor.

"Something the matter with him?" Niccoli asked.

"He drinks," Nadine answered shortly. "He's been
drinking this morning."

The elevator groaned and creaked.

"What's that?" Stefanich asked.

"The elevator," Nadine said. "Mr. Reid must have
rung for it."

"He drinks?" Niccoli repeated interestedly. "How does
he keep his job?"

"I don't know why that should interest you. It has
nothing to do with why you're here."

Niccoli shrugged. They waited silently until the
elevator descended and Reid shambled into the room.

Niccoli asked him the same questions he had asked
Nadine, and Reid gave the same answers.

"You never heard Bright say anything about a man
named Dearborn Pinch?"

"No."

"You never heard any of those other names, either?
Fannie Tyler, Stella Gresham, Dolly . . . er . . ." Niccoli
snapped his fingers.

"Dolly Fairchild," Stefanich filled in.

"Or James Bell?"

"No."

"Fannie Tyler's an old-time actress. You never heard
of her?"

"You didn't ask me if I'd ever heard of her," Reid
replied. "You asked me if I know her."

"So you have heard of her."

"Certainly."

"But she was never here?"

"None of the people you mentioned have been here.
Unless they were here under aliases."

"Why do you say that?"

"What?"

"Aliases," Niccoli snapped. "Why would they use
aliases?"

225

"That's your question to answer, Lieutenant," Reid snapped back. "I never met them. How would I know why they'd use aliases."

Benjamin, who had tiptoed partway down the hall and flattened himself against the wall beside the switchboard, breathed easier. Reid was going to be all right. But there were still the Smiths. The minute Niccoli spoke to them the jig would be up. Benjamin moved to the employees' lounge and slipped through the half-open door. "Dad?" he whispered.

Dearborn wasn't there. Benjamin looked around the room in bewilderment. Where had he gone? He hadn't come past Benjamin hiding on the back stairs. He couldn't have gone to the front door or up the front stairs without being seen. Had he climbed out the window? Benjamin went over to look. The windows were open, but when he looked out he spotted the policeman standing a few feet away and quickly withdrew his head. Obviously Dearborn hadn't left through the window. Benjamin went back to listen at the door. The door to the lounge was only a few feet from the parlor entrance. Niccoli, Nadine, Reid, and Stefanich were standing less than five yards away.

"Would you call the cook and the handyman, please?"

"What for?"

"I'd like to ask them a couple of questions."

"They're not going to know any more than we do," Nadine said.

"Suppose you leave that up to me?"

"I'm not certain they're here. They might have gone into town."

"If they have, then we'll wait."

Nadine walked slowly out into the hall. She began moving toward the elevator. As she came abreast of it, the gears meshed and it began to rise. She glanced back over her shoulder with a scared face and then up at the receding elevator cage. Benjamin opened the lounge door and hissed at her. She turned and saw him. He crooked his finger and beckoned to her. She crossed the hall and he pulled her into the room.

"What'll I do?" she whispered frantically.

"Never mind that. Who's coming down in the elevator?"

Benjamin peered out the crack in the door and felt the sweat break out on his forehead. Niccoli had come into the hall with Stefanich and Reid. They walked to the elevator shaft.

"That's an old-timer," Stefanich commented. "They still got a few of them in the old brownstones. Maybe in a couple of the old hotels over by the West Side."

The elevator started back down. Benjamin and Nadine watched with horror as trouser legs and nylon stockings were revealed, then knees, hips, shoulders, and faces. They belonged to James and Dolly. James looked like he'd been in a brawl. His shirt was wrinkled and pulled out from under his belt, his sleeves were rolled up, and he wasn't wearing a jacket. Dolly wasn't in her wheelchair. She looked as scruffy as James, with a scarf around her head and bedroom slippers instead of shoes on her feet. Oddly enough, she was carrying a monkey wrench. The elevator ground to a halt and they got out. Benjamin took a deep breath and put his hand on the doorknob.

"I'm Roscoe Smith," James announced. "This is Mrs. Smith."

Benjamin froze. He stared at Nadine, who mirrored his startled expression.

"I was helpin' Roscoe with Miss Garrett's toilet," Dolly explained waving the wrench at Niccoli.

"My plumber's assistant," James said with an artificial but passable grin. " 'There is always work, and tools to work withal, for those who will; and blessed are the horny hands of toil.' Lowell. 'A Glance Behind the Curtain.' "

Niccoli regarded James with mistrust. "What'd you say?"

"I was commenting on the rewards of physical labor," James explained.

227

Dolly stepped on his toe. "Nobody wants ta listen to your recitin'," she drawled. She poked the wrench in James's stomach. "My husband went ta college. If he wasn't so lazy he coulda been a lawya . . ."

In the lounge Benjamin screwed up his face and shook his head in despair. She sounded like Katherine Hepburn imitating Ruth Gordon.

"Where are you from originally, Mrs. Smith?" Niccoli asked.

"Biloxi," Dolly promptly improvised. "I was born in Biloxi in—well, I'm not tellin' you when. But it was the year they found the Cullinan diamond. The same year C. P. Snow was born."

"Oh, yeah," Stefanich noted. "C. P. Snow. The Hollywood director."

"Could you come in here a minute," Niccoli directed. He walked back into the parlor.

Benjamin motioned desperately to Nadine. She slipped out into the hall, tiptoed to the back stairs, then reversed direction and walked noisily back down the hall to the parlor. "I see you've already met Mr. and Mrs. Smith, Lieutenant."

"I'm just about to ask them a few questions."

"Fire away," James said confidently.

"You ever heard of Dearborn Pinch or Benjamin Pinch?"

"No," James replied.

"No, suh," Dolly added.

"Fannie Tyler? Stella Gresham?"

"Never heard of them, Lieutenant," James declared.

"James Bell?"

"Now," James ruminated, "do you mean James Bell, the poet? It seems to me I have heard of him. Pretty well-known in literary circles."

"You know him personally?"

"I haven't had that pleasure."

"What about Dolly . . . er . . . ah . . . Dolly . . ."

"Fairchild?" Dolly supplied.

Niccoli's expression closed up. He studied Dolly from

narrowed eyes. "How did you know who I was going to say?"

"I . . ." Dolly reddened.

"She got it from me," Nadine cut in smoothly. "I explained to Mr. and Mrs. Smith what information you're after."

"Why couldn't you tell me that?" Niccoli demanded of Dolly.

"You looked so . . . frightenin' glarin' at me like that. We Southern gals frighten so easily. Don't we, Roscoe?"

James wasn't looking at Dolly. He was watching Niccoli to see how he was reacting to their answers.

"Don't we, Roscoe?" Dolly repeated, tugging at James's arm.

"Who? What? Oh yes," James declared. "Um, ah, Mrs. Smith frightens very easily. Faints occasionally. Rather inconvenient when she's dishing up the *foi gras.*"

Niccoli shook his head and switched subjects. "How long have you two been working here?"

"About a year," James answered.

"Where's Mr. Bright?"

Dolly's eyes made an involuntary sweep of the floor at their feet. "Gone," she answered.

"You know when he'll be back?"

"No, they don't," Nadine interrupted severely. "Now that's really enough. These people aren't involved in the business end of the clinic. Their jobs are domestic and they answer to me, not to Mr. Bright. Mr. Bright's comings and goings are no concern of theirs."

"I'd like to take a look around," Niccoli said unexpectedly. "Would that be okay?"

Benjamin, out in the hall, had all he could do not to groan aloud. He covered his face with his hands and waited.

"Do you mean you want to search the place?" Nadine responded stiffly.

"I wouldn't put it that way."

"I'm afraid I would. Answering questions is one thing. But the people you're looking for are strangers to us and

229

I can't see any reason why, now that we've answered your questions, we should submit to having our privacy violated. Do you have a search warrant?"

"No, I don't," Niccoli admitted. "But I can get one."

"Then you'd better do it," Nadine stated flatly. "Though why you'd want to waste your time looking around a deserted old people's home I can't imagine."

Niccoli said patiently, "I told you, Miss Garrett, we understand that Dearborn Pinch, this guy we're after, was asking questions about the place. We're following up on the information."

"You're very conscientious. Maybe a little bit too conscientious."

Niccoli looked annoyed. "That's what I'm paid for."

"Okay. But if you want to search the place," Nadine said firmly, "you'll have to come back with a search warrant."

"Maybe I'll do that."

"Suit yourself."

"Come on, Stefanich," Niccoli said. "Let's make tracks."

"Goodbye, Lieutenant."

"Wish we could help you more," Dolly cooed.

Niccoli and Stefanich went to the door. James held it open for them. "Don't despair," James tossed out, 'If you can keep your head when all . . .' "

Dolly gave James another sharp jab with the monkey wrench and pushed the door shut.

Thirty

Dearborn emerged from the back hall. Fannie and Stella hurried down the front stairs.

"Worked, did it?" Dearborn exclaimed exultantly. "Knew it would."

"Thanks to Nadine," Benjamin said admiringly. "Nadine, you were terrific!"

"It would have worked better if you'd let *me* play Mrs. Smith," Fannie complained. "James, who ever heard of a handyman spouting poetry. And Dolly, Stella and I were sitting on the steps up there. We heard everything you said. Where *did* you get that accent?"

"What was wrong with my accent?"

"Had I been there I would have lent at least a degree of authenticity to the impersonation."

"I'm sure you would have been marvelous," Stella said. "But those policemen know you. They would have recognized you!"

"Then *you* should have done it. I'm sure you would have been better than Dolly. And you certainly look more like a cook."

"I would have done it," Stella said agreeably, "if I could have gotten this ridiculous emerald off my finger."

"Let's not quibble," Dearborn said. "All that matters is that it succeeded."

"Up to a point," Benjamin said pessimistically.

"Why?" Nadine asked, looking up at Benjamin anxiously. "Don't you think he bought it?"

"Sure he bought it. But that doesn't mean he won't come back."

Nadine shivered. "I kept wondering what would happen if Roscoe had come upstairs while Lieutenant Niccoli was questioning Mr. Bell."

"I was prepared for that," Dearborn said. He reached into his bulging jacket pocket and pulled out a sausagelike object.

"What is that, Dad?" Benjamin asked.

"A cosh."

"A what, Dearie?" Stella asked.

"A cosh. I made it out of one of Robert's socks. Filled it with sand from the potted cactus. A friend of mine used to carry one."

"Dad, getting Dolly and James to pretend they were the Smiths was a brainstorm."

"Nothing to it. When Reid rang for the elevator, I slipped into it. Went up to the second floor. Told Dolly and James what was required and sent them into the fray."

"Dearie," Fannie said, "what do we do now? Suppose Benjamin is right? Suppose that policeman does come back?"

Dearborn consulted his watch. "It is now eleven o'clock. We are going to have to be patient for a few more hours."

"Why?" James asked. "What are we waiting for?"

"We are waiting, James, for the pieces to fall into place."

"What do we do in the meantime?" Dolly fretted.

"Now that you've shown your true mettle, Dolly," Dearborn encouraged, "don't waver."

"I did do well, didn't I?"

"We can get on with the poker game now," Fannie suggested.

"I'm not good at poker," Dolly objected. "I can't remember the combinations."

232

"I don't know how I feel about socializing with you, Fannie," James added in a formal voice. "You've made accusations against Dolly and me that are uncalled for."

"What about your accusations against me?" Fannie retorted. "What about going through my personal belongings?"

"We're stuck with one another," Stella interrupted. "We're also safer with one another. So I suggest we make the best of it."

"Safer?" Dolly murmured. "I hadn't thought about that."

"Stella may be right," James conceded. "Perhaps we are better off sticking together."

"Well, then?" Fannie pursued impatiently. "You're playing?"

"We'll play."

"It's getting dark in here," Stella noted. The sunlight had dimmed. A gust of wind brushed a flurry of leaves against the window. "It's going to rain again."

"The classic setting," Fannie reflected. "A rainstorm, a mansion, a group of frightened guests. *The Cat and the Canary.*"

"That's silly," Stella remonstrated. "You're letting your imagination run away with you. Come on, Fannie, I'll help you pass out the chips."

"You're exhausted, Dolly-O," James said tenderly. "Would you like for me to go for your wheelchair?"

"No," she answered. "I can do without it. I'm feeling quite well. Are you coming, Dearie?"

"Not just yet, Dolly. I'm going to get a cup of coffee."

"I'll go with you, Dad," Benjamin volunteered quickly.

"I know the way to the kitchen."

"I haven't anything else to do."

"Then find something else to do."

No one recognized the danger better than Benjamin. He had the sore shoulder to prove it. The murderer was there. And desperate. If there was a move to make, he'd make it soon. "I'm going with you, Dad. Don't give me any of that 'find something else to do' business. Until this is over we're inseparable. And I mean inseparable."

"Come ahead, then. But don't tax me with your theorizing or advice. Useless prattle is the last thing I'm in the mood for."

They found Mrs. Smith sitting at the kitchen table wearing her hat and holding her pocketbook.

"What's this?" Dearborn asked. "Going out?"

"Not out. Away. Roscoe is packing. He saw the policemen. He's afraid we're going to be dragged into a sex scandal."

"A what?" Benjamin asked in disbelief. "Why a sex scandal?"

"The police," Dearborn said, "were making routine inquiries regarding the annual renewal of licenses and permits. I happened to be in the parlor with Miss Garrett when they arrived. I was witness to the entire interview."

"I *told* Roscoe that it wasn't anything. But he said it was."

"In that case," Dearborn returned, "how does he account for the fact that the police left without arresting anyone?"

"He says you paid them off."

"He doesn't lack for imagination, does he?" Benjamin noted.

"I assume that Smith has not given notice?" Dearborn went on.

"He isn't going to. We're just going to leave."

"What about your wages?" Benjamin asked.

Mrs. Smith toyed with her pocketbook. "Roscoe wouldn't let money interfere with his principles."

"It's a pity his principles are so misdirected," Dearborn said wryly.

Mrs. Smith bit her lip. "Roscoe said . . ."

"What?"

"I'm afraid Roscoe is going to report you to the . . ."

"The police," Benjamin supplied. "The police?"

Mrs. Smith looked apologetic. "He thinks you're part

234

of a sex cult. He says he's seen pictures of that naked gentleman somewhere. He thinks you're hiding drugs in the basement. In the freezer."

"Wait a minute," Benjamin said. "You mean he saw us bring in Mr. Br—"

"Where is Smith?" Dearborn broke in. "In your room?"

"Yes."

Dearborn went to the door. "I shall have a word with him."

"Not without me, Dad."

"We don't want to intimidate the fellow," Dearborn objected. "You wait here."

"Not on your life. I'm not letting you out of my sight."

Dearborn was exasperated. "If you insist, you may stand in the hall."

Benjamin accompanied Dearborn partway down the hall and stopped. "It might be better for me to talk to him," Benjamin whispered. "He's not crazy about you, Dad."

"And what, may I ask, would you say to him?"

Benjamin looked blank. "I'd think of something."

"There isn't time for you to think of something. This situation requires split-second mental agility. Agility that—and I say this without rancor—you do not possess."

"It's nice to know I can count on you for the straight goods, Dad."

"My paternal responsibility, Benjamin."

Dearborn left Benjamin and knocked loudly on Smith's door.

"Who is it?"

"Dearborn V. Pinch."

"What do you want?"

Dearborn turned the knob and opened the door.

"I didn't invite you in!" Smith shot out.

"I cannot carry on a conversation through a closed door." Dearborn stepped into the room and closed the door behind him.

235

"What do you want?" Benjamin heard Smith ask again in an unpleasant voice.

Dearborn's reply was inaudible.

"I don't care what you want. We're leaving!" Smith's voice cracked out.

Benjamin listened to the steady drone of Dearborn's voice, insistent, reasonable, a trifle imperious.

"No!" Smith shouted.

Dearborn persisted. Benjamin wondered what he had thought to say.

"Don't try and sell me that bologna!" Smith yelled. "I seen what's going on around here!"

More of Dearborn's subdued monologue. Benjamin was impressed by Dearborn's self-control. He was implacable. His tone remained calm.

"Buzz off!" Smith finally shouted. "I'm going to give you to the count of three! One! Two!"

Benjamin readied himself to rush in. Then suddenly he heard a dull thump behind the door. An instant later the door opened and Dearborn strolled back into the hall, closed the door, extracted a key from his pocket, and turned it in the lock.

"Dad! What was that! Listen, you didn't . . ." Benjamin's eyes traveled to the bulge in Dearborn's jacket pocket. The cosh. "You didn't . . ."

"A temporary measure," Dearborn said calmly.

"He'll come to in a couple of minutes! Then what are you going to do!"

"There is one window in the room," Dearborn said. "And it's barred. The only way out is the door. I now have the key."

"Are you crazy? You can't keep him locked up in there!"

"It will only be for a few hours."

"The door won't hold him!"

"Yes, it will," a voice behind them said. It was Mrs. Smith. "It's the same kind of door as the infirmary. Once when Mr. Reid lost the infirmary key Roscoe tried to break it down and couldn't."

"You're siding with my Dad?" Benjamin exclaimed.

"It serves Roscoe right. Trying to run off like that without giving notice. Accusing Mr. Pinch of such awful things! Spoiling everyone's fun! I've always said to Roscoe, Roscoe, some day God's going to punish you! and now, you see, he has."

"It was my idea entirely," Dearborn returned ungraciously.

Thirty-One

It was a downpour, with thunder, lightning, and winds slamming against the house and all but drowning out conversation. The rain poured in sheets down the windowpanes and trickled in under the doors on the south side of the house. In the game room the players huddled around the big card table under a hanging lamp that swung back and forth gently in the draft from the north windows.

When Dearborn and Benjamin returned, Fannie induced them to join the poker party, insisting that there must be at least six to make the game worthwhile. It was a surprise to Benjamin that Dearborn agreed, and even more of a surprise when, after a recess for lunch, Dearborn rejoined the game as if there were nothing else he had to do. They played all afternoon.

Occasionally Dearborn dispatched Benjamin, with raised eyebrow and a subtle nod of the head, to check on Smith, but he remained at the table himself, enduring

Dolly's ineptitude and Fannie's aggressiveness with something akin to patience.

Smith, downstairs, wasn't so stoical. He established a demonstration pattern consisting of fifteen minutes of door pounding and yelling, alternating with fifteen-minute intervals of full-volume radio. Fortunately the walls and floors were thick and Smith's bedroom far removed from the game room.

Mrs. Smith remained unperturbed. She took off her hat, put on her apron, and began baking lemon meringue pies. Each time Benjamin came downstairs she greeted him with an amiable smile, a floury wave, and another assurance that Roscoe was "learning his lesson good."

By three o'clock, except for Fannie, who was as fresh as ever, everyone had tired of game-playing. Dearborn, during the final hour, got up four or five times to pace the hall near the wall phone, regarding it with an expression of tense anticipation. By four, over Fannie's objections, the game broke up and the players transferred to the parlor. Benjamin succeeded in filling in as bartender without raising too much comment as to Smith's whereabouts, and Dearborn intensified his telephone vigil.

The rain continued. It settled into a steady, undramatic drizzle that dimmed the twilight into early darkness and impelled the group to pull their chairs into a close circle as far from the windows as possible. At four-thirty Dearborn made his dozenth trip to the phone. This time he picked up the receiver. Simultaneously Nadine, flushed and upset, emerged from the back stairs.

"Mr. Pinch, I was just downstairs. Mrs. Smith says that you locked—"

"Ssh," Dearborn commanded. "No need to shout, Miss Garrett."

She glanced into the parlor as she passed and then walked up closer to Dearborn. "But how could you have—"

"It was unavoidable. Now see here. This telephone

238

doesn't seem to be connected. Would you mind fiddling with the wires and plugging me in?"

"That telephone is plugged in," Nadine said.

Dearborn jiggled the phone. There was no response. Nadine crossed back to the switchboard. She stood for a moment with her back to Dearborn. Then she turned.

"What is it?" Dearborn asked, seeing her distraught face.

She stepped aside and pointed. Everything looked normal. It took Dearborn a full thirty seconds to comprehend what it was she was pointing to. The yellow and black telephone cords were neatly plugged into the board, but they had been severed about six inches below the plugs.

Dearborn hung up the phone and went over to the switchboard. "The board's been pulled from the wall," he noted, circling the switchboard. "The wires have been cut in back, also."

"What are you doing, Dad?" Benjamin called from the parlor. Dearborn didn't answer. A moment later Benjamin came into the hall. It took him even longer to take it in.

"Not a word of this to anyone," Dearborn cautioned in a low voice. "We shall carry on as if it hadn't occurred."

"Are you kidding? Weren't you expecting a call? You've been hanging around out here for hours."

"Never mind. It's inconsequential."

"Inconsequential?" Benjamin shook his head. He'd bided his time as long as he could. He'd humored the old man longer than he should have. "Okay, Dad. This is it. I'm taking over. And I say we get out of here. Now. Right now."

"We cannot leave now, Benjamin."

"Oh, no? You'll see if we can or not. The nearest house is a half-mile down the road. We're cut off here without a phone."

"I do not intend to be defeated by an act of vandalism," Dearborn insisted.

239

"You can blame it on me."

"We shall carry on as before," Dearborn persisted haughtily. "With one minor concession—we shall dispense with the proprieties. We shall not dress for dinner."

"Forget it! Forget it, Dad! Sorry! No, sir! Not this time!"

"What's going on out there!" James called.

"Nothing," Dearborn called back. "We're discussing dinner."

"Nadine," Benjamin instructed in a low voice, "get Reid. Tell him to get his stuff together. I'll tell the others."

"Benjamin," Dearborn declared imperiously, "we must not lose our heads."

"Dad," Benjamin returned in a strained whisper, "my only excuse for going along with you this far must be that I've got a crazy streak I inherited from you. Well, no more. If I have to flatten you, I'll flatten you. If I have to truss you up and carry you out of here, I'll do it. But you're going. We're all going."

Dearborn stopped arguing. He said suddenly, "All right. I agree."

"We're going?" Nadine asked nervously.

"For once Benjamin is right," Dearborn declared magnanimously. "My safety is one thing. But there are others to consider."

Benjamin regarded his father suspiciously. "Now what?"

"What what?"

"What have you got up your sleeve?"

"Nothing. Not a thing."

"No funny business?"

"No funny business. I bow to the inevitable."

"What *is* going on out here?" Stella asked, coming into the hall.

"We are leaving, Stella," Dearborn explained. "I am going to fetch Reid, and then we shall leave."

"Leave? Why?"

"Benjamin will explain." Dearborn stepped into the elevator, shut the door, and pressed the button. "Tell her, Benjamin." Slowly he rose from sight.

"I don't understand," Stella said in a baffled voice.

"My father thinks it's foolhardy to stick around any longer," Benjamin stated flatly.

"What about Roscoe?" Nadine asked. "You'll have to let him out."

"Who's Roscoe?" Stella demanded.

"Mr. Smith. He's locked in his bedroom."

"What about Smith?" Fannie asked, wandering in from the parlor.

"That's what I'd like to know," Stella said. "Miss Garrett says he's locked in his bedroom. Good Lord!" she exclaimed. "Don't tell me it's Smith!"

"Smith?" James cried from the parlor. "Dolly, I think I heard Stella say it's Smith!"

"No, no," Benjamin intervened. "Smith's got nothing to do with this."

"Then why's he locked up?" Stella asked in bewilderment.

"It's a long story."

"He isn't going to come out of there smiling," Nadine pointed out. "He's very angry at your father for locking him in."

"Why did Dearie lock the man up?" Dolly asked. She came into the hall leaning on James's arm. "He must have done *something* wrong!"

"He quit," Benjamin explained desperately.

"That hardly justifies locking him up," James observed.

"Could we talk about this later? Right now we've got to get out of here."

"We're going?" Fannie burst out. "Why?"

"It's not safe," Benjamin said.

"We all know that," Fannie declared. "The point is that it's not safe anywhere. That's what Dearie told us."

"It's just as safe as it was an hour ago, isn't it?" Stella asked.

241

Benjamin held out his hands in a helpless gesture.

"Isn't it?" Fannie picked up insistently. "Isn't it?"

They faced Benjamin challengingly.

"The switchboard's out of whack," Benjamin mumbled.

All eyes darted to the switchboard. James disengaged himself from Dolly's arm and stepped across the hall to inspect the switchboard at closer range. He nodded slowly. "It is certainly out of whack."

"How so?" Fannie moved closer and leaned over his shoulder. "What's wrong with it? It looks fine to—" She shrieked suddenly, causing Dolly to clutch at her heart and lean back against the wall.

"What is it?" Stella cried.

"Cut," James said succinctly. "The wires have been cut."

As he spoke the elevator descended. Reid, heavy-lidded and dazed, was slouched on the seat inside. He got up slowly and fumbled with the cage door.

"The wires have been cut!" Fannie cried agitatedly. "Someone has cut the switchboard wires!"

Reid's eyes moved from Fannie to the switchboard, then to Nadine, with a vague questioning look.

"It's true," Nadine told him.

"We're leaving," Benjamin added. "Are you in any shape to . . ."

"Of course," Reid muttered. But he wasn't able to pronounce the *s* cleanly and it came out *coursh*.

"What about Roscoe?" Nadine asked again.

"What's the matter with Roscoe?" Reid asked blearily. "Nothing's happened to Roscoe, has it?"

"No," Benjamin snapped. "Smith's okay."

"He's locked up," Fannie explained. "Benjamin and his father locked him up."

"I'll take care of Smith," Benjamin declared.

"Why did you lock up Roscoe?" Reid demanded.

"Let's see," Benjamin speculated. "There are ten of us. Nadine, you can handle six in the station wagon. Four of us can go in my car. I'll have to take the Smiths and one

242

other. Not my dad, obviously. Maybe Miss Gresham. That okay, Miss Gresham?"

"I guess," Stella said.

"Nadine, you can take Mr. Reid, Mrs. Tyler, Mr. Bell, Mrs. Fairchild, and my dad."

"Where is Dearie?" Stella asked.

"Yes, where is Dearie?" Fannie echoed.

Benjamin looked at the empty elevator, then turned to Reid. "Where is he?"

Reid shrugged. "I have no idea."

Benjamin didn't bother with the elevator. He ran for the front stairs, taking them two at a time and shouting "Dad!" at the top of his voice. The others could hear him run down the second-floor corridor and bang on Dearborn's door.

"Oh," Dolly wailed, "now what's happening? I don't understand it at all. Don't tell me Dearie is gone again. Where *is* Dearie?"

Thirty-Two

"He took the car."

Benjamin cursed himself for having left the car keys in his room. By the time he had reached the garage, Dearborn was gone.

"What do we do now?" Fannie wailed. "Why has Dearie run away?"

"Who would have thought it of him," Dolly said in wonderment.

243

"Don't be silly," Stella snapped. "Dearie did not run away."

"He would take my car," Benjamin muttered. "Every cop between here and Hoboken must have a description of my car."

"Where do you suppose he's gone?" James asked.

"He had something in mind," Stella declared. "He may have gone for the police."

"If that's what he had in mind," James disagreed, "he would have said so. I don't like to be the one to point it out, but there was a furtive quality to Dearborn's departure."

"He's stalling for time," Benjamin explained shortly. "He figures I won't leave without him."

A new sound intruded on their conversation—sharp, quick footsteps running down the hall. They turned to see Mrs. Smith coming into the room.

"What's the matter?" Fannie exclaimed.

"Where's Mr. Pinch?" Mrs. Smith asked agitatedly.

"He's not here," Nadine answered. "Why?"

"Roscoe has set fire to his room!"

Nadine drew in her breath and jerked her head around to stare at Benjamin. "My God!"

Benjamin leaped out of his chair. "He what!"

"Smoke is coming through the cracks in the door."

"Maybe he's blowing cigar smoke at you," Fannie suggested.

"He set the room on fire. He did it to force Mr. Pinch to open the door."

Reid, who had been supporting himself by leaning against the back of Benjamin's chair, pulled himself shakily upright. "Where's the key?" he demanded.

"My father's got it," Benjamin answered.

"But Dearie isn't here!" Dolly squawked.

Benjamin ran toward the back stairs. The others fell in behind him, Nadine and James first, Reid, staggering, at the end of the line.

"Tell him to smother it with blankets!" James shouted.

"Let him lie on the floor with his mouth to the door!" Stella called.

"It *could* be a sham," Fannie suggested shrilly.

"We could squirt water in the window," Dolly cried desperately.

"I think we should call the fire department," Mrs. Smith burst out as she hurried to keep pace with Fannie.

"We can't," Fannie informed her, gathering her skirts around her knees as she clattered down the back steps. "Phone's out."

"Phone's out. Key's gone," Dolly puffed. She had paused halfway down the steps to lean on the wall and catch her breath.

"You're not getting one of your attacks, are you?" Fannie demanded as she and Mrs. Smith flew past.

"I don't think so."

"Well, don't. There's no time for it."

The downstairs hall was smoky, and they could hear Smith coughing inside the bedroom.

Benjamin pounded on the door and yelled, "Can you put it out? Listen, we don't have a key. Can you put it out?"

"Get me out of here!" Smith cried hoarsely.

"There's an extinguisher on the wall behind you," Mrs. Smith cried excitedly.

"The extinguisher's no good until we get in the room. What we need is an axe."

Reid was the last to arrive. He ran unsteadily for the kitchen, calling that there was a hatchet in the woodshed. Benjamin dashed after him, passing him at the kitchen door, throwing the door open and bursting outside. The woodshed was a lean-to next to the basement entrance. It had no door. The wood was stacked inside on open shelves and the hatchet was propped up on two nails hammered onto the inside wall. Benjamin cleared the ten yards there and back in a few seconds, pushing Reid aside as he barreled back into the house.

"Hurry!" Stella cried.

"He's suffocating!" Nadine shouted. "I heard him fall."

Benjamin told them to stand clear, then swung at the door. The hatchet blade dug into the wood and stuck. Benjamin tugged at it with both hands, freed it, and struck again. This time the wood splintered above and below the jagged gash. He pulled the hatchet free and aimed his next blow at the same spot trying to break the middle section of door. It took almost three minutes to accomplish the breakthrough, minutes during which the acrid stench burned his nostrils and stung his eyes.

The rest of the group retreated to the kitchen and then, as the smoke thickened, out the back door, coughing and holding their hands in front of their mouths. But even in his inebriated state Reid had the presence to take constructive action. He went back upstairs and returned with two additional fire extinguishers. Nadine, who had stayed with Benjamin, took one of them, and Reid laid the other at Benjamin's feet, then disengaged the third extinguisher from its holder and held it ready.

"That'll do it," Benjamin declared finally. He dropped the hatchet and reached through the hole he'd torn open. The room was dense with smoke. Smith was crumpled against the inside of the door. Benjamin, lifting and pulling, managed to drag him out into the hall. "Mr. Bell!" Benjamin shouted. "Mr. Bell!"

James heard and charged valiantly back into the smoke-filled hall. "Here!"

"Pull him out," Benjamin yelled to Reid. "Grab his hands and pull him out into the air. Give the extinguisher to Mr. Bell!"

James pulled the extinguisher out of Reid's hands. Reid took hold of Smith's wrists and dragged him away.

Benjamin, wielding the hatchet, continued to hack at the door until he broke the lock. Then he directed the nozzle of the extinguisher toward the interior of the room. "Where's the fire? I don't see anything burning!"

"Over by the window," Nadine said in a strangled voice. "The curtains and bedding."

"I can't see if the window's open."

"You can't get to it, anyway. It's behind the bed."

Nadine and James crowded into the room behind Benjamin. They sprayed the end of the room blindly. Fortunately the blaze was confined to the far end of the room, and it didn't take long to put out. Benjamin checked the window. The bottom sash was open. He used the extinguisher cylinder to smash out the upper panes. "Let's get out of here!"

Nadine dropped the extinguisher, untucked her blouse and lifted the hem to mask her nose and mouth. She darted out of the room with James gagging at her heels. Benjamin picked up the hatchet on his way out and stumbled down the hall, dropping the hatchet on the grass outside.

Reid had revived Smith, who lay on the grass with his head on his wife's lap. His eyes were dull and his face and clothing were black with soot.

"Is he all right?" Benjamin asked.

"Not even singed," Reid answered. "But he inhaled a lot of smoke."

"Shouldn't we get him to a hospital?"

"He'll be all right."

"I'm not sure *I* shall be," James said weakly.

"Oh, Jimmy," Dolly cried, "you look terrible. Come and sit down."

James lowered himself onto the edge of a stone urn outside the kitchen door.

"You all right?" Benjamin asked Nadine.

"I'm all right. A little sick to my stomach."

"I'm queasy myself."

"Why did you do it!" Dolly suddenly demanded of the limp Smith.

"He might have killed himself," Stella observed.

"And us as well," Fannie joined in. "As if we aren't in enough difficulties already." She frowned. "Come to think of it, that would have been one way to get rid of us." She moved closer to Smith and looked down at him with fierce eyes. "That isn't what you had in mind, is it?"

Smith's mouth was agape and he sucked in air noisily as he stared up at her.

"That's silly," Stella pointed out. "He wouldn't set fire to *himself* in order to get rid of *us*."

"Roscoe doesn't approve of you," Mrs. Smith said, rallying to his defense, "but he wouldn't try to kill you."

"He doesn't approve of us?" James said wonderingly. "Why not? Is he talking about Dolly and me?" James scowled at the recumbent and uncaring Smith. "I'll have you know that Mrs. Fairchild and I do not take kindly to your insinuations."

"Have you been eavesdropping?" Fannie demanded of Smith.

It was doubtful whether Smith was capable of registering the question, much less of formulating the answer. He stared vacantly at Fannie's kneecaps while he inhaled fresh air raspingly through his open mouth.

"The man is a fanatic," James declared. "A religious zealot!"

"The man is suffering from smoke poisoning," Reid interrupted impatiently. "Can't you see that?"

"It's his character we're discussing," Fannie stated flatly. "Not his physical condition."

"What you're telling us is that Smith has no idea what we're saying to him and that he cares even less?" asked Stella.

"Exactly."

"Then I suggest we turn to more pressing questions. Dearie, for instance."

"Where is Dearie?" Dolly promptly picked up.

"Yes," Stella said. "Where *is* Dearie?"

"Well?" Dearborn demanded. "Let's not waste time. What did you find out?"

"I went to the bank," Hector began.

"Are you eating something?"

"Yeah. A hot dog and a glass of orange juice."

"Stop chewing in my ear."

"I haven't had any food since this morning."

248

"You went to the bank," Dearborn prompted.

"Bingo. A bank account showing thirty thousand dollars deposited over the last two years."

"Excellent. Did you tell the bank manager that you represent a credit agency, as I suggested?"

"How far do you think I would of got with that?" Hector replied. "My numbers contact has a sister who works for one of the branches. I give him forty and said I'd get her on 'Blank Check.' "

"Give her a blank check? Are you mad?"

"Not give her a blank check. Get her on 'Blank Check.' It's a quiz show. My cousin's nephew is a—"

"Never mind that, Toole. Go on. Did you succeed in getting the initial deposit date?"

"Two years ago September."

"Ah. That's the lead we needed. So?" Dearborn urged. "Were you able to use the information to good advantage?"

"You bet," Hector answered confidently. "I checked the record files downtown in case it turned out to be a cinch type operation." Hector paused to gulp down some orange juice. "Then when that didn't pan out I checked the back issues of the papers at the library, like you said. And I called *Newsday* and the *Long Island Press*. No soap. That left New Jersey and Connecticut. Lucky I hit it on the first try. I called one of my customers, Larry Baker. He's the assistant manager of the Drift Inn Motel chain up in Connecticut. He's got a lot of contacts himself. Now the interesting thing about Larry Baker is that he cheats on his old lady. He meets all his broads in front of my place. You know, two innocent-looking people buying *Cue* or *Vogue*. They waltz off in the same direction—"

"Skip the romantic embellishments."

"I'm just explaining how come he was willing to cooperate . . ."

There was a clicking sound in Dearborn's ear. "Wait a minute, Toole. I have to deposit another coin."

"Where are you calling from? Sounds like you're far away."

249

Dearborn looked over his shoulder at the handful of patrons in the Islip Diner. "Not far enough for comfort, Toole. You were talking about this Baker individual. . . ."

"So I went up there around three and him and me gabbed a little. Get it? Then he says he'd be glad to help and he checks around all the hotels, motels, and he comes up with the answer."

"Which is?"

"Norwalk, Connecticut."

"You are sure?"

"Positive."

Dearborn began to hum. He drummed on the side of the phone box and repeated thoughtfully, "Norwalk, eh?"

"But that's as far as I could take it. So I never got the last question answered. I mean I'd have to be there to do any good in Norwalk. I know a guy in Ridgefield . . ."

"Not necessary, Toole. I know a gentleman myself in Fairfield County, a very straitlaced gentleman named Edward Dill. Once married to a dear, umm, friend of mine, now deceased. It's a little late in the day, but I don't think he'll object to pulling a few wires. I'll call him. Thank you, Toole. You did your job well."

"So when do I get paid?"

"Tomorrow. I think it's safe to assume that I'll be home by then."

Thirty-Three

"The respiratory system is delicate," Reid said. "Smith was suffocating. The larynx, the pharynx . . ."

"The what inks?" Dolly asked.

". . . the windpipe, the lungs, the nose, when their functions are interfered with—the sinuses especially—"

"Oh, please," Fannie pleaded. "Stop talking about respiratory systems."

"I'm talking about my patient," Reid returned lugubriously.

"I suspect," James said, "that even Smith would find an analysis of his sinus cavities irrelevant."

"Jimmy's right," Dolly agreed. "This is not the right time to discuss noses."

"There is never a right time to discuss noses," James said.

"What about Cyrano?" Stella returned.

"All the great bravura roles were written for men," Fanny digressed wistfully.

"If you ask me," James went on, "even theatrically, the nose lacks clout."

"One does blow it, of course," Dolly suggested vaguely.

Benjamin's feelings of weariness and concern were mirrored in Nadine's face. And Smith, pallid and weak, reflected the ordeal he'd been through. Even Mrs. Smith looked worried. But to Benjamin's wonder the others digressed on noses as if they hadn't anything else to think

251

about. He didn't know whether to chalk it up to nerves or to the absentminded ramblings of old age. "I think we'd better go inside," he suggested tactfully.

"The nose," Stella argued, "is very symbolic. We win by a nose. We put it on the nosebag. We hit it on the nose. We're nosy parkers. We cut off our noses to spite our faces."

"And what," Fannie challenged, "could be more theatrical than that?"

"We also bob our noses," Stella said. "I wonder what Freud would have made of it."

"Castration," James returned. "There's the connection. He would have seen it for the aberration it is."

"I'd like to move Smith indoors," Benjamin broke in hopefully.

"Yes," Nadine seconded. "We can put him into one of the empty rooms on the second floor."

"Don't you think cosmetic surgery is frivolous?" James asked Reid. "Altering the physiognomy according to whim?"

"No," Reid mumbled. "It's not frivolous." The word frivolous came out mushy and indistinct.

"It is frivolous," James insisted.

"Remember Countess Ambeil," Dolly said. "I wouldn't call her operation frivolous. It was disastrous."

"So was Caroline," Reid said unexpectedly.

"She met her match in Jack Rogers," Fannie reflected. "Poor Jack. I guess he wasn't cut out for a surgeon."

"She knew the operation was experimental," Reid muttered.

"What?" Stella asked. "Did you say something about Caroline Ambeil?"

"Raymond," Nadine interrupted, "I think we should get Roscoe upstairs."

"I said she knew the operation was experimental."

"Then you *knew* Countess Ambeil?" Stella asked.

"You must have known Jack, too," James said curiously. "Did you?"

"No," Reid said shortly.

Nadine tried again. "Really, this is no time to talk about that. We've got to take Roscoe inside."

"You think Caroline was at fault?" Dolly asked. "For wanting her nose bobbed, I mean?"

"She begged me," Reid answered indistinctly.

"Wait a minute," Stella said. "She begged *you*?"

"I didn't say me."

"You did. And you referred to Smith as your patient."

"A slip of the tongue."

"What had you meant to say?"

"I don't remember."

"My God!" Stella cried. "It isn't possible that you . . ."

Reid glared at her. "I don't know what you're talking about!"

"All that discussion of larynxes. How do you know all that?"

"Stella!" Fannie bellowed. "Are you thinking what I think you're thinking?"

"Yes, I am. Of course I am."

"Please!" Nadine cut in. "Couldn't you save all this until later?"

"Jack!" James trumpeted. "Jack, you say!"

"He said it himself," Stella came back excitedly. "It's true, isn't it? You're a physician. A plastic surgeon?"

"No wonder Bobby hadn't a wrinkle on him," James exclaimed.

"What have Bobby's wrinkles to do with anything?" Dolly asked.

"You heard him," Fannie said. "Don't you understand? Don't you realize who the man is?"

"A doctor?" Dolly repeated. "What doctor?" She gasped and dug her fingers into James's hand. "Jack? Jack Rogers?"

"Oh, this is all nonsense," Nadine exclaimed. "Ben," she pleaded, "can't you reason with them?"

Benjamin, standing on the sidelines, was shocked. They knew Reid? He was someone they knew? He looked at Reid. Reid was trying to face them down. Benjamin shook his head at Nadine and held his fingers to his lips.

"I didn't say she begged me," Reid insisted desperately.

"Look," Nadine whispered suddenly into Benjamin's ear. "I'm going to get the medical bag. I don't know what's going on, but I'm willing to bet we're going to have to break out the tranquilizers before it's over." She dashed back into the house.

"I knew you looked fa-familiar," Dolly stammered. "I sa-said so from the first . . ."

"Now, Dolly," James warned, "don't go to pieces. Get hold of yourself."

"Would somebody spell it out for me," Benjamin demanded.

"This man is Jack Rogers," Stella explained. "A doctor, one of the Rotten Apples. Don't you understand?"

"Don't deny it," James added. "It's too late. The cat's out of the bag!"

"All right! So what if I am!" Reid barked defiantly.

"So what if you are?" James returned excitedly. "May I remind you that I was the one who shoveled you onto the *Queen Mary* one step ahead of Jacques Ambeil? And this is how you repay me? Repay us?"

"Really, Jimmy," Dolly intervened, "I don't think he did it to spite us."

"I'm not talking about spite, Dolly. Why do you think Jack persuaded Miss Garrett to sell the clinic? Why do you think he pretended that poor old Bobby was touring the Orient all the time he was locked up in his room? Why do you suppose he forged Bobby's name to those contracts?"

"Why?" Dolly asked.

"Listen," Benjamin interrupted. "Let me try and get this straight—"

"We told you about Jack Rogers," Stella said. "He's been pretending to be Raymond Reid all these years."

"Biding his time!" Fannie cried out. "Waiting for the time when Bobby would . . . would . . ."

"I thought you were dead!" James proclaimed. "No one's heard from you since you left the country."

"What about Bobby?" Stella asked. "Didn't Bobby realize?"

"Private physician to the Longevity King," Reid mumbled in an ironic tone. "He kept my secret and I kept his."

"What was *his* secret?" Dolly asked in bewilderment.

"It would never have done for Bobby to advertise his face lifts to the general public," Fannie said. "Jack must have been Bobby's plastic surgeon."

"Loyalty obviously played no part in your arrangement," James admonished Reid. "You tried to sell the clinic out from under Robert."

"That's a lie," Reid said shakily. "We were friends. I did what I did in good faith."

Mrs. Smith, still cradling her husband's head in her lap, gazed from one to the other of them in confusion. "Did somebody say the clinic was sold? Did Mr. Bright sell the clinic? No one told Roscoe or me about it."

"Ben!"

There was a flurry in the kitchen doorway. Nadine came out carrying the medical bag in one hand and a narrow shining object in the other. "Ben! Look!"

"What is it?" Benjamin asked.

"I found it in Raymond's bag. It's a scalpel. Look at it!" She held out the slender instrument and Benjamin bent over it. It had clearly been put to some use other than its intended one. The tip was broken and there was a nick near the end of the blade. Caught in the nick were a few yellow and black strands. "This must have been used to cut the telephone cords!"

Reid took a hesitant step forward. "What are you suggesting, Nadine?"

"While we were playing poker, of course," Fannie said.

"Raymond," Nadine exclaimed in horror, "I thought you were trying to protect Mr. Bright."

"You've been used, Miss Garrett," James declared. "Ill-used. The real reason this man enlisted your aid in selling the clinic was so that he could collect a share in the profits. He wasn't stretching the law for altruistic reasons. He was committing a deliberate crime for his own benefit."

"More than a single crime," Stella elaborated. "Fraud was the least of it . . ."

"The least of it?" Dolly chimed in questioningly. "What else . . ." She suddenly recognized the import of Stella's remark. "Oh-h-h," she shrieked.

"Dolly! Now Dolly!" James shouted. He reached out with both hands to take her arm, but she slipped through his grasp and slithered to the ground.

Benjamin dashed over and dropped to his knees. "Is it an attack?"

"I don't know."

"Let me see," Reid ordered. He crossed the grass and knelt next to Benjamin. He lifted one of Dolly's wrists.

"Let her alone!" James thundered. "Don't lay a hand on her!"

"She may need medication," Reid advised.

"Not from you!" James bawled.

"Don't be a fool! I'm trying to help her."

"You're a killer!"

Reid's face was white. "No," he said. "No, I'm not."

"A killer!" Fannie echoed dramatically. "The man is a killer!"

Reid was still holding Dolly's wrist. James darted to the kitchen door and picked up the hatchet. "Release her!" he shouted. "Get away from her!" He raised the hatchet and rushed forward.

"Drop it!" Benjamin shouted. He leaped forward and grabbed James's arm. "Are you crazy? You'll kill him with that!"

Fannie loyally rushed to James's aid, scooped up a small rock, and thrust it at him.

"Quit it!" Benjamin slapped the rock out of James's hand. It flew through the air and struck Reid on the side of the head. Reid dropped Dolly's wrist and struggled to his feet. He clawed at Benjamin and threw an ineffectual punch at James. Benjamin released James and caught Reid in a bear hug, but Reid broke the hold and butted

256

Benjamin with his head. Then he reached out and pressed his thumbs against Benjamin's Adam's apple. Benjamin's response was automatic. He lifted his knee and kicked Reid in the groin.

As Reid keeled over, James reached down, picked the rock up from the ground, and smashed it over Reid's head. Dolly raised herself onto one elbow and screamed. James, galvanized by the scream, raised the rock for a second blow, but Benjamin intervened, shouldering James aside.

Reid lay sprawled on the grass, his arms outstretched, his eyes closed, his body still.

"You've killed him," Stella whispered.

"Is he dead?" Nadine asked.

"He's not dead. It's okay. He'll be okay."

Mrs. Smith had risen when James grabbed the hatchet. She stood between her husband and the rest of the group. "Roscoe wouldn't like any of this," she said mildly. "Luckily, he's passed out."

"Passed out?" Benjamin exclaimed. "Hell. We'd better get him in the house."

"Are you all right, my dear?" James asked Dolly.

"I think so," Dolly answered in a weak voice.

"Jack Rogers," Stella murmured. "Who even knew he was alive?"

"Remarkable," Fannie agreed weakly. "Thank God we found out in time."

"Please go for the police," Nadine said in a strained voice. "I don't think we should wait any longer."

"There's nothing left to wait for," Benjamin agreed. "Let me just carry Smith upstairs."

Thirty-Four

Benjamin used some rags from the ragbag to tie Reid's wrists, and Stella slipped a sofa pillow under his cheek.

"How shall we handle this?" James asked.

"There isn't much choice," Benjamin replied. "It's a hike to the garage and I don't relish carrying him. I'll bring the police back."

"It shouldn't take long to get to town, should it?" Dolly asked nervously.

Her question was addressed to Nadine, who was leaning against the piano gazing down at Reid with a preoccupied expression.

"What? Oh, no. Ten or fifteen minutes."

"Are you okay, Nadine?" Benjamin asked with concern.

"I'm fine."

"Because you're going to have to hold the fort. Look after everybody until I get back."

Nadine took a deep breath and said shakily, "I can handle Raymond. It might be better, though, if you take everyone else with you."

"We wouldn't leave you here," Stella said quickly. "Besides, we're quite all right. Aren't we, group?"

"I, for one," Fannie announced, "am better than I have been in days."

"True, true," James chimed in. "I feel quite relieved myself. The worst is over."

Benjamin leaned over to tug at the bindings on Reid's wrists. "Don't let him con you into anything when he comes to."

"Like what?" Fannie asked.

"Like having to go to the john. Or saying that I cut off his circulation. Anything like that."

"Or that you've made a terrible mistake," Nadine added tensely. "You know he's going to deny everything."

"That won't cut any ice with us," Fannie declared. "We're not imbeciles."

"What are you going to tell the police, Benjamin?" asked James. "It won't be easy to explain."

Stella, pacing up and down in front of the French doors, said, "The truth. The truth up to a point, that is."

"We shall tell them," Fannie stated firmly, "everything we know except the details concerning the Rotten Apples. We shall tell them it was a social club and leave it at that. If Jack says otherwise, we shall simply deny it."

"I wish Dearie were here," Dolly said plaintively.

"What about Bobby?" Stella asked. "Do we tell them how he was? That he was senile?"

"If we don't," James speculated, "Jack might."

Benjamin said, with a sideways glance at Nadine, "Miss Garrett's right. Reid's going to issue a blanket denial to everything, which may be to your advantage."

"Why?" James asked.

"The police won't believe anything he says. Including any claims he makes about Bright being senile."

"But we'll be making ourselves accomplices to the fraud," Dolly pointed out. "Won't we?"

"For what it's worth, Miss Garrett's no more a criminal than any of you. She did what she did out of kindness."

"That's true," James allowed. "And don't forget that if we tell the police about the fraud, we'll lose our share of the profits."

"I say we forget about it," Fannie promptly voted. "After all, the essential point is that Jack has been killing off Rotten Apples. The rest is of no concern to anyone."

259

"You're right," Stella agreed. "What's the difference what condition Bobby was in when he died?"

"Especially considering the condition he's in now," Fannie concluded reasonably.

"I knew it all along," Dolly murmured, gazing down at Reid. "Didn't I say he looked familiar?"

"You said," Fannie corrected, "that he looks like John Gilbert."

"He does look like John Gilbert."

"I wonder why he didn't burn his shirt," James reflected, "instead of sticking it in the ragbag?"

"It was a mistake," Benjamin conceded. "I imagine he thought the clinic was the last place in the world anyone would look for the murderer. Listen, I'd better get going. The sooner I get the police, the sooner we can get out of here. Nadine, where are the car keys?"

"Hanging on a hook near the back stairs," Nadine answered. "You can get them on your way out."

"What about the Smiths?" James asked.

"What about them? They'll be okay upstairs until I get back. Smith's starting to come around. His wife's up there with him."

"But what are they going to say? Smith has a peculiar notion of what's been going on here."

"Not as peculiar as what *has* been going on here," Benjamin suggested wryly.

"Maybe I could talk to Roscoe," Nadine said. "While the rest of you pack."

"Pack?" Stella repeated. "That's right. I hadn't thought about it. We *had* better pack, hadn't we?"

"Do you think you can straighten Smith out?" Benjamin asked Nadine hopefully.

"I don't know. I'm willing to try."

"It would be one less complication," Stella said. "The man is such a troublemaker. Maybe you could threaten to accuse him of arson."

"We shouldn't leave Jack unguarded," Fannie declared. "I don't think we should go upstairs and leave him alone here."

"Why?" James asked. "He's harmless enough now."

They contemplated the recumbent Reid, eyes closed, wrists bound, breath heavy and deep.

"Jimmy's right," Stella concluded matter-of-factly, "we've nothing to fear anymore from Jack Rogers."

Benjamin skirted the shed, circled the swimming pool, and arrived at the garage two or three minutes after leaving the house. He threw open the door on the side of the garage and was about to step inside when he stopped and cocked his head. From down the road he heard the noise of a motor. The sound was familiar and distinct. He listened as the volume increased. The car was traveling fast—faster than a car should have been traveling on that winding back road without street lights or room to maneuver.

The hum became a drone, then a roar. There was a loud screech, the crunch of tires on the gravel drive, and, a second later, the reverberating slam of metal against wood. Benjamin shut his eyes.

A car door slammed and Dearborn's voice carried through the still night. "Damned fools! Asses! Mechanical dimwits!"

"Dad?"

There was a momentary silence, then the sound of footsteps coming around the corner of the garage. Dearborn appeared, looking out of sorts but otherwise intact. "What are you doing here?" he demanded.

"I'm going for the police."

"You're going for the police? Without waiting for me? Without knowing where I was? You are taking it upon yourself to summon the police?"

"Dad, there's no time for long explanations."

"A short one will suffice."

"We found out that Raymond Reid isn't who he says he is," Benjamin rattled off. "He's a guy named Jack Rogers. He's the one. The murderer."

"He is not," Dearborn stated flatly.

261

"He's the murderer, Dad! I've got him tied up back at the house and I'm going for the police."

"You have the wrong man."

"Hell, Dad. You want to come with me or you want to wait here?"

"I am not going with you and you are not going without me," Dearborn declared vehemently.

"Now listen—"

"*You* listen. Reid is not the murderer. On the contrary, unless I miss my guess he is in imminent danger of being the next victim."

"You're wrong, Dad," Benjamin argued. "You don't know what happened awhile ago. I'm telling you—"

"Stop telling me!" Dearborn turned his back on Benjamin and dashed across the grass. He disappeared into the fog while Benjamin listened in shocked silence to the sound of his feet drumming across the soft earth.

"Dad, I tell you you've got it all . . ." As the gap between them lengthened, Benjamin gave up talking and broke into a run that was at first an easy lope, then an energetic sprint. He came abreast of Dearborn at the edge of the swimming pool. "He confessed," Benjamin puffed. "He came out and told us who he is! From his own lips!"

"He told you who he is, not what he is," Dearborn wheezed.

"What?" Benjamin panted. "What did you say?"

Dearborn didn't answer. He passed the shed and made for the kitchen door. "Where is he?" Dearborn shouted hoarsely over his shoulder.

"Upstairs. Front parlor."

Dearborn flung himself through the kitchen door and ran toward the back stairs. Halfway up the stairs he halted and waved Benjamin past him. He put both hands on the wall and rested against his outstretched arms.

"Dad, you okay?"

Dearborn released one hand long enough to point upward. Benjamin went past him, taking the steps two at a time, and raced down the hall to the parlor. He paused in the doorway. Nadine was helping Reid sit up. She whirled and gave an involuntary yelp.

"It's all right," Benjamin reassured her. "Don't panic."

"What's wrong?" she cried out.

"How's Reid?"

Reid's face was gray and his eyes were glazed. There was a purple welt on the side of his head and a swelling under his eyes, but he was conscious.

"I was going to give him some smelling salts." Nadine pointed to the open medical bag on the arm of the couch. "What's wrong, Ben?"

"I ran into my father out by the garage. He says Reid's not the one."

"He's not the one? What does your father mean?"

"We didn't have time to discuss it."

"I don't understand," Nadine said in bewilderment.

"He's gabbling something about Reid being in danger. If you ask me, the old man's beginning to show the strain."

"But you came back."

"I guess the strain's getting to me, too." Benjamin turned his head and looked back down the hall. "Maybe I'd better see if he's okay."

"Who?"

"Dad."

"Where is he?"

"That's what I want to know!" another voice interrupted. Benjamin turned. Roscoe Smith was standing next to the switchboard, a malevolent expression on his face, both hands clenched, his blackened face and clothing adding to his look of menace.

"Roscoe!" Nadine exclaimed. "You shouldn't be downstairs!"

"Where is he?" Smith snarled. He pivoted quickly as if he expected Dearborn to pop up behind him.

"He's not here," Benjamin said.

"Oh, no?" Smith strode past Benjamin and Nadine to make a quick survey of the parlor. Reid, shaking his head blearily, attempted to get up from the couch but couldn't quite make it. He mumbled a few incoherent words, gestured toward Nadine, and then slumped back against the cushions. Nadine, following Benjamin into the room, grabbed his arm and whispered, "Keep Roscoe here. I'll warn your father." She went quickly back into the hall.

"Wait a minute!" Smith yelled. "Where'd she go!" He started after Nadine. Benjamin intercepted him, throwing out his arms to prevent Smith from leaving the room.

"Get out of my way!" Smith roared. He aimed a fist at Benjamin's chin, and Benjamin lifted one of his hands to ward off the blow. Smith's fist smashed into Benjamin's open palm.

"Ow!" Benjamin's hand snapped backward so sharply that he thought Smith had broken his wrist. In the first moment of shock, he let Smith push past him and rush out the parlor doors.

"Son of a bitch." Benjamin caught up with Smith in the hall. "Hold it!" he cried, throwing himself between Smith and the back stairs.

"Out of my way!" Smith rushed toward the back stairs, stamping on Benjamin's foot as he plowed past. Benjamin cursed, tried to grab him, missed, and began hobbling after him. As he came abreast of the elevator, his ankle was abruptly jerked backward.

"What the . . ."

"Get in."

"Dad?"

"Get in," Dearborn hissed. He was squatting toadlike behind the folding seat.

"Smith's after you," Benjamin hissed back.

"Never mind that," Dearborn said. "Get in."

Benjamin got in and Dearborn pressed the button for the basement.

"We're not hiding in the basement, Dad."

"Correct. We are not hiding in the basement," Dearborn returned querulously. "One person hiding in the basement is sufficient."

"What do you mean?"

"I mean that a moment ago I heard the elevator in motion. When I investigated, I found that the elevator had descended to the basement. I rang for it. When it ascended, it was empty. What does that mean to you, Benjamin?"

"That someone's in the basement."

"*Hiding* in the basement," Dearborn corrected. "The basement door is locked. I saw to that myself. It cannot be used as a means of escape. Therefore someone is hiding in the basement."

"What someone?"

"*The* someone, of course. *The* someone. Why must you be so dense?"

Thirty-Five

The elevator dropped past the kitchen floor; Benjamin peered through the bars as they slid by. He could see a wedge of kitchen and smell the acrid odor of smoke that permeated the lower hall.

"What's that?" Dearborn demanded. "That stink."

"Smith set his room on fire."

"Ah. That's how he got out, was it. He's sharper than I gave him credit for, the baboon."

The elevator descended the last few yards to the bottom of the shaft. The light bulb in the cellar corridor swayed slightly, its pale reflection casting moving shadows on the damp walls.

Dearborn held up a warning hand and started to get

out of the elevator, but Benjamin, anticipating the move, barred the way with his arm and slipped out first. "I'll handle this," he whispered.

Dearborn slapped Benjamin's arm aside and followed him into the hall. He took up a position against the wall halfway between the wine room and the two storage rooms at the opposite end of the corridor. "Check the cellar door," Dearborn commanded.

Benjamin tiptoed to the end of the hall and tested the door. "Locked," he called in a loud whisper. "Still locked."

Dearborn grunted and gestured toward the wine room. Benjamin walked back, moving as quietly as he could, and slipped through the door into the wine room. He felt for the light switch. It wasn't until he flicked the switch up and down a couple of times that he remembered the light wasn't working. It couldn't be a fuse; the light was on in the hall. It must be the light bulb. He stood and listened.

Something was dripping—a faucet, or a leak in a pipe. He eased sideways toward the left end of the room, keeping his back to the wall and feeling his way down each row, stopping to listen every four or five steps so that there was no chance he could be caught unawares. The wine racks, some stocked, some empty, yielded nothing to his exploring hands but their honeycomb pattern and a thick coating of dust and grime. When he reached the last row on the far right, he located the source of the drip, an ancient tin sink attached to the back wall with a bucket set under the leaking faucet. He rubbed his wet fingers on his chinos, returned to the door, and rejoined Dearborn.

Dearborn raised his eyebrows. Benjamin shook his head. Together they walked down the corridor toward one of the two storerooms. Dearborn opened the door to the one nearest them. There was another brief scuffle as he attempted to slither into the room in front of Benjamin and was elbowed aside. Benjamin stepped into the room and switched on the light. He was in the cold-storage room. A floor-to-ceiling divider lined with shelves divided the room. Rows of five-gallon-size tins lined the walls and the divider shelves. Five barrels, three sealed, two open, stood near the door. One barrel was empty. The other was filled with dried beans. A burlap sack containing sprouted potatoes hung from a wall hook.

Benjamin circled the wall divider. Partway around, he tripped over a wicker basket full of onions and saved himself by leaning against one of three large freezer chests that lined the back wall. He eyed the one he was leaning on, then gingerly lifted his arm away. It was the one containing Robert Bright's body. The floor next to it was stacked high with dripping juice cans and soggy packages of frozen soup. He lifted the second freezer lid. The freezer held ice cream, sacks of frozen vegetables, and a tower of frozen cakes and pies. He lowered the lid, shifted his weight, and lifted the third lid. Inside were packages of frozen beef, poultry, and fish.

"What are you doing?" Dearborn called from the doorway.

"I'm checking the freezers."

"Come back here!"

"I'm coming." Benjamin closed the lid and returned to the door.

"Would you deliberately shut yourself up in an ice box?" Dearborn asked testily.

"Anything's possible."

"Anything is *not* possible." Dearborn crossed the hall to the second storage room. "In the interests of time I shall take over from here," he announced.

"That's what you think." Benjamin fastened his fingers in Dearborn's lapels and attempted to shift him to one side. Dearborn was ready for him. As Benjamin pushed, Dearborn brought his fist down smartly on the top of Benjamin's head, then quickly opened the door and dodged inside.

"Dad, are you crazy?"

Dearborn felt for the light. His fingers came into contact with the switch and he flicked it up. Nothing happened. He opened the door wider to let in as much light from the hall as he could and gazed into the darkness while Benjamin slid into the doorway behind him.

"Lights out here, too," Benjamin whispered.

"Did you expect it would be otherwise?" Dearborn muttered.

The large room was filled with equipment. Gym apparatus, carpentry and plumbing tools, party and banquet decorations, the bulky reserves necessary to the running of a hotel were piled everywhere. Most of the center of the room was blocked by furniture. They strained their eyes, trying to see into the blackness.

"No one in here!" Dearborn suddenly announced loudly.

"Ssh."

"You can see the place is empty!" Dearborn boomed.

"Ssh, Dad," Benjamin repeated impatiently.

Dearborn touched Benjamin's sleeve and pointed. In the middle of the room, lying across a bureau, was an exercise bicycle. The wheels were rotating gently. Benjamin took a step forward. Dearborn put out his hand to restrain him.

"Let me take a look, Dad . . ."

There was a grating sound. Something heavy in the back of the room was dislodged and crashed to the floor, precipitating a brief avalanche of slipping, falling objects. Then, from nowhere, something hit the door between them and thudded to the floor. They looked down. It was an old-fashioned clothes iron.

"Watch out!" Benjamin pushed Dearborn to one side and leaped to the other, then dashed toward the side of the room, circling a pile of packing cases and flattening his back against the wall in front of a stack of wooden bed frames. With a loud crack the door behind Dearborn slammed and the room was plunged into sudden darkness. Benjamin jerked back his head and cried out as his head struck something sharp hanging on the wall.

"Benjamin?" Dearborn called out anxiously.

"Don't talk, Dad. Don't move."

A second later Benjamin felt something fly past his face, then heard it bounce against the bed frames and clatter to the floor.

Dearborn, opposite, moved a few feet deeper into the room, then slid down behind a stack of chairs. He stumbled over what he guessed was a lumpy pile of table linens and sank down on top of it. He struck out with his hands and explored his position. The chairs formed a barricade. Carefully he reached into his breast pocket and pulled out a pack of matches.

Benjamin, about ten feet from the door, could hear the sound of heavy, uneven breathing. He stared into the room, straining to see the figure he knew was there. He wondered whether he should take the initiative and attack, but he knew the killer was desperate and that the room was full of potential weapons. He took a tentative step forward, but when the breathing stopped he stopped too, fixing his eyes unblinkingly on the spot where he knew his adversary waited, alert and watchful.

Dearborn also listened to the breathing as he slowly lifted the match cover and with exacting care disengaged one of the matches. He cupped his hand around the packet and lit the match. He was holding it so close to the palm of his hand that he burned himself and dropped the packet, but he held onto the match and it flared. He was surrounded by Christmas decorations, from papier-mâché trees to plump plaster angels. He couldn't see more than a foot in any direction. He looked up. The pile was about five feet high. If he rose and lit another match, he might be able to light the doorway.

The match wavered and died. He leaned over and felt around for the packet he'd dropped. His fingers crept along the floor on either side of him and into the space in front. They moved across something between his feet— part of the mound he was sitting on—and paused to assess it; soft, fleshlike. Dearborn's mouth went dry. He found the matches and lit another one, holding it low as he examined the lump he was sitting on. He pushed away some loose fabric and found himself staring into a face that was flat, white, with red spots for cheeks, pouting red lips, open eyes, painted eyelashes and a polka-dot jester's cap. Before he registered the fact that it was a dummy, he burst out from behind the pile with a strangled cry.

The eruption was so unexpected and volatile that Benjamin, with a shrill cry, also bolted forward, his momentum carrying him across the space that separated him from the figure at the door and pitching him against the dark hulk. They crashed to the floor.

Dearborn hopped across the room, tripped over the sprawling bodies, and, in the process of disentangling himself, received a resounding blow on the head. He got up reeling and slapped the wall blindly until his hand came into contact with the door knob and he succeeded in pulling open the door.

The light, dim as it was, had the same effect as a pail of cold water. Benjamin, wrestling with the figure on the floor, froze with his fist in mid-air while the person under him, stiff with shock, stared blankly up into his face.

No one spoke for a long, horrified moment. Then Benjamin broke the silence. "Nadine," he said wonderingly. "Nadine."

Thirty-Six

"But, Dearie," Stella protested, "you couldn't have realized who Jack was. None of us did, and we were better acquainted with him than you."

"I knew almost from the first, Stella," Dearborn replied calmly. "He looked familiar. I couldn't place him. I thought for a minute he was Robert. Then it struck me that he resembled Ronald Colman. The lack of hair put me off, but once I visualized him with a full head of hair I made the connection. Always thought Jack Rogers looked like Ronald Colman. I simply put two and two together."

"John Gilbert," Dolly interjected.

"What?"

"He looks like John Gilbert, not Ronald Colman." Dolly nodded toward Reid, propped up on the couch, sipping coffee.

"Never mind who he looks like," Fannie said impatiently. "Finish your story, Dearie. You put two and two together."

"I saw that the man was an alcoholic," Dearborn went on, "and remembered that Jack always carried a flask. I remembered that distinctly. It all added up. So I called an acquaintance of mine, a pillar of the American Medical Association, and asked him if he could verify Jack Rogers's handwriting. He replied in the affirmative. The records are all there—the unsavory proceedings involving the malpractice suit, the loss of Jack's medical license."

"How did you get a sample of his handwriting?" Stella asked.

"The note to the druggist," James broke in.

"Exactly. The note to the druggist was a ruse." Dearborn conceded.

"Why didn't I think of that?" Benjamin muttered.

"Everything the man did pointed to him being a physician," Dearborn went on. "Health directors dispense vitamins and direct sitting-up exercises. They do not work out of an infirmary equipped for major surgical procedures or diagnose uncommon diseases."

Reid lowered his coffee cup. "I couldn't ignore Dolly's symptoms."

"Nevertheless, it was a giveaway," Dearborn informed him.

"But you didn't think Jack was the murderer?" James pressed.

"In the beginning I had no reason to believe he had a motive. I thought he had sought out a safe haven here at the clinic, that Robert probably knew who he was, and that Reid was, no doubt, instrumental in maintaining Robert's youthful . . . um . . . externals. My only concern was that Reid might be in danger, like the rest of you."

"But then what did you think when you realized that Jack did have a motive?" Stella asked.

"There is nothing devious in the man's makeup. His professional ethics are unassailable. He aided me when I was hurt. He revived Dolly when he might easily have taken advantage of the opportunity to do away with her. Even his drunkenness is a point in his favor. One might, in an analytic flight, say that his detonator is faulty." Dearborn nodded at Reid. "To be blunt about it, you're a dud, Reid."

"He did ruin Caroline Ambeil's nose," Dolly reminded Dearborn.

272

"I was not drunk when I operated on Caroline Ambeil's nose," Reid declared.

"Which only strengthens the case," Dearborn returned.

Stella turned to Reid. "Why did you want us here? You're the one who suggested we come. We thought you inveigled us here to kill us."

"I thought I was protecting you," Reid replied. "I believed you'd be safe, that Nadine wouldn't dare try anything here at the clinic."

"When did you first find out she had committed a murder?" Dolly asked timorously.

"Nadine knew about me, but not everything. A few months ago we got into an argument. I don't remember about what. But I told her I had a stake in the clinic, that I'd get a percentage of the profits if it were sold. I told her about the Rotten Apples. It was after that that she persuaded me to help her arrange the sale. I wanted the money and I agreed. There was plenty to go around. But when Dearborn came looking for Robert and I found out that the members of the Rotten Apples were being killed . . ."

"You knew Nadine had to be responsible."

"And that, like it or not, I was part of it. But I made up my mind not to let her hurt any one else . . ." Reid shook his head and buried his face in his coffee cup.

"When did *you* begin to suspect her, Dearie?" Fannie asked.

"As soon as I learned about the clinic sale," Dearborn answered. "I had already asked myself why a young, beautiful woman who might be better occupied almost anywhere else . . ." Dearborn eyed Benjamin speculatively, "would remain here. Then I took it upon myself to examine Robert's room and decided he was not off gallivanting, as advertised. That he might have been murdered didn't occur to me. I drew what seemed to me a more reasonable conclusion. Robert made a prime suspect but he couldn't be working alone, not with letters arriving from the Orient, not with business deals being transacted. I concluded that Miss Garrett was in on it. Then after poor Robert showed up I realized that Miss Garrett was the only one in on it and that the "it" in question was murder. She showed signs of having already reaped the benefits of an intimate association with Robert. She claimed to be poor, but she wore a bracelet that appeared to me to be more Cartier than Woolworth. I borrowed that bauble—"

"You're the one who took the bracelet?" Benjamin asked incredulously.

"Certainly. I have it upstairs with the rest of the evidence. Miss Garrett's manner was, from the first, secretive. It seemed odd to me, among other things, that she kept her bedroom door locked, not only during the night, which might have been reasonable, but during the day. I was certain she was hiding something. At the first opportunity I picked the lock and searched her room. The first thing I noticed was the arrangement of the rooms. Almost all of the bathrooms and bedrooms on the second floor are joined railroad fashion, so that each bedroom is accessible to either of two bathrooms and can be arranged and rearranged in any way the management finds convenient. That is not true of Miss Garrett's room, which is next to the elevator. Miss Garrett's room adjoins only one bathroom—Robert's. Also, her bedroom is the twin of Robert's. The same carpet, matching drapes and bedspread, the same furniture. In essence, her room is part of Robert's suite."

Benjamin tried to picture Nadine's room. He couldn't remember anything about it.

"The next assumption is obvious," Dearborn continued. "She shared more with Robert than a common bathroom. When I discovered a wedding ring among her possessions, I reached the logical conclusion—"

"Married?" Dolly declared. "To Bobby? There must be fifty years difference in their ages!"

"The old lecher!" Fannie exclaimed. "There's nothing

less appealing than a lecherous old man lusting after a young girl."

"That point, you may be sure, was not lost upon Robert. No doubt that is why the marriage was kept secret. I obtained the proof today. They were married two years ago in Fairfield County, Connecticut. Since they married, Miss Garrett, or should I say Mrs. Bright, has made several substantial deposits to an account maintained under her unmarried name."

"How did you find that out?" Benjamin asked.

"Miss Garrett mentioned that her bank is lodged in the same building as the firm of Corbett, Rubin, and Bonnell," Dearborn answered with composure. "There is only one bank in the building."

"How clever of you, Dearie," Stella remarked.

"I mentioned that I found Miss Garrett's wedding ring when I searched her room," Dearborn stated. "But that is not all I found. Her jewelry case also contained a diamond wristwatch inscribed AO from AO, 1946."

"Antoinette Dill," James said.

"Ormacht," Dolly corrected.

"Yes. Miss Garrett took it from Toni, not, as I first suspected, to simulate a robbery, but because her greed is all-consuming. She coveted Toni's wristwatch enough to risk stealing it."

"What about the fabric Dolly found in the ragbag?" Stella asked.

"It was a piece from Miss Garrett's blouse. Mrs. Smith identified it for me."

"Talk about your number-one numbskull," Benjamin muttered. "Talk about being duped . . ."

"Don't feel badly," Dolly sympathized. "Miss Garrett certainly acted the young innocent."

"Like butter wouldn't melt in her mouth," Fannie commented.

"Everyone makes mistakes," Stella added kindly.

"The girl married Robert for his money," Dearborn said. "Robert's health was probably already failing. She no doubt hoped that Robert would do her the favor of dying, but I suspect that she was prepared from the first to help matters along if necessary. It was probably you, Reid, who stood in the way of killing Robert a long time ago. She was afraid you would realize what she was up to. But then, once the clinic began to deteriorate, it became imperative to get rid of it. Once she realized it would be to your benefit to cooperate, she enlisted your aid in perpetrating the fraudulent sale. Am I correct?"

Reid nodded morosely.

"And then she proceeded to eliminate, one by one, those members of the Rotten Apples who stood to share in the profits along with her. I would guess that you and Robert were intended to be the final victims, but she was forced to alter the sequence when matters went awry."

"Matters, as you call them," Benjamin remarked, "went awry once you got involved, Dad. You're damned lucky she didn't bump you off somewhere along the line."

"That was never a possibility," Dearborn said smugly. "I was in command of the situation from the first."

"Mr. Pinch?"

Lieutenant Niccoli stood in the parlor door, Officer Stefanich peering out from behind his shoulder.

"Well?" Dearborn responded rudely.

"We'd like you to ride back to town with us."

"Certainly not. I do not ride in police cars."

"We have to get this mess straightened out. Put something on paper. Get a few statements down. That kind of stuff."

"I will stop in tomorrow morning after breakfast," Dearborn proposed. "Or perhaps after lunch."

"You don't get it. Technically speaking you're . . . er . . ."

"What?"

Lieutenant Niccoli looked pleadingly at Benjamin.

"Hey wait a minute, now," Benjamin objected. "We're all going to the police station anyway. My father can ride with me. What's the difference how he gets there?"

"The difference is that he's under arrest," Stefanich piped up. "He can't take himself to jail."

Niccoli jammed his elbow into Stefanich's ribs. "It's just routine. Nothing to get worked up over."

"You intend to incarcerate me?" Dearborn asked politely.

"Let's say that we've got some questions to ask you," Niccoli amended.

"Mr. Pinch found your murderer for you," James pointed out. "He has enough evidence to convict her three times over."

"And you have us as witnesses," Fannie added. "There's no reason to arrest Mr. Pinch."

"There's the little matter of Kenneth Keck," Stefanich announced. "Right, Lieutenant?"

"Who," Dearborn inquired, "is Kenneth Keck?"

"The guard you konked out at Roosevelt Raceway."

"How droll," Stella said. "I can see the headlines now. Dearborn V. Pinch, heroic citizen . . ."

"Or," James interpolated, "as he shall hereafter be known, the man who konked Kenneth Keck . . ."

"Arrested by New York City police. Irate citizenry protest!"

"It still remains that you're a fugitive, Mr. Pinch," Niccoli appealed. "You've got a lot of explaining to do. It was your cane that killed Vernon Tree."

"My *favorite* cane," Dearborn amended. "Let us not overlook that fact. I expect my cane to be returned to me in mint condition."

"I don't think you're getting the point," Niccoli pursued doggedly.

"I am most assuredly getting the point," Dearborn interrupted. "The point is that your reasoning defies logic, rationality, consequence, applicability, appropriateness, or relevancy."

"Yeah, well, maybe. But you're still going to have to come in the car with us."

"Forget it, Lieutenant," Benjamin urged. "I'll be responsible for him."

277

"You forget it, Benjamin," Dearborn announced, suddenly capitulating. "I'm not a novice at the game. The only practical course is compliance." Dearborn got up from his chair and crossed the room. "Am I to be handcuffed?" he asked.

Niccoli reddened. "No reason for that," he mumbled.

Dearborn walked past him and Stefanich and paused at the front door. "If you don't mind, I shall wait in the car."

"The car's out by the gate," Stefanich protested. "You better wait for us. Right, Lieutenant?"

"I have no intention of running away."

"We got to go according to the book," Stefanich insisted.

"Lieutenant," Dearborn said, turning to Niccoli, "my honor is in question."

Niccoli rubbed his hand across the nape of his neck. "No, sir. It's got nothing to do with your honor."

"I beg to differ."

Niccoli looked at Benjamin's set expression, then back at Dearborn. "Okay. It's against regulations, but considering you're Benjamin Pinch's father . . ."

"Benjamin Pinch," Dearborn returned coolly, "is my son."

"Yeah. Well. Right. Whatever. I guess it'll be okay."

Dearborn opened the door, bowed slightly, and stepped outside.

"I'm sorry about that," Niccoli said to Benjamin after Dearborn closed the door. "If it was up to me, I'd forget the whole thing. But there's a routine we've got to follow."

"I know," Benjamin said. "You're doing your job. I know the speech. If you don't mind, I'd like to call my father's lawyer."

"Sure, go ahead. We'll wait. You can tell him to meet us down at Homicide in an hour or so."

"But Benjamin . . ." Stella began.

Benjamin shook his head warningly and she fell silent.

278

He went into the hall and picked up the phone. He held the receiver to his ear, dialed Otto's number, and waited.

It wasn't going to ring. Not unless the switchboard had repaired itself during the last hour. But Benjamin held onto the receiver anyway. He figured it would take Dearborn three or four minutes to walk around back to the garage and another three or four minutes to back out the car. Add another five minutes as a safety precaution—thirteen minutes at the outside—and Dearborn would be gone.

Benjamin eyed the dangling cords and useless plugs on the switchboard, then said in an eager voice, "Hello, Otto? How the hell are you, old buddy? It's me. Ben Pinch. Sorry to bother you. Know you've had a busy day. So have I, as a matter of fact. Called to talk about a little problem that's come up. It's about the old man. What about him? Well, I think he's going to need some advice . . . me too, come to think of it. . ."